MacCallister:
The Eagles Legacy:
Ten Guns from Texas

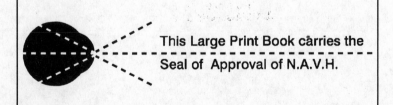

MacCallister:
The Eagles Legacy:
Ten Guns from Texas

William W. Johnstone
with J. A. Johnstone

WHEELER PUBLISHING

A part of Gale, Cengage Learning

GALE
CENGAGE Learning®

Farmington Hills, Mich • San Francisco • New York • Waterville, Maine
Meriden, Conn • Mason, Ohio • Chicago

Following the death of William W. Johnstone, the Johnstone family is working with a carefully selected writer to organize and complete Mr. Johnstone's outlines and many unfinished manuscripts to create additional novels in all of his series like The Last Gunfighter, Mountain Man, and Eagles, among others. This novel was inspired by Mr. Johnstone's superb storytelling.
Wheeler Publishing Large Print Western.
The text of this Large Print edition is unabridged.
Other aspects of the book may vary from the original edition.
Set in 16 pt. Plantin.

LIBRARY OF CONGRESS CATALOGING-IN-PUBLICATION DATA

Names: Johnstone, William W., author. | Johnstone, J. A., author.
Title: MacCallister : the eagles legacy: ten guns from Texas / by William W.
   Johnstone with J. A. Johnstone.
Other titles: Ten guns from Texas
Description: Large Print edition. | Waterville, Maine : Wheeler Publishing, 2017. |
   Series: Wheeler Publishing large print western
Identifiers: LCCN 2016044493| ISBN 9781410495556 (softcover) | ISBN 1410495558
   (softcover)
Subjects: LCSH: Large type books. | GSAFD: Western stories.
Classification: LCC PS3560.O415 M33 2017 | DDC 813/.54—dc23
LC record available at https://lccn.loc.gov/2016044493

Published in 2017 by arrangement with Pinnacle Books, an imprint of Kensington Publishing Corp.

MacCallister:
The Eagles Legacy:
Ten Guns from Texas

CHAPTER ONE

Chugwater, Wyoming

Duff MacCallister was having a Scotch with
Baldy Johnson at the Fiddler's Green saloon
when Wang Chow came in.

"Hey!" someone shouted. "What's that
Chinaman doin' in my drinkin' bar?"

"This isn't your drinking bar. It is mine,"
Baldy said. "You may have noticed on the
sign out front, just under the name Fiddler's
Green. It says Baldy Johnson, Proprietor."

"Yeah? Well, it seems to me like you would
have more consideration for your customers
than to allow a stinkin' Chinaman to come
into a bar where white men are drinkin'. I
think you should throw him out."

"Throw him out yourself," Baldy replied,
smiling across the table at Duff.

"Really? You mean it's all right with you if
I throw him out?"

"Sure, go ahead."

Wang Chow looked at Duff, who, with a

7

smile, nodded at him.

"Hood, you really plannin' on throwin' that Celestial outta here?" one of the other saloon customers asked.

"Yeah." With a malevolent smile, Hood left the bar and started toward Wang Chow. "What's your name, Chinaman?"

"My name is Wang Chow."

"Well, Wang Chow, you got two choices. You can either turn around and leave now, or you can let me mop up this floor with you and throw you out. Which will it be?"

"I do not wish to do either," Wang Chow replied.

"Well, then, we'll do it my way." Hood swung, putting everything into a wide right cross.

Wang Chow ducked easily under the wild swing, then shot out his hand, palm forward, striking Hood in the chest. The return blow surprised Hood, and drove him back several steps.

"Why, you — !" Hood swung again, missing as badly as he did the first time.

Wang Chow hit Hood on his forehead with the heel of his hand.

"Stop playing around with him, Hood," someone said.

Hood decided to try a straight jab and shot his left fist forward. Wang Chow moved his head to one side easily, and with no show of effort, hit Hood in the side, just under his arm.

Hood punched and swung again and again, never once making contact with Wang Chow, who with movements as graceful as those of a dancer, responded to every one of Hood's attempts with a counterpunch that scored. It soon became very evident that Wang Chow was carrying Hood and could, at any time, have dealt him a fight-ending blow.

Hood was getting more and more frustrated, and more and more exhausted. Finally, breathing heavily, he stopped, and held up his hand. "What did you say your name was?"

"I am Wang Chow."

"Well, Wang Chow, come over here and let me buy you a drink. I need to make friends with anybody who can fight the way you do."

"Why don't the two of you come over to my table?" Baldy called out to them. "I'll get the drinks. You've probably worn yourself out."

"You've got that right," Hood said.

The two men walked over to sit at the table with Duff and Baldy.

"Where did you learn to fight like that?"

Hood asked.

"I am a priest of the Shaolin Temple of Changlin," Wang Chow replied.

"A priest? I'll be damned if I've ever seen a padre who could do that."

"Wang Chow isn't the kind of priest you are thinking of," Duff said. "A Shaolin priest is a most unique individual. Wang Chow entered the temple as a boy of nine, and left when he was twenty-eight years old, a master of the Chinese martial art of *Wushu*."

"How did you wind up in America?" Hood asked.

"Some evil men killed my mother and my sister," Wang Chow said. "When I went to the temple to burn incense to honor my family, the master of the temple told me to seek no revenge. I was told that if I did so, it would bring dishonor to the temple."

"Damn, but you done it anyway, didn't you?" Hood asked.

"Yes. I cut the topknot to my hair, which distanced me from the temple, then I went to the tong of the men who had done the evil thing. Six men were there, laughing about having killed my family." Wang Chow stopped.

"Well, go on," Hood said. "What happened?"

"I killed them."

"Wait a minute. You said there were six of them."

"Yes."

"And you killed all six?"

"I am ashamed to say that I let my temper control me."

"So you shot all six of them?"

"I do not use guns," Wang said.

"Then how did you kill them?"

"I killed them with the sword."

"What happened then?"

"I was expelled from the Changlin Temple and the Empress Dowager Ci'an issued a decree ordering my death. I left China with a group of laborers, and came to America to work on the railroad," Wang said in conclusion.

"Damn," Hood said. "I'm glad I didn't really make you mad."

Duff and Baldy laughed.

"Say, Duff, is it true you're going to be taking some of your beeves to Texas?" Baldy asked.

"Aye, 'tis true. I've been dealing with a man named Jason Bellefontaine. He owns the Slash Bell Ranch at Merrill Town, which is near Austin. He wants some Angus to improve his herd."

"How soon will you be going?"

11

"I expect it'll be at least another month before we've got everything worked out. I've checked with the railroad. 'Tis five hundred of the creatures I'll be takin', so 'tis twenty cars I'll be needing."

"You're takin' cows to Texas?" Hood laughed. "Here, now, 'n if that ain't 'bout the funniest thing I've ever heard. I thought cows come out of Texas, not go in."

"These are Angus cattle. 'Tis a special breed from Scotland they are, and far superior to the Longhorns 'n aye, even the Hereford."

"Superior how?" Hood asked.

"Oh, in about ever' way you can count," Elmer Gleason said, joining the conversation. "They have lower calf weights, so the birthin' is a lot easier, which means you don't lose as many during calving season. They produce a quality carcass, 'n that means a better beef.

"But now, you take a Hereford, they have a higher birth weight, 'n they got white faces, which could cause the pinkeye. Also, they ain't as calm as the Angus is, neither."

"What about the Longhorn?" Hood asked.

"Anyone who is still raisin' Longhorns don't even deserve to be called a cattleman," Elmer said.

"What do you know 'bout bein' a cattlemen?" Hood teased. "I mean, seein' as you ain't nothin' but a cowboy your ownself."

"Oh, on the contrary, Mr. Hood," Duff said. "Mr. Gleason owns a substantial piece of Sky Meadow. He is every bit a cattleman, and has a personal stake in the safe delivery of these cows to Mr. Bellefontaine."

Near Phantom Hill, Texas

As Duff and the others were having a pleasant gathering in Fiddler's Green, some eight hundred and fifty miles south, two outlaws, Al Simmons and Hugh Decker, were on the run.

"They're a-comin'. I can feel it in my gut. They are out there, and they're close." Simmons climbed down from a rock and walked over to his horse, where he slipped his rifle out of the saddle holster.

"What is it you're a-plannin' on doin' with that rifle?" Decker asked.

"When they get here, I'm goin' to commence shootin'. It looks to me like we don't have no other choice."

"Yeah," Decker agreed. "Yeah, you're prob'ly right."

With rifles in hand, the two men climbed back up onto the rock that afforded them not only a good view of the approaching trail but also some cover and concealment.

They checked the loads in their rifles, eased the hammers back to half-cock, then hunkered down on the rock and waited.

"Let 'em come up to about fifty, maybe seventy-five yards away," Simmons suggested.

He and Decker weren't career outlaws. Until earlier that day, they had never done anything against the law. But they'd held up the Abilene stagecoach. During the robbery they took nothing from the passengers, stealing only the money being transported by the coach. They believed they had every right to do that because, until the week before, they had worked for the stage company, keeping the coaches in good repair. However, their supervisor had come in drunk and offensive. They'd gotten into a row with him, and he fired them. When they took their case to the station manager, he upheld his supervisor. To make things worse, they were each due two weeks' pay, and the company withheld their pay, claiming it was a *fine*.

They had moped over the unjust treatment for a few days. When they learned that the bank was expecting a shipment of money, they made up their mind to rob the coach.

Even though they had worn masks during

14

the holdup, the driver had recognized them and a posse, hastily formed, had chased them into a dead-end canyon.

As the thieves waited, the posse came into view over a distant rise.

"There they are," Decker said.

"I see 'em!" Simmons raised his rifle to his shoulder.

"Wait a minute," Decker cautioned. "Don't shoot!" He reached up to pull Simmons's rifle down. "They don't have no idea we're here."

"You're right. I'll wait until they get closer," Simmons agreed.

They waited as the distant riders came closer, sometimes seeming not to be riding, but rather floating as they materialized and dematerialized in the heat waves rising from the ground. On they rode, across the long, flat plain.

"It's takin' 'em forever to get here," Simmons complained.

"Yeah, well, what else have we got to do?" Decker asked with a chuckle.

"Nothin', I suppose," Simmons replied, also chuckling.

The two men waited until the posse closed to less than one hundred yards.

Simmons lifted his rifle again and rested it carefully against the rock, taking a very careful aim. "Wait until they get just a little closer," he said quietly. "I'll give you the word, then we'll both fire at the same time."

"No," Decker said.

Simmons looked at him in confusion. "What do you mean, no?"

"Think about it, Al. Do we really want to do this?"

"What do you mean, do we want to do this? Seems to me like we don't have no choice. 'Case you ain't noticed, this here is a dead-end canyon. We ain't got no way out 'cept through them."

"There's at least twenty of them. There's two of us," Decker said. "What difference does it make how many we shoot? We'll still be dead in the end."

Simmons nodded. "That's prob'ly true."

"And consider this. Some of them men is our friends," Decker said. "Hell, me 'n you had Thanksgiving dinner with Phil Burke and his wife. And how many times have we pitched horseshoes with Danny Mitchell? If we start shootin' now, we'll wind up killin' some of our friends. I don't mind goin' to meet my Maker as a thief, but damn if I want to meet Him with murder on my conscience."

"What do you propose that we do?"

"I say we give up."

16

"We'll be goin' to prison."

"Yeah, well, at least we'll be alive, 'n we won't be murderers. Besides, they'll feed us there, 'n we'll have a place to sleep. It ain't like we don't know no one that's there. How bad can it be?"

"Yeah," Simmons said. "Yeah, you're right. So, what do we do now?"

"We give up. I'll call down to 'em." Decker cupped his hands around his mouth. "Phil!" he shouted. "Phil Burke!"

Burke, Burke, Burke echoed back from the canyon.

"What do you want?" Burke called back.

"Me 'n Al want to give up!" Decker shouted.

Give up echoed several times.

"That's up to the sheriff!" Burke called back up.

"Sheriff, tell them boys not to shoot. We're comin' down," Decker shouted.

Down, down, down echoed.

"All right. Toss your guns out, then come down with your hands up," the sheriff replied.

Simmons and Decker responded to the sheriff's order, then, with their hands up, climbed down from their perch behind the rocks.

17

Two weeks later, tried and convicted, they were delivered to the prison at Huntsville.

CHAPTER TWO

Slash Bell Ranch — Travis County, Texas

Six mounted men materialized out of the darkness, riding slowly and quietly. Of the six men, only their leader Dirk Kendrick was not carrying a large wire cutter tool. When they reached a long stretch of barbed wire, he held up his hand. More than a hundred calves were on the other side of the wire. Most were sleeping, but many were moving around anxiously, searching for their mothers, for though they had been physically weaned away from the teat, they were not yet emotionally ready to be alone.

"Cut from here to there," Kendrick said, pointing to locations on the wire fence. "Cut all five strands."

When the wires were cut, five horsemen looped their ropes around the posts standing between the two cuts and urged their mounts on. The horses easily pulled the posts from the ground then dragged the section of fence away, leaving a twenty-foot opening.

Aware that something had happened, even the calves that had been asleep were on their feet.

"All right, boys, let's get the creatures out of there," Kendrick ordered.

All six men went into the pen and, within less than a minute, every calf had been moved out, each content to move as long as all the others were moving.

Merrill Town, Texas

When Jason Bellefontaine, owner of the Slash Bell Ranch, left the theater, he decided to have a few drinks over at the CSS *Alabama* Saloon before returning home. Owner Ken Prescott had been a crewman onboard the Confederate raider and had honored his saloon with the name. He had lived in Mobile before the war and was signed on to the ship by Admiral Semmes, who, at the time, was also a resident of Mobile.

"Tell me, Ken, do the folks back in Mobile actually live in houses?" Bellefontaine teased.

"Not just houses, my friend, but mansions," Prescott replied. "You will find some of the most beautiful mansions in all of America on Adams or St. Anthony, Claiborne or Conception Streets, right there in Mobile."

"Then why did you leave, if there are such beautiful homes in Mobile?"

Prescott smiled. "Because I didn't live on any of those streets. I lived on Telegraph Road."

Bellefontaine laughed. "Good enough reason. Besides, if you had stayed in Mobile, we wouldn't have the *Alabama* Saloon, and where would I go when I have a thirst for a beer?"

"You could always go to the Hog Pen," Prescott suggested, mentioning one of the other saloons in town. Whereas the CSS *Alabama* was a very pleasant saloon with a convivial atmosphere, the Hog Pen catered to a considerably more crude clientele.

"Ha. I would be real welcome in the Hog Pen now, wouldn't I?" Bellefontaine finished his drink, then set the glass down on the bar. "Take care, my friend. I'll see you later."

"Bye, Jason," Prescott said as Bellefontaine started toward the door.

Bellefontaine rode through the dark to return home, thinking of the unbranded calves that had been rounded up over the last two days. Tomorrow his crew would be branding them, then turning them back into

21

the herd. It promised to be a busy day, so reason told him he would be better served by returning to the ranch and going to bed.

It took him no more than half an hour to cover the five miles between his ranch and Merrill Town, and though he had no watch, he was certain it had to be after eleven o'clock by the time he dismounted in front of the barn. He was about to unsaddle his horse when someone came toward him, moving out of the shadows. It was so dark he couldn't see who it was, and for a moment he thought the worst. Cautiously, he let his hand slip down to rest on his pistol.

Recognizing Sam Post, his foreman, he relaxed. "Hello, Sam. I thought sure you and the others would be in bed by now. Especially given how hard you all worked today," Bellefontaine said as he returned to the job of unsaddling his horse.

"We've got a problem, boss."

"What kind of problem?"

"When I stepped out of the bunkhouse about an hour ago, I heard the calves we had cut out for brandin' today all bawlin' 'n such, so I rode out to check on 'em just to make sure they were all right."

"And?"

"They're gone, boss. Ever' damn one of 'em."

22

"Damn. How did they get away? Did the fence fall?"

"No, sir, the fence didn't fall. It was cut."

"Cut? You mean by the Fence Busters?"

"Oh, it was the Fence Busters, all right, Mr. Bellefontaine. Ain't no doubt in my mind about it."

"Dirk Kendrick?"

"Yes, sir. That's what I figure all right. That's why I've got all the men up and dressed," Sam said.

"What for?"

"So we can go after him. Don't forget, boss, those were some of the newly born Hereford calves. You don't want to lose any of 'em, do you?"

"Sam, suppose we did go after them. What good would it do? Remember, we aren't dealing with your average rustler here. The Fence Busters are as well organized a group of men as I have seen since Robert E. Lee surrendered my regiment to the Yankees at Appomattox. If we go after them with no more than a handful of cowboys, we're are going to wind up getting a bunch of good men killed."

"Does that mean we don't do anything at all?"

"We can go see Sheriff Wallace," Bellefontaine suggested.

"Dirk Kendrick has Sheriff Wallace in his pocket, you know that. Deputy Bullock is so slimy I don't see how even Wallace can put up with him."

"Yeah, well, I tend to agree with you," Bellefontaine said. "But right now, what other choice do we have?"

"You've got those Angus beeves comin' in before too much longer," Sam said. "I'd hate to see some of them get stole like these was."

"We'll just have to be extra careful," Bellefontaine said.

"How many?" the ranch owner asked.

"One hundred and nine," Kendrick replied. "Eighty-five are Herefords and twenty-four are Longhorns."

"It will cost you five dollars a head to keep them here, same for the Longhorns as for the Herefords."

"The Longhorns are worth only half as much as the Herefords," Kendrick complained.

"Whatever the cattle are worth on the market means nothing to me," the ranch owner replied. "I run the same risk in holding stolen Longhorns that I do stolen Herefords. The law makes no difference, so far as stolen property is concerned."

"I didn't say I wasn't going to pay it. I need someplace to keep them, and right now your ranch is the only place I have."

"Yeah, it is. Listen, I was thinkin'. Maybe you had better cut some of my fence and run off a few head of Longhorn. I'll claim I had several head of Herefords stolen. I wouldn't want people getting suspicious because my fence wasn't cut 'n I wasn't losin' cattle just like ever'one else is."

Kincaid chuckled. "I see what you mean. It is to our mutual benefit to maintain a degree of secrecy with regard to our business arrangement. All right. Soon as we get the cattle we acquired tonight remanded to an area that offers the least chance of discovery, we run off a few of your Longhorns."

"Just what is it you expect me to do?" Sheriff Wallace asked when he was approached by Bellefontaine the next morning.

"Well, you are the sheriff and I did have some of my cattle stolen. The correct thing to do when you have some of your property stolen is to report it to the sheriff."

"Yeah, well, first of all, how do you know your cows was stole?"

"What do you mean, how do I know? The

25

calves were gathered in a pen to be branded. They were there, now they aren't there."

"And you say it was the Fence Busters?"

"It had to be. The fence was cut."

"Was the fence on public or private land?"

"It was on public land. I run a lot of my cattle on public land and fence off my cattle to keep them separated from other brands. All the cattlemen do that. The only thing we do is make sure that everyone has equal access to the water. Hell, you know that, Wallace."

"Yes, I do know that, and therein lies the rub," Sheriff Wallace said.

"What do you mean?"

"You know damn well, Bellefontaine, that there is no law against cutting fences that are on public land. If it was the Fence Busters, there's nothing I can do about it. They have every right to be cutting the fences. In fact, they have been hired by a legitimate company in New York to do that very thing."

"Yes, but I don't think they have been hired to steal my cattle," Bellefontaine replied. "No legitimate land company would do that. Besides which, I'm not the only one having cattle stolen. I checked with some of the other ranchers before I rode in here this morning, and a few of them lost cattle last night, too."

"You said it was calves, didn't you?"

"Yes."

"Then how do you know they were stolen? If it was calves, it's more 'n likely they just wandered off on their own, lookin' for their mamas. That's what calves do, you know."

"It wasn't calves that were taken from Chris Dumey or Tom Byrd or Donald Dobbins. It was cows, full grown and ready for market. Whether you are willing to admit it or not, the Fence Busters are nothing more than cattle thieves. They might try and pass themselves off as legitimate businessmen, but nobody in the entire state believes that."

"I wouldn't be so quick to make that accusation, if I were you," Sheriff Wallace replied. "You may not realize it, but you are setting yourself up for a lawsuit. Big companies like the New York and Texas Land Company have lots of money, and they can afford very expensive lawyers. It wouldn't be good for them to be accused of association with cattle rustlers. I'd lay off if I was you."

Bellefontaine sighed. "Sam told me I was wasting my time coming here, and he was right."

"Even if what you say is true, how do you expect me to do anything about it? There are at least forty Fence Busters. I've just got

Deputy Bullock."

Disgusted, but not really surprised, Bellefontaine left the sheriff's office and rode back out to his ranch.

"What did the sheriff tell you?" Sam asked when Bellefontaine returned.

"You were right. He isn't going to do anything."

"We need to get rid of him come the next election," Sam said. "He's worthless as tits on a steer."

"I would suggest that you run for sheriff . . . except that you are too good a foreman, and I wouldn't want to lose you."

Sam grinned. "I'm not goin' anywhere, boss. I like ridin' for the brand."

CHAPTER THREE

Blowout, Texas

The town was a scattering of flyblown, crumbling adobe buildings laid out on the east side of the Blanco River about three miles below the origin of Blanco Creek. The name came from Blowout Cave, located in a hillside east of the river about a mile above the spring. At one time, the cave had been home to thousands of bats, and over at least a hundred years, a huge deposit of guano had accumulated. Ammonia and other gases from the decomposing guano had built up to such a degree in the cave that it was impossible for anyone to breathe, thus no one could even stand to be there long enough to mine it for fertilizer.

During a thunderstorm, lightning struck at the cave mouth and ignited the gases. The resultant explosion carved away almost one third of the mountain and gave the town its name.

It had no city marshal nor sheriff and had trouble filling those positions since three law officers had been killed over the last two years. Those hapless victims of Blowout's lawlessness lay buried in a part of the cemetery known as the "Lawman's Corner."

Blowout wasn't an outlaw town as such. There were still decent citizens and merchants who were trapped in the town by circumstances. Occasionally, they would hold secret meetings and plan ways to attract someone willing to put on a badge.

At the moment, such a meeting was taking place.

"Who is going to give his life to be the sheriff in this town?" asked Wes Long, owner of the mercantile. "We didn't do anything to help any of the previous lawmen stand up to Kendrick, and we aren't likely to show any more courage for the next sheriff."

"Besides, we already got law." Fred Matthews owned the wholesale and freight company.

"What are you talking about, Fred? You call Dirk Kendrick law?"

"Yeah, I do. I mean, when you think about it, he keeps his men sober 'n won't let any of 'em run roughshod over the citizens of the town. He keeps the peace."

"It's a hell of a peace is all I've got to say," Long added.

As had all previous meetings, that one ended in frustration and failure. They had not been able to come up with one suggestion to deal with the problem at hand — the occupation of the town by Dirk Kendrick and the Fence Busters.

Wheatland, Wyoming

Wheatland was twenty-five miles north of Chugwater and more than twice as large. The greater population had brought Duff to town, for it was there that he was able to make arrangements to have enough cattle cars delivered to the railhead in Chugwater to accommodate the cattle he would be shipping.

Once he had completed all the arrangements, he stopped at Nippy Jones Tavern to have a beer before he started home to Sky Meadow Ranch. Only one other customer was at the bar, standing at the opposite end. Duff got the distinct impression that the man was looking at him. More than looking, the man was studying him.

Duff started to walk down and introduce himself, but before he could do so, the man left the saloon. He also left a beer mug that was more than three quarters full.

As Duff was mulling this over, Nippy Jones, the owner of the saloon, came down to speak with him. "Hello, Duff. What brings you to town?"

"Hello, Nippy. I came to town so that I might lease twenty stock cars."

Over the years since he had arrived in the United States, Duff had done a considerable amount of business in Wheatland. As a result, he knew several of the local businessmen. As it so happened, Nippy Jones and Baldy Johnson, owner of Fiddler's Green, were also very good friends.

"Ah, shipping some stock to Kansas City, are you?"

"Nae, to Texas. I've sold some cattle to a rancher there."

"Ha, it's about time Texas started improving their ranches with good Wyoming cattle."

"Scottish cattle," Duff corrected. " 'Tis true that they'll be coming from Wyoming, but the breed is from Scotland."

Nippy laughed. "I'll not argue with you. By the way, how is the old Sergeant Major doing?" Nippy asked.

"Baldy is doing quite well, and 'tis his own regards he asked that I bring you."

"And give him my best as well," Nippy replied.

"Nippy, the gent that just left your establishment, would ye be for knowin' his name?"

Nippy shook his head. "I never laid eyes on 'im 'til he come here today." Suddenly he brightened and held up hand. "But I think he must know you. No more 'n fifteen minutes before you came in, he asked about you."

"What did he ask?"

"He asked if you came here often. He said he was wantin' to meet you. And that's funny, now that you think about it. If he actually did want to meet you, I wonder why it is that he didn't stay and talk?"

" 'Tis enough to make a man wonder now, isn't it?"

"Don't you find that a little peculiar?" Nippy asked.

"Aye, 'tis peculiar all right, but I've lived long enough to have seen many a peculiar fellow. If ye nae mind, I'll be for takin' my drink over to the table."

"Go find your table, 'n I'll bring your drink m'self," Nippy offered.

Shortly after Duff's drink was delivered to him, two men came into the saloon, talking with each other as they stepped in through the swinging batwing doors. Once they were inside, they separated. The big bearded man

33

went to one end of the bar, while the smaller of the two, who had a handlebar mustache but no beard, went to the opposite end. Both of them appeared to take no notice of Duff, but he couldn't help but notice that both were studying him in the mirror.

To most people, the fact that those two men had come in together, talking as if they were old friends, then taking up positions far apart from each other would mean nothing. But for Duff, it activated a little signal of alarm. He had the feeling they were setting up an ambush, and he had an even stronger feeling that he was the target.

Deliberately and as unobtrusively as he possibly could, Duff slid his pistol out of his holster, then held it on his lap under the table. He had never developed the skill of the fast draw, which seemed so prized by all Westerners, but did whatever needed to be done to give him an even chance anytime he was forced into a confrontation. For that reason, he held the pistol on his lap.

He had one additional advantage, one that required no manipulation of the situation in order for it to be effective. He was an exceptionally accurate shot, and his prowess extended with equal skill to the pistol and the long gun.

Even as he wondered about the strange

34

behavior of the two men who had just come in, the same man who'd left a few minutes earlier returned and walked right to the center of the bar.

He was met by Nippy Jones. "You left your beer more 'n half full last time you was here, Mister. I can replace it if you like, but it'll cost you the price of a new beer."

"I'll do my drinkin' after," the man said.

"After?"

"After me 'n this feller over here finish up with our business." The man turned to face Duff.

Here it is, Duff thought. He almost felt a sense of relief, not only because it was proof positive that his natural instincts were still active and correct in the assessment of danger, but also because the threat was imminent and he could deal with it right away.

"Would you be the Scotsman they call Duff MacCallister?" the man asked.

"Aye, Duff MacCallister 'tis my name."

"Is that a fact? Well, Mr. Duff MacCallister, my name is Deekus Pollard, and I'm calling you out, now."

With that announcement, a sudden repositioning of all the other patrons in the saloon occurred as most everyone moved to get out of the line of fire, should shooting begin.

Duff noticed that neither of the two men who'd come in just before Pollard had moved. In fact, they seemed to be studying their beer, which seemed very strange, given the possibility that they might be in the line of fire.

"Mr. Pollard, would you be for telling why you wish to pick this fight with me?"

"What difference does it make? You'll be dead in another couple minutes, 'n once you're dead, how or why you was kilt won't make no difference at all."

"Ah, so you are a philosopher, as well as a gunman. I have found that philosophers are some of the most interesting men I have ever encountered. 'Tis a shame I'm going to have to kill you."

Pollard's smile disclosed crooked, yellow teeth. "I ain't the one that's goin' to be kilt. You see, I got me what you might call an edge."

"An edge, you say? Do you think that's fair?"

"Fair? What do you mean, fair, you damn fool? I'm here to kill you. Fair ain't got nothin' to do with it."

"Well, in that case, I shall feel nae compunction about acquiring my own edge, and you'll have nae cause for complaint, seeing as you have already established the parame-

36

ters for our tête-à-tête."

"For our what?"

"You're right, *tête-à-tête* would nae be the correct word, would it? I mean, of course, because a tête-à-tête normally refers to a head-to-head encounter between two people, and 'tis obvious that isn't to be the case here."

"I don't know what you're a-talkin' about, but I can tell you right now, you won't be a-drinkin' no tea."

Duff chuckled, though instead of humor, there was a raw, almost dangerous edge to his laughter. "This is a life-or-death situation, wouldn't you agree?"

"Yes."

"And in a life-or-death situation, one should take every advantage, should they not?" Duff cocked the pistol he was holding under the table.

"Yeah," Pollard said.

"I'm glad to hear you say that. Oh, and you two gents standing at either end of the bar . . . I suspect that you are a part of this. If you are, you will die along with Mr. Pollard. If you aren't, then you need to leave now, while you can."

"Draw!" Pollard shouted.

Duff didn't squeeze the trigger until Pollard had his gun in hand.

Pollard's victorious smile changed to an expression of shock when he heard the roar of a gunshot and felt the bullet tear into his stomach. He dropped his own unfired pistol and slapped his hands over the bleeding wound in his stomach.

"What the hell? Where'd that gun come from?" shouted the big, bearded man standing at the bar. He put his hands up, as did the smaller man standing at the opposite end of the bar.

"Don't shoot, don't shoot!" the bearded man shouted. "We ain't in on this!"

Duff pulled the still-smoking pistol out from under the table. "Would the two of you be good enough to take your guns out of your holsters 'n lay them on the bar?"

"Why? I told you we ain't goin' to do nothin' "

Duff cocked his pistol, the sound of the hammer drawing back making a loud, metallic click in what had become a very silent room. "I'll nae be askin' again."

"All right, all right. I'm a-doin' it!" the bearded man said. As he slowly drew his pistol to put it on the bar, the other man followed suit.

Duff nodded to the owner. "Mr. Jones, if you would be so good as to remove the bullets from the two guns, I would appreciate it."

Nippy Jones did so.

"Now, if you two gentlemen would be for joining me, I would like to buy you a drink."

"You want to buy us a drink?"

"Aye."

"Why?"

"Have you ever heard the expression, *Keep your friends close, but keep your enemies closer*?"

"Nah, ain't never heard nothin' like that," the bearded man said as he and his companion joined Duff at his table.

"Well, 'tis an old Chinese proverb. To that end, would you be for tellin' me your names?

"I'm Tremble," the larger of the two men said. "He's Harrison."

"Mr. Tremble, Mr. Harrison, why did you want to kill me?"

The two men looked at each other for a second, then Harrison spoke. "We didn't want to kill you. There ain't neither one of us ever even heard of you before today. It was Pollard that wanted to kill you. He seen you when you was down at the depot, 'n he said he'd give us twenty dollars apiece if we'd come along with him."

"Oh, that's most disheartening to think

39

that my life would be worth no more than forty dollars."

"Yeah, well, here's the thing," Tremble said. "We wasn't supposed to have to do anythin' but just be standin' there 'n sort of back him up. Pollard said he'd be able to kill you all by his ownself."

"And why is that? Why did he want to kill me, I mean."

"He said you kilt his brother."

Duff shook his head. "He was mistaken. I have nae killed anyone named Pollard."

The sheriff and his deputy had arrived, and after interviewing several eyewitnesses, informed Duff that the killing of Pollard was justifiable homicide, and that he needn't be present for the official inquiry.

"What about these two?" Duff asked, indicating Tremble and Harrison. "Can we charge them with attempted murder?"

"I'm not sure that we can," the sheriff replied. "As I understand it, neither of them actually even drew their guns. I think it would be hard to make a case against them."

"That's right, Sheriff. We just happened to be standin' there when it all happened."

"Uh-huh," the sheriff replied, showing his disbelief. "I'll say this for you. You are a couple very lucky men."

"You mean 'cause you can't charge us

with nothin'?" Tremble asked.

"No. I mean you are lucky that you didn't actually take part in the shooting. I know you didn't, because if you had been a part of, it you would both be dead now."

"What makes you think that?" Tremble charged. "I mean, don't get me wrong, we wasn't a part of it, but if we hada been, there woulda been three of us to his one. More 'n likely, MacCallister would be the one that would be dead now."

The sheriff chuckled cynically. "Of course he would be," he said, sarcastically. "Now, I want you two to get out of my town before I change my mind."

"You got no right to run us out of town," Harrison said.

"I don't have to run you out of town. I can put you in jail."

"How are you goin' to put us in jail? We ain't neither one of us done nothin'. You ain't got no reason."

"I'll keep you in jail till I think of a reason," the sheriff replied.

"No need for that," Tremble said. "We're leavin'.

"Hey, Tremble," Harrison said as the two men rode out of town. "Why don't me 'n you wait here, 'n when MacCallister rides by, we'll shoot 'im."

"What would be the advantage of that?" Tremble replied. "Pollard's dead. We wouldn't make any money from it."

"Yeah, well, maybe not. But we could get some satisfaction out of it."

"How about getting satisfaction and a lot of money?" Tremble suggested.

"What do you mean? Do you have an idea?"

"Yeah."

CHAPTER FOUR

Blowout

Carl Peabody pushed through the swinging batwing doors of the Four Kings Saloon. "We cut fence where Jim Crockett was pennin' in some of his cows, 'n we got fifty Herefords," he said as he approached the table near the back of the room where Dirk Kincaid was sitting.

Kincaid was playing solitaire. He held a card, studying the board for a play. "Any trouble?"

"No, trouble. We took 'em to the Double D, 'n he said you'll owe him two hunnert 'n fifty dollars for parkin' the cattle there."

"It's worth it," Kendrick said as turned up the queen of hearts. "Ah, good. I've been looking for that one."

"Are you sure it's worth it? Seems to me like we're payin' an awful lot of money just to park our cattle there. I mean, at five dollars a head, for as many as we've got there, it's beginnin' to add up."

"Tell me, Peabody, do you think we could buy cattle for five dollars a head?"

"What? No, you know we couldn't do that."

"Then look at it as if we are acquiring a rather sizeable herd at an exceptional bargain. In addition, we have a place for them to graze, as well as a place to hide them out. The Double D is one of the most respected ranches in the whole area. Nobody is ever goin' to think to look for stolen cattle there."

"Yeah," Peabody said. "Yeah, I reckon I can see that."

"Now go away and let me finish this game," Kendrick said. "Tell Weasel to give you a drink on me."

"Thanks." Peabody headed toward the bar.

Northern Colorado

The snowcapped peaks of the Rocky Mountains were white against the night sky. Four men waited in the darkness, gathered in a shallow depression behind a water tower. Before them twin rails gleamed in the moonlight.

"It'll be easier than eatin' a piece of apple pie. All we got to do is wait for the train to stop for water, then we'll take it over."

44

"You know the cattle will be on this train?" Abner Grant asked.

"Yeah, when I was in Wheatland, I seen him get twenty cars. Twenty cars with twenty-five head on each one of 'em is five hunnert head. And oncet we take the train, the cows will belong to us."

"I hope you're right. If you are, this'll sure be easier 'n rustlin' them," Moe Sutton said.

"Tremble's right. I was in Wheatland, too. Me 'n him both seen MacCallister orderin' the cars," Harrison said.

They heard a distant whistle.

"There it is, boys," Tremble said with a wide smile. "We're about to be rich."

Cephus Prouty, the engineer, was leaning out of the cab, looking ahead at the long beam of light cast by the mirrored headlamp just forward of the smokestack. He held his eyes squinted against the eighteen-mile-per-hour wind being generated by the speed of the train. Behind him was the tender, twenty stock cars filled with cattle, a car that was carrying three horses, a private passenger car, and a caboose.

"I always get nervous during this part of the run," the fireman said. "They got this water tank just about as far from the last one as you can possibly go before the tank runs plumb dry. And if that happens, we sure as hell can't get out and push."

Cephus laughed. "You worry too much, Doodle. It's only a couple more miles." He checked the gauge. "Pressure is holdin' up pretty good. We could damn nigh coast from here on in."

Doodle laughed. "Yeah? Well ever' time we get to this part of the road, I get to thinkin' we may need to. And one of these days, if the tank ain't that good 'n full from the last time we took on water, we damn near may have to coast."

Back in the private car, each in their own bedroom compartment, Duff, Elmer, and Wang were sound asleep. When the train began slowing, the change in the motion awakened Duff, and he sat up to have a look out his window. They were coming to a stop, and at first he wondered why, then he realized they must be approaching a water tank.

He lay there for a few minutes, then decided to take advantage of the stop to check on Sky and the other horses. Pulling on his boots, he hopped down, then walked up to the car that was just forward of the private car. Looking ahead, he saw that the spout had been brought down from the

46

tank. The fireman was standing on top of the tender taking on water.

Satisfied that nothing was amiss, Duff peered in through the slats on the side of the car and saw the three horses standing calmly, no doubt asleep. He was about to return to his car when he heard someone speaking.

"That's it, Mr. Fireman. You just keep on pumpin' in that water till you got the tank good 'n full," someone said. "We'll be a-needin' that."

Startled not only by the voice, but by the fact the voice was familiar, Duff looked toward the front of the train, where he saw four men silhouetted against the glare of the headlamp. With drawn pistols, they were advancing toward the engine.

Train robbers? But what would they be robbing? The train has neither express car, nor passengers, so what do they want? As soon as he thought the question, the answer came to him. They weren't robbing the train . . . they intended to steal the train and the cattle.

Duff hurried back to the private car. "Elmer! Wang! Wake up!"

"What is it?" Elmer asked, sticking his head through the door to his room.

"The train is being robbed!"

"Robbed? What do you mean, robbed? What are they stealin'?"

"They're stealing the whole train," Duff said.

Even as he was talking, Duff was strapping on his pistol. It took but a moment for Elmer and Wang to join him.

The train was still stopped, still in the process of taking on water, when the three men left the car.

"How do we want to do this?" Elmer asked.

"I'll advance up the right-hand side of the train, Elmer, you go up the left side."

"I will go on top," Wang said.

"Aye, 'twas hoping you might suggest that."

"Wang, if this train gets started a-fore me 'n Duff get up there, it's up to you to get it stopped. Elsewise, we're likely to get stranded, and it'll be a mighty long walk into the next town," Elmer said.

Wang nodded his understanding, then the three men, each in their respective positions, started forward. Duff and Elmer were carrying pistols, but Wang, who was leaping adroitly from car to car, was without a weapon.

When Duff reached the front of the train, he saw two men standing there, both directing their attention toward the engine. He wondered where the other two had gone but couldn't worry about that. He had these two to contend with.

He recognized one of the men and realized at once why he had found the voice familiar. "Hello, Mr. Harrison. I dinnae think I'd be seeing you again. I'd be obliged if you and your friend would drop your guns."

"What the hell? How does he know your name?" the other man asked in alarm, startled by Duff's unexpected appearance.

"Oh, Mr. Harrison and I are old friends, aren't we? Where is Tremble?"

"I'm right here, MacCallister, holdin' a gun on you," a voice said from the top of the tender. "Drop your —" That was as far as Tremble got before he let out a cry of alarm and pitched headfirst from the top of the car.

Wang stepped up to the edge of the car and nodded toward Duff.

Duff's attention had been directed toward the top of the car, giving the two men he had accosted an opportunity to fire. Wide flame from the muzzle flash lit up the night. They shot first, but their shots were hurried and inaccurate. Duff returned fire, and both his shots found their target, as the two train

49

robbers went down.

Duff heard another shot from the other side of the train.

"I got the one in the cab, Duff!" Elmer shouted.

"Cephus, are you and Doodle all right?" Duff yelled into the cab.

"We're both fine, Mr. MacCallister," Cephus replied, stepping to the edge of the cab and looking down toward Duff.

Elmer appeared beside the engineer. "This 'n up here's dead."

Duff examined the three that lay on the ground before him. It took but a moment to ascertain that Tremble had broken his neck in the fall and was as dead as Harrison and the other man he had shot. "So are the three down here."

"That makes four," the engineer said. "And four was all we saw."

"All right. Let's get the bodies loaded," Duff said. "We can dump them off at the next station."

Pierce, Colorado
The sun was well up when the train arrived in town. Although it would have normally passed on through the station without stopping, Doodle jumped down and turned the switch plate so that the train was taken off

50

the through line and switched over to a sidetrack.

By the time the train had rumbled to a stop, the stationmaster was coming across the track toward them. "Here, what are you doing takin' a sidetrack? No need for that. I've got you cleared to pass right on through."

Duff hopped down to meet the depot manager. "We have some bodies that we must off-load here, and I expect by the time the sheriff is through with us, it'll be too late for us to pass on through."

"I expect you're right. You have bodies, you say? Whose bodies? Was there an accident somewhere? How did you come by them?"

"We'll explain it later. For now I would like to borrow one of your baggage carts, so we can get them off my train."

Five minutes later, the four bodies were laid out on the depot platform. Each one had his arms folded across his chest. Three of them had their eyes open. The one exception was Harrison, whose eyes were closed, the result of having had his lid muscles destroyed by the bullet that hit him right between the eyes. Soon, there were more than three dozen people who had been drawn to gawk at the grisly scene, including

51

the sheriff.

"And you say they was tryin' to rob the train?" the sheriff asked.

"Yes," Duff replied.

"Well now, that don't make no sense atall, does it? I mean, how are you goin' to rob a freight train?"

"Obviously, Constable, their intent was to steal what the train is carrying," Duff replied.

"And that was?"

"Five hundred head of purebred Angus."

"How were they agoin' to do that?"

"I believe they was plannin' on takin' the whole train," Cephus said. "Leastwise, that's what the man that climbed into the cab told me."

"Yeah, that's what he said, all right," Doodle added.

"That still don't make no sense to me," the sheriff said. "Just where is it that they planned to take the train? I mean, you can't take it nowhere, where you ain't got track."

"No, but by the time you get to LaSalle, there is track going east," Cephus said.

"Aye, and it wouldn't be hard to take the cattle to Kansas City and sell them to a broker there," Duff said.

The sheriff studied Duff for a long moment. "These here is your cows, are they?"

52

"Not entirely mine."

"What do you mean, not entirely yours?"

"Mr. Gleason," Duff said, nodding toward Elmer, "and a lady named Megan Parker back in Chugwater are partners with me in the cattle. We have them sold to a rancher down in Texas."

"But you are the one who killed these men?" the sheriff asked.

"Aye."

"That ain't entirely true, Sheriff," Elmer said. "Duff only kilt two of 'em. I kilt one of 'em myself."

"That only accounts for three."

"I killed one of the men," Wang said.

"You? How'd you do that? You ain't wearin' no gun."

"Mr. Wang does not require a gun," Duff said.

"All right, Gleason here owns part of the cattle, so I can see how he mighta had some reason to kill one of 'em." He looked at Wang. "You don't own any of the cattle, do you?"

"No."

"Then why did you kill one of 'em? 'N with your bare hands, too?"

"He was pointing a gun at MacCallister *Xian shen*."

"He was pointing a gun at what?"

53

"At me," Duff said.

"Yeah, I caught that part of it. I just don't know what else it was that he said, the zing zang thing."

"Xian Shen," Duff repeated. "It's like using *mister,* only it conveys a little more respect."

"Respect, huh? You demand a lot of respect, do you?"

"Only when it is due. Constable, I can't help but get the impression that you are somewhat hostile toward my friends and me."

"Hostile? Yeah, you might say that. As far as I'm concerned, there's somethin' fishy 'bout this whole thing."

"Do you intend to present a bill of charges to the solicitor?"

"Do I what?"

"Do you intend to prosecute us for murder or manslaughter, or any similar charge?" Duff clarified.

"No, I don't plan to do nothin' about it, on account of, for one thing, it wasn't even in my jurisdiction where it happened. But I'm tellin' you right now that I don't believe anyone would actual try and steal an entire train. Besides which, I know two of these men. That's Abner Grant and that's Moe Sutton. I've known both of 'em for a long time, 'n there ain't neither one of 'em ever really give me too much trouble before. Oh, they get a little rambunctious ever now 'n then, but it's hard for me to believe they'd ever do somethin' so foolish as to rob a train. I don't have no idea who them other two are."

"The big fellow with the beard is Tremble. The one with the handlebar mustache is Harrison."

"I see. Friends of yours, are they?"

"I only know their names, and just their last names at that," Duff said. "And they are nae friends."

"Well if they aren't friends, that means they are enemies. Would you say they are enemies enough, that you might want to kill them?" the sheriff asked, somewhat triumphantly.

"Of, for heaven's sake, Sheriff Weldon. What is it you are getting at? You got me 'n Doodle, and C.G. the brakeman, as well as these three gentlemen here, 'n all six of us is tellin' you the same thing," Cephus said. "These four men was tryin' to steal the train. Now, if you know these here two fellers like you say you do, then you know we're tellin' the truth."

The sheriff nodded. "Yeah, now that I think back on it, I reckon I could see Abner

55

Grant stirrin' the rest of 'em up." He sighed. "Seems I ain't got nothin' I can actual charge none of you with, so I'd be just as happy if you would just get that train on out of here. If there's goin' to be anyone else tryin' to steal the train, I'd just as soon it be somewhere else. How soon is it before you reckon you can get gone?"

"We'll prob'ly have to spend the night here," Cephus said.

"Spend the night here? What for?" the sheriff asked, surprised by the engineer's response. "I told you, there's no need in any of you stayin' here, 'cause there ain't goin' to be no charges."

"I can answer that, Sheriff," the station-master said, speaking for the first time since the sheriff had arrived. "Their staying here has nothing to do with whether or not you're planning on charging them with anything. They are not part of a regularly scheduled run, you understand, which means they have to have track clearance before they can go anywhere. Since circumstances have brought them here, their initial clearance is no longer valid. They will have to apply for a new clearance. I expect that will take at least another day before it is granted, and they'll have to wait right here until that time. They dare not go back out

56

on the high iron until everyone knows to look out for them."

"All right. Go ahead 'n get your clearance, but do it as soon as you can. The sooner you get your train out of my town, the better I'll feel."

CHAPTER FIVE

The private car was spacious enough and livable enough to provide Duff, Elmer, and Wang with comfortable quarters as they were waiting for Cephus to get track clearance for them to continue on their journey. They put the window up and were playing cards when Elmer began sniffing audibly.

"Damn. Smells like someone is bakin' bread. That's about the best-smellin' thing I've ever smelt."

"There's a bakery just down the street." Duff tossed his cards down. "Why don't I just go get us a couple loaves of bread?"

"Whoa. Why do you want to do that? Another couple hands, 'n there's no doubt in my mind I'll wind up ownin' all of Sky Meadow," Elmer teased.

"In that case, that's all the more reason I should go," Duff replied with a chuckle. "Besides, wouldn't you like to have some hot bread?"

"Yeah, well, if you're goin' to do that, get some butter and jam as well, or it won't be worth eatin'," Elmer said.

"That's all right. I'm sure Wang and I will find your share worth eating."

"No, now, don't get me wrong," Elmer said. "I don't pure dee have to have butter 'n jam, but you gotta admit yourself that it would make the bread a heap better."

Duff chuckled again. "I'll see what I can do."

Leaving the car, he walked across the tracks, then stepped up onto the depot platform. The four bodies were still laid out where they were before, and he wondered why they hadn't been moved or at least covered. He thought about stepping into the depot to say something about it, but decided against it. He had no wish to get into any entanglements. His primary purpose was to deliver the cattle to Mr. Bellefontaine at the Slash Bell Ranch. And the best way to do that was to just stay in the private car until they were able to get under way again.

The initial crowd around the bodies had dissipated, so that only one man remained. He was a very large man, at least six feet five or more, and well-proportioned to his size.

Duff wondered why he seemed to be so interested in the gruesome display. Despite his earlier thought that he would not get any further involved, he stepped into the depot to speak with the stationmaster about the bodies.

"You think I like having them lying out there?" the stationmaster replied to Duff's inquiry. "Sheriff Weldon said that he would have Lonnie Welch . . . never mind, here he is now."

Lonnie Welch was a rather tall, thin, almost cadaverous man, wearing a cutaway jacket, striped pants, and a top hat.

"It's about time you got here, Welch. If these bodies lay out there much longer, they're likely to commence smelling," the stationmaster said.

"I'm very sorry for the delay, Mr. Lester, but I had a subject that needed my attention. I've brought a couple men with me. We can move them now."

"Yeah, well, you might have to move Big Tom out of the way. He's been out there, just starin' down at his brother, for the last fifteen minutes."

"I have a great deal of experience dealing with the bereaved. I can deal with Big Tom," Welch replied.

"Yeah, well he" — Lester stopped in mid-sentence, then continued — "doesn't appear to be there right now."

Duff watched as Welch directed a couple of his men toward the bodies, then, leaving the depot, he continued on his original mission of buying bread. He was halfway across the street when he sensed a sudden movement behind him. Before he could turn, he felt a blow to the side of his head. He saw stars, but even as he was being hit he was reacting to the movement, and though it didn't prevent the attack, it did prevent him from being knocked down.

When his attacker swung at him a second time, Duff was able to avoid him. It was also when he saw that it was the same big man he had seen standing over the four bodies. The man the stationmaster had identified as Big Tom.

"Mister," the big man said with a low growl, "one o' them men you kilt was my brother, 'n I aim to settle accounts for 'im."

"You must be Big Tom," Duff said.

"You've heard of me, huh? Well, if you've heard about me, you ought to have know'd that I wasn't goin' to let you kill my baby brother 'n not do nothin' about it."

"I'm sorry about your brother," Duff said, coming up on his toes and moving about to be ready for Big Tom's next attempt.

"Maybe he should have considered another line of business besides robbery. Which of them was your brother?"

"It was Abner Grant, is who it was," Big Tom said, then he swung wildly at Duff.

Duff slipped the punch easily, then counterpunched with a quick, left jab to the big man's face. It was a good, well-hit blow, but Big Tom just flinched once, then laughed a low, evil laugh.

"I'm goin' to kill you with my bare hands. It's goin' to be a fair fight, all right, but you're goin' to wind up gettin' yourself kilt. That way they can't nobody say it was murder." He topped off his long dissertation with a rush toward Duff.

Duff stepped aside, avoiding him as gracefully as a matador might sidestep a charging bull. And like a charging bull, Grant slammed into a hitching rail, smashing through it as if it were kindling.

He turned and faced Duff again. "You're kind of a slippery one, ain't you? Well, you can dodge all you want. You ain't gettin' away from me."

The fight had drawn several onlookers, and they stood out in the street watching as the two men circled around for a moment, holding their fists doubled in front of them, each trying to test the mettle of the other.

Grant swung another club-like swing, which Duff was again able to avoid. Duff counterpunched and he scored well, but again, Grant shrugged it off."

"Who's that feller Big Tom's afightin' with?" someone in the crowd asked.

"I don't know. All I know is, whatever he done to get Big Tom mad wasn't very smart of him."

As the fight continued, Duff managed to avoid the wild swings while scoring easily with his counterpunches. And though Grant laughed off his early blows, Duff was a big, strong man in his own right, and his punches were starting to have a cumulative effect. Both of Grant's eyes began to puff up, and there was a nasty cut on his upper lip. Duff landed a hard, well-placed left on the bridge of Grant's nose, and it began bleeding heavily as the blood streamed in rivulets down his teeth and chin.

Except for the opening blow, he hadn't managed to connect with any of his wild swings.

"I believe that feller is a-winnin' this fight," one of the onlookers said. "Look at Big Tom. Damn. He's bleedin' like a stuck pig."

"Big Tom ain't give up, though. You know what a strong sumbitch he is. Chances are, he's only got to hit that feller one time, 'n it'll be all over," another answered.

Grant continued to swing, and after four or five such swinging blows, Duff saw an opening that he could use. He timed it, and on Grant's next swing, Duff threw a solid right, straight at the place where he knew Grant's sore nose would be. The blow was timed perfectly and Duff had the satisfaction of hearing a bellow of pain from his opponent for the first time.

Grant was obviously growing more tired, and he began charging more and swinging less. Duff got set for one of his charges, then stepped to the side as Grant rushed by with his head down. Like a matador thrusting his sword into the bull in a killing lunge, Duff sent a powerful right jab to Grant's jaw. Grant went down and out.

"I'll be damned! Look at that! I never thought I woulda seen anyone whup Big Tom."

Duff was a little winded from the exercise, and he could still feel the effects of the opening blow. He held his hand up to his ear, but pulled it away quickly because of the tenderness of the ear.

"What's your name, mister?" one of the men in the crowd asked.

"MacCallister. Duff MacCallister."

"Well, Mr. MacCallister, you just done somethin' there ain't nobody else ever been able to do. Big Tom Grant has lorded it over ever'one for 'bout as long as I can 'member."

"This oughta take 'im down a notch or two," another said.

"Wait a minute. I seen you down at the depot. You're the one that kilt them four boys for trying to rob the train, ain't you?"

"Yeah, he is," another said. "Abner Grant was one of 'em, don't you know? That's why Big Tom come after 'im the way he done."

Big Tom groaned, then sat up. Duff reached down to offer his hand, to help him to his feet, and the offer was accepted.

"Is it over between us?" Duff asked.

The big man held his hand to his jaw. "Yeah. Is it true, what they're sayin'? Did my brother try to rob the train?"

"Aye, 'tis true."

"I knew he was goin' to wind up like this someday. Pa knew it, too. He told me a long time ago that my little brother warn't no good."

"I'm sorry I was a part of his demise."

"His what?"

"I'm sorry I'm the one who had to kill him."

"Yeah, well, it's done now, 'n if it hadn'ta

65

been you, it woulda been someone else. At least I won't have to be worryin' 'bout him anymore."

"I'm sorry," Duff repeated.

Bit Tom nodded. "I reckon I'd best go tell Pa what happened."

"Big Tom?" said one of the men who had come to watch the fight."

"Yeah?"

"Why don't you step into my office and let me take a look at that nose for you? And get you cleaned up. I don't expect you would like to see your father with blood all over your face."

Big Tom put his hand to his nose gingerly, then winced. "Yeah. Thanks, Doc. I'd appreciate that."

Duff watched Big Tom and the doctor walk off, then he continued on his own task, which was to buy a loaf of freshly baked bread.

"What took you so long?" Elmer asked later as Duff returned with bread, jam, and butter."

"I had to find a place where I could buy butter," he said, holding up the container.

Blanco County, Texas
Somewhere in the predawn darkness a calf

66

bawled anxiously and its mother answered. In the distance, a coyote sent up its long, lonesome wail, while out in the pond, frogs thrummed their night song. The moon was a thin sliver of silver, but the night was alive with stars . . . from the very bright, shining lights, all the way down to those stars which weren't visible as individual bodies but whose glow added to the luminous powder that dusted the distant sky.

Around the milling shapes of shadows that made up the small herd rode three cowboys known as "nighthawks." Their job was to keep watch over the herd during the night.

Considerably younger than the other two, Billy asked, "Fendall, do you mean to tell me you've actually been up in one of them balloons?"

"Yep, I sure did. Back in Dallas, it was," Cooter answered. "This aeronaut —"

"This what?" Billy interrupted.

"Aeronaut. That's what they call a feller that flies through the air in one of them balloons. Anyhow, he come to the fair in Dallas 'n he brung his balloon with 'im. If you gived him a dollar, why he'd let you go up in the balloon with 'im. So, I give 'im a dollar, then I clumb into the basket, then me 'n him went up in that balloon. So, I reckon you can say I'm one o' them aeronauts, too."

"How high did you go?"

"Hell, we went all the up to the end of the rope."

"The end of the rope?"

"Yeah, the balloon was tied to a rope, you see, 'n when we went up, why, we went to the end of the rope."

"Then you didn't really go up in the balloon, did you? I mean, not way up to float free in the sky."

"Well, that woulda been kinda foolish, wouldn't it? I mean, how would we a-got back to the fair?"

"Well then, you ain't really no aeronaut. I mean, not if you was tied down to the ground the whole time. Hell, that ain't no different from climbin' up on the roof of a barn 'n havin' yourself a look aroun'. I thought you had really done it. I mean, gone way up into the sky as high as the clouds."

"Well, I'm a lot more of a aeronaut than you or anyone else I know. Are you a-tellin' me you wouldn'ta done it if you'd been there?"

Billy smiled. "Yeah. I would rather go all the way up to the clouds, but I woulda done that, if that was all I could do."

The calf's call for his mother came again, with more insistence. The mother's answer had a degree of anxiousness to it.

"Sounds like one of 'em's wandered off," Billy said. "I'll go find it."

"Hell, why bother? It'll find its own way back."

"I don't mind." Billy slapped his legs against the side of his horse and rode off, disappearing in the darkness.

"Cooter, did you really go up in that there balloon or was you just a-funnin' the boy?" the other rider asked.

"I done it all right, but I wouldn'ta done it if it hadn't been tied down by that rope."

Suddenly, from the darkness came a loud, blood-curdling scream, filled with such terror that both cowboys shivered all the way down to their boots.

"What the hell was that?"

Billy's horse came running by then, its saddle empty.

"Sumbitch! That was Billy!"

Though both were wearing guns, neither man was actually a gunman. Nevertheless, their friend was in trouble, and feeling the unfamiliar weight of pistols in their hand, they rode to his aid.

A moment later, gunshots erupted in the night, their muzzle flashes lighting up the herd.

"Jesus! What's happening? Who is it? They're all around us!" one of the cowboys shouted in terror, firing his gun wildly in the dark.

The two men tried to fight back, but they were young, inexperienced, scared, and outnumbered. In less than a minute, both had been shot from their saddles and then the night grew still, save for the restless shuffle of the herd of cattle.

At some distance away, a man with dark hair, dark eyes, and a purple scar slashed down his left cheek sat his saddle. Dirk Kendrick had brought men there specifically to steal cattle, but he had not been personally involved.

One of his men, with the smell of death still in his nostrils, rode up to him. Like Kendrick, the rider had a blue kerchief tied around his neck. "That's it. We kilt all three of them cowboys and took a look all around the herd. There ain't no one else ridin' nighthawk."

"Good. Now, take the cows," Kendrick said.

CHAPTER SIX

*San Saba County Courthouse, San Saba,
Texas*

"Here ye, hear ye, hear ye! This here trial is about to commence, the Honorable Anthony Craig presidin'," the bailiff shouted. "Everybody stand respectful."

Judge Craig came out of a back room. After taking his seat at the bench, he adjusted the glasses on the end of his nose, then cleared his throat. "Would the bailiff please bring the accused before the bench?"

The bailiff, who was leaning against the side wall, spit a quid of tobacco into the brass spittoon, then walked over to the table where the defendant, Roy Kelly, sat next to his court-appointed lawyer, Robert Gilmore. "Get up, you," the bailiff growled. "Present yourself before the judge."

Roy was handcuffed and had shackles on his ankles. He shuffled up to stand in front of the judge. Gilmore went with him.

71

"Roy Kelly, you stand accused of the crime of ridin' for that butcherin', thievin', rapin' Bloody Bill Anderson," the judge said. "How do you plead?"

"Judge, what the hell are you talkin' about? The war's over! Hell, it's been over for twenty years now!" Kelly replied.

"There is no statute of limitations on murder."

"It ain't murder when you are in a war," Kelly said.

"How do you plead?" the judge asked again.

"Your Honor, if it please the court," Gilmore said.

"You got somethin' to say to this court, Mr. Gilmore?" Judge Craig asked.

"Yes, Your Honor. Bloody Bill Anderson did most of his murderin' and thievin' up in Kansas and Missouri," the lawyer said.

"What's your point, Mr. Gilmore?"

"Well, Your Honor, I don't know why we're trying Mr. Kelly in Texas for any murdering and thieving he may have done while he was up in Kansas. I move that this case be dismissed for lack of proper jurisdiction."

"Is that the best you can do?" Kelly asked his lawyer. "How about sayin' somethin' like Bloody Bill Anderson didn't do any murderin' or thievin' on account of murderin' 'n thievin' when you're at war don't count."

"Your Honor, my client has a point. If we were to try everyone who participated in a war which saw hundreds of thousands killed, we would have to try half of the male population of the entire United States."

The prosecutor, Abel Hawkins, said, "Your Honor, I would like to point out that Bloody Bill Anderson held no commission recognized by the Confederate government. Even they thought that what killing he did was indeed murder. And by extension, anyone who rode with Bloody Bill Anderson is also a murderer."

"Your point is well taken, sir," Judge Craig said, slapping his gavel on the bench. "If even the Confederate government didn't recognize him, any killing he did is murder."

"But, Your Honor, if he did kill anyone, it was in Kansas or Missouri," Gilmore said again. "As far as we know he never killed anyone in Texas. With all due respect, Your Honor, that means you have no jurisdiction over him or anyone who rode with him."

"Your Honor," Hawkins replied quickly. "We know that Anderson was in Texas at least once, during the war."

"Come on, Abel, you know damn well Bloody Bill Anderson didn't kill anyone down here," Gilmore said. "Texas was part of the Confederacy."

"Kelly rode with Bloody Bill Anderson, which brings us right back to the initial charge," Dempster said. "Your Honor, the very fact that Bloody Bill Anderson was once in Texas puts the case under your jurisdiction."

"Even if Bloody Bill Anderson was here, there is no proof that my client was with him at the time," Gilmore said.

"It doesn't matter whether Kelly was with Anderson when he was here or not. Kelly is here now, and he rode with Bloody Bill Anderson, who was also here, at least once. That means I do have jurisdiction, and this case shall proceed.

"Mr. Gilmore, how does your client plead?"

"Your Honor, my client pleads not guilty."

"Did you, or did you not, confess before several assembled men in the Brown Dirt Saloon, that you rode with Bloody Bill Anderson?" Judge Craig asked Kelly.

"That wasn't a confession, Judge. I was just drinkin' and talkin' and tellin' war stories with some of the other fellas. Hell, we was all tellin' war stories, 'n more 'n likely half of what we was a-tellin' was lies."

"Were you lying when you bragged about

riding with Bloody Bill Anderson?" the judge asked.

Kelly looked at his lawyer.

"Your Honor, my client respectfully declines to answer that question," Gilmore said.

"It doesn't matter whether he answers the question or not. Anyway, the charge is murder, not simply riding with Bloody Bill Anderson. Riding with Bloody Bill Anderson is merely a means to establish the charge. Mr. Prosecutor, are you prepared to make your case?"

"I am, Your Honor," Abel Hawkins said. "I call Merlin Harris to the stand."

Harris was a short, rather rotund man with a pockmarked face and thinning hair.

"Oh damn," Kelly said under his breath.

"What is it?"

"Me 'n him got into a fight oncet. He don't like me, 'n I don't like him. I shoulda kilt him, instead of just knockin' him down."

"Was he present when you were telling your" — Gilmore paused for a moment — "war stories?"

"Yeah, he was there," Kelly said.

Harris walked up to the witness chair.

"Raise your right hand. Do you swear to tell the whole truth, and nothing but the truth?"

"Yeah," Harris said.

The clerk who administered the oath returned to his seat, and Dempster approached Morris. "Mr. Morris, do you know the defendant?"

"Yeah, I know him."

"And were you present in the saloon when Mr. Kelly was discussing his war exploits?"

"Yeah."

"What was he talking about?"

"He was talkin' about how he rode with Bloody Bill Anderson, 'n how he kilt lots of people while he was with him."

"Cross, Mr. Gilmore?"

"No, Your Honor."

"Any more witnesses, Mr. Dempster?"

"I don't need any more, Your Honor. I've made my case," Dempster said.

"Mr. Gilmore, you may call your first witness," Judge Craig said.

"We will present no witnesses," Gilmore replied.

"Have you a case to present?"

"Yes, sir, I do. Your Honor, I know that you are not native to the South, but I am. If you would just look out into the gallery, you'll see men and women who were born and raised here. There are many in this courtroom who participated in that war, and even more who are old enough to remember it. They were all loyal to the South. Now you are about to ask them to pass judgment against a man simply because twenty-three years ago he fought for what he believed in, as did many who are here now. I don't believe you are going to find much agreement in your zeal to prosecute."

The gallery broke into applause, and the judge angrily banged his gavel until they were quiet. "Is that your case?"

"It is, Your Honor. The defense rests."

The judge looked to the jury. "You gentlemen of the jury, will you be able to set aside your normal loyalty to the South in order to serve the law?"

The jurors looked at each other, then held a few quick conversations among themselves.

"Your Honor, like the feller said, the war was over more 'n twenty years ago," one of the jurors said. "And they's at least seven of us that fought in that same war, 'n we fought for the South. It don't seem to us like we'd be accomplishin' anything by findin' a man guilty of murder now, just because he fought for what he believed in durin' that war."

"Very well, you are dismissed," Judge Craig said.

"Yeah, well, I would thank you, but the

truth is, I don't think you had no business tryin' me in the first place," Kelly said. "Now how 'bout gettin' these chains offen my ankles?"

"I have dismissed the jury, sir, not you!" the judge said. "I will decide the case."

"Your Honor, you have no legal authority to decide this case. My client is entitled to a jury of his peers," Gilmore said.

"This trial has already begun, and the jurors have been dismissed," Judge Craig said. "In the interest of expediency, I will decide this case. As a matter of fact, I have already made the decision. Roy Kelley, I find you guilty as charged. Now, you stand there, while I administer the sentence."

"Do your damndest, you pig-faced, four-eyed —," Kelly said angrily before Gilmore interrupted.

"Kelly," Gilmore hissed.

Judge Craig cleared his throat.

"Roy Kelly, you have been tried before me, and you have been found guilty of the crime of riding with the butcher Bloody Bill Anderson, and aiding and abetting in the atrocities of murder, arson, and robbery that he visited upon innocent people," Judge Craig said. "Before this court passes sentence, have you anything to say?"

Kelly started to speak again, and Gilmore

pulled him aside. After a hasty consultation, Kelly spoke.

"All I got to say is that I was a soldier doing my duty."

"Did that duty include the burning and sacking the town of Lawrence, Kansas?" Judge Craig asked.

Kelly didn't answer.

"My father was murdered that day. And you, you miserable, damn Confederate *soldier,* whether you personally did it or not, were there when it happened."

"Your Honor, I beg that you decide this case on the law, and not on your personal feelings," Gilmore said. "Remember, you have no direct evidence that Mr. Kelly actually killed anyone, that day or any other day during the war."

"Roy Kelly, it is the sentence of this court that you be taken from this courthouse to the prison at Huntsville, there to serve a term of no less than twenty years," Craig said.

"No!" some in the court shouted. "You can't put him in prison, you damn Yankee! He ain't guilty of nothin' but bein' a soldier!"

"Constable!" the judge said. "Arrest the man who just made that outburst and hold him in contempt of court!"

The constable stood and looked out over the gallery. "Arrest which man, Judge?" the constable asked. "I didn't see who it was."

To a man, every person in the courtroom at that moment was quiet.

"Who was it?" the judge asked. "Who made that outburst?"

There was no response to his inquiry.

Craig glared at the gallery for a long moment, then brought his gavel down with a loud bang. "Court is adjourned." He and the bailiff hurried out the back door, leaving the courtroom under the control of the county sheriff.

"Damn, Tom, you ain't actually goin' to take this man off to prison, are you?" someone called.

"The judge has made the decision. I don't have any choice," the sheriff replied.

"Mr. Kelly, I will appeal," Gilmore said.

"What good will that do?" Kelly replied.

"I will appeal," Gilmore said again.

"Come, Kelly. Don't give me any trouble now," the sheriff said.

"You got my wrists and ankles cuffed. Just what the hell trouble can I give you?"

Chapter Seven

Austin, Texas

Even as Roy Kelly was being transported to prison in Huntsville, Duff MacCallister was in Austin, the nearest railhead to Merrill Town and the Slash Bell Ranch. It had taken six days to make the trip from Chugwater, which was one day longer than the original estimate because of the full day they had been forced to lay over in Pierce, Colorado.

They were shunted to a sidetrack so the cattle cars could be off-loaded. Duff arranged for a pen to hold the cattle until he was ready to move them out to Slash Bell Ranch.

A young man wearing a weathered Stetson, a cotton shirt, and denim trousers stuck down into well-worn boots came up to Duff shortly after the cattle were transferred from the train to the holding pens.

"Would one of you gents be Duff MacCallister?"

"Aye, that would be me."

"I'm Tim O'Leary, Mr. MacCallister, ridin' for the Slash Bell brand. Mr. Bellefontaine sent me into town to meet you 'n lead you on down to Merrill Town. It's only about two miles from the ranch. We'll keep the cattle there tonight, then take 'em on out to the ranch tomorrow."

"Wish you had caught me earlier. 'Twould have saved me the time and expense o' renting the pens."

"The pens won't cost you nothin'," O'Leary said. "I'll talk to Mr. Chambers. If there's any charges, he'll send the bill to Mr. Bellefontaine. He does business with Mr. Chambers all the time."

"Well then, I've nae complaint, do I?" Duff replied. "How far is it out to the ranch?"

"It's ten miles from here to Merrill Town, then two miles from there on to the ranch."

"You'll be with us for the drive?" Duff asked.

"Yes, sir, I will be."

"Then the drive bein' no longer than that, 'tis sure I am that the four of us can make the drive ourselves."

"Yes, sir. I told that self-same thing to Mr.

82

Bellefontaine," O'Leary replied.

"O'Leary? So 'tis an Irishman you be?"

"Just the name, Mr. MacCallister," O'Leary answered quickly. "It was my grandparents who first came to America. I've never even seen Ireland. So I've nothing against the Scots."

"And I've nothing against an Irishman who wasn't born there," Duff replied with a broad smile. "But 'tis a pity you've never seen Ireland, for though the entire country be loaded with black-hearted heathen, 'tis a beautiful land."

"So my grandpa used to say," O'Leary replied.

"Ten miles to Merrill Town, is it? Tell me, ye heathen Irishman, is there a holding pen there . . . for the cattle?"

O'Leary didn't reply right away, and Duff laughed. " 'Tis teasing you I am, lad. Sure 'n I mean nothing by it."

O'Leary laughed nervously, not sure yet how to take Duff. "Uh, yes, sir, there's a holdin' pen there. Mr. Bellefontaine has already made the arrangements."

"Then what do you say we get started, so we can get the cattle taken care of, then get some supper before it's too late?"

O'Leary smiled. "I'd say that's a good idea."

Duff showed O'Leary a collar big enough to encircle a cow's neck. A bell was attached to the collar. "We'll be for putting this bell on Brother Ben. He will lead the cows, 'n it'll be nae more than a nice ride for the rest of us."

"You don't say? All right. Let's bell the critter," O'Leary replied.

"Better let me do it," Elmer suggested. "Brother Ben knows me." He went into the pen, found the proper steer, hung the bell on him, then led him out.

The cattle were so relieved to be out of the close confines of the cattle cars that they were a little skittish when the drive started. Nevertheless, Duff and the others soon had them gathered and moving in an orderly procession out of town. O'Leary rode point, as he knew the way. Brother Ben, the bell clanging with every step, was at the head of the herd, and the five hundred head of cattle, including fifty heifers and five bulls, followed dutifully behind.

Duff and Elmer rode on either flank, and Wang Chow brought up the rear. With a very large herd, riding drag was the most uncomfortable and least desirable position as it was necessary to eat a lot of dust.

But with only five hundred cows, riding drag wasn't bad. Even so, Duff had offered to rotate the duty between the three of them, but Wang Chow told him that such an arrangement wouldn't be necessary.

Merrill Town

They reached the town just a little after five, then once again put the cattle into a holding pen, which, as O'Leary had promised, was pre-arranged by Jason Bellefontaine.

With that taken care of, the next move was to board their horses. O'Leary led them down to the Merrill Town Livery.

"Heckemeyer," O'Leary said. "These men brought some cattle in for Mr. Bellefontaine. Board their horses along with mine in Mr. Bellefontaine's private section."

"All right, Tim," the liveryman said.

"We'll be wanting them at first light on the morrow," Duff said. "Will that be a problem?"

"No problem at all," Heckemeyer replied. "I have a man who spends the night here, keeping watch over the horses. He'll be able to let you have your mounts no matter how early you may be."

"Thanks." Duff turned to O'Leary. "You know this town, Mr. O'Leary. Would you be so kind as to lead us to an establishment where we might partake of drink and something to eat?"

85

"Yes, sir, I can do that. The best place in town would be a saloon called the CSS *Alabama* Saloon."

"Mr. O'Leary, as you have seen, one of my men is Chinese. I've nae wish to be wanting to enter a place where Mr. Wang would nae be welcome."

"Don't worry. Ken Prescott is a good man," O'Leary replied. "There'll be no problem with your friend."

The false front of the saloon featured a painting of a brigantine-rigged sailing ship, with the name CSS *Alabama* painted just after her bow.

"Look at that," Elmer said, pointing to the painting. "That's the finest warship ever to go to sea."

"You mean there really was a ship called the *Alabama*?" O'Leary asked.

"Of course there was. What do you think that is?" Elmer said, pointing to the picture.

"I just always thought it was somethin' that Prescott was makin' up," O'Leary said.

"With that name, I take it the *Alabama* was a ship for your South," Duff said to Elmer. Duff had not arrived in America until after the Civil War had ended, but the war was often enough on the tongue of many of his friends that he was well aware of the conflict between the states. And his

86

closest confidant, Elmer Gleason, had fought with the South.

"Yes. 'N I'll tell you the truth. Iffen I had know'd about the *Alabama* at the time, I most likely woulda gone to sea rather than riding with Raiders, Bushwhackers, or Ghost Riders."

Duff chuckled. "Did all the Southern units have such picturesque names?"

"Ha! What do you have to talk about? Weren't you with something called the Black Watch?"

"Aye, the Royal Highlanders, and 'tis no finer a military regiment ever formed, as we were never defeated," Duff said.

"Yes, well, the Ghost Riders was never defeated, neither," Elmer said. "The South may have been, but we wasn't. As it turns out, I was a better sailor than I was a soldier anyhow," Elmer said.

Elmer's allusion to being a good sailor was not without some justification. Before he came to work with Duff, he had sailed the Pacific on the great clipper ships.

When the four men stepped into the saloon, they heard the sound of piano music coming from the back of the room. The piano player, Duff noticed, was a cut above the average piano player.

O'Leary led them up to the bar, then

called out to the bartender, who was standing at the opposite end of the bar talking with one of the customers. "Prescott, you've got four thirsty men here."

"O'Leary, what are you doing in town?" Prescott asked. "Don't normally see you until the weekend. Did you quit working for Mr. Bellefontaine?"

"No, I come in town to meet these men. They've brought some cattle down from Wyoming for the Slash Bell."

"Texas cows aren't good enough for Bellefontaine?"

"This is a special breed of cow," O'Leary said. "You going to serve us or are you going to just stand around here and yap all day?" The question was asked in jest, the words ameliorated by O'Leary's smile.

Prescott returned the smile. "Yes, gentlemen, what can I do for you?" Seeing Wang, he got a surprised look on his face.

Duff was glad to see, though, that it was one of surprise, rather than belligerence. "That depends on whether or not you can serve all of us. For if it be a problem for you to serve my Chinese friend as easily as you serve us, we'll be on our way."

The bartender nodded. "I've no problem with serving the Celestials as long as they've the money to pay for it. Anyway, where else would you go? It's more 'n likely I'm the only one that would serve him, except Ma Ling's Chinese Restaurant."

"Good," Duff said. "In that case I'll have a Scotch, and though I'll be for letting my friends order for themselves, 'tis I who'll be paying for it. And I'll be paying for Mr. O'Leary as well."

"What is that accent, mister?"

"Why 'tis nae an accent m' lad, but 'tis music to the ear of the Scotsman."

"From Scotland, are you?"

"Oh Lord, don't get him started," Elmer said. "For if you do, like as not he'll haul out his pipes 'n give you a tune."

Prescott laughed. "And what'll you have?"

Elmer ordered bourbon, Wang ordered wine, and O'Leary ordered a beer.

As the bartender turned away to get the drinks, Duff happened to see an iron bar attached to the wall alongside the mirror. "Elmer, I'll be thinkin' that you've seen one of those before."

As Prescott noticed Duff and Elmer's interest in the iron bar, he commented, "I'll bet you don't know what that is." He set the drinks before them.

"If I were guessing, I would say that 'tis a Flinders bar," Duff said.

"That's what it is, all right," Elmer said.

"That's what you use to orient a ship's compass."

"By damn, the two of you do know," the bartender said with a big smile. "I take it you gentlemen have both been to sea, for it would take a sailor man to know what that is."

"Aye, we've both been to sea," Duff said. "What is it doing here, if I may ask? It seems to me that we are a long way from the sea."

"That we are, friend, that we are. And you're right, it is a Flinders bar, but it isn't just *any* Flinders bar. It's the Flinders bar off the greatest fighting ship ever to sail the seas. I grabbed it off the CSS *Alabama* just before I abandoned ship. I knew it was going down, 'n I wanted a souvenir."

"So you sailed on the *Alabama,* did you? I understand the name of the saloon now."

"I more than just sailed on her. I was her helmsman. Do you know anything about the *Alabama*?" Prescott asked.

"I've heard of her. She was some sort of a raider, wasn't she?"

"She was much more than a mere raider. The *Alabama* captured or burned sixty-five Union merchant ships and took more than two thousand prisoners before we run into the *Kearsarge.* We woulda sunk the *Kearsarge,* too, but for the fact that a hundred-pound shell we lodged in her rudder post didn't explode."

" 'Tis good to see that you survived," Duff said.

"Yes, but I'm sorry to say that nineteen of my shipmates died that day."

"To your lost shipmates," Duff said, lifting his glass.

The others, including Wang, lifted their glasses with him.

Duff had put a dollar bill on the counter to pay for the drinks, and the bartender pushed it back to him.

"No, my friend, for your sentiments, your first drinks are on the house."

"My thanks to you, and 'tis a foine man you be." Duff tossed the drink down, then ordered another. Ordinarily, one drink would be his limit, but since the bartender had bought the first drink it seemed only right that he buy another.

"Tell me, Mr. Prescott, you got 'ny grub in this place?" Elmer asked.

"I sure do," Prescott replied. "How would fried potatoes, eggs, and biscuits suit you?"

"Sounds like somethin' my old mama woulda cooked for me," Elmer replied. "If she had been sober long enough to cook it," he added with a chuckle.

"Mr. Wang, if you would like, I can send

someone down to Ma Ling's for a Chinese dinner for you. I've done such a thing before."

Wang, who most of the time kept his expressions neutral, allowed a smile to spread across his face. He put his hands together, prayer like, and dipped his head slightly. "One thousand thanks."

"You're welcome," Prescott said. "I know a few Celestials, and I've always known them to be good people."

Seeing the headline RIDER WITH BILL ANDERSON SENT TO PRISON at the top of one of the stories, Elmer picked up the newspaper and began to read. "I'll be damned. Roy Kelly's done got hisself throwed in jail."

"I beg your pardon?" Duff said.

Elmer thumped the newspaper. "Roy Kelly. He's a feller I rode with some back in the war. Says here they sent him to prison just for ridin' with Anderson. Hell, maybe I better not say nothin' 'bout who I rode with, seein' as lots of times me 'n Kelly was ridin' side by side."

CHAPTER EIGHT

Over at the Hog Pen Saloon, Pete Jaco and Clem Dawkins were having a beer at a table in the back. It had been chosen so they could have a private conversation, but they needn't have worried. The noise level was such — discordant notes coming from the out-of-tune piano, loud guffawing of the men, and the high-pitched cackles of the women — that they could have been talking anywhere in the saloon without the likelihood of being overheard.

"I seen 'em comin' in 'n I heard somebody say they was five hunnert of 'em," Jaco said. "Black Angus they was, too, 'n them is some of the most expensive cows they is. I say we snatch 'em up."

"From the pens?"

"No, not from the pens. We'd never get away with it if we tried takin' 'em from the pen. I'm talkin' 'bout after they leave town, while they're out on the trail," Jaco said.

"Where is it do you think they're a-goin'?" Dawkins asked.

"Well, I seen O'Leary lookin' 'em over, 'n bein' as he rides for the Slash Bell, I reckon that's where they'll be a-goin'."

"How many men are there?"

"Well, with O'Leary, there'll be four of 'em, but seein' as one of 'em is a Chinaman, I reckon that's near 'bout the same thing as there bein' only three of 'em."

Dawkins frowned. "Still, we'd be outnumbered if we hit 'em with just the two of us. Besides which, even if we was to take 'em all out, there ain't no way we could move five hunnert cows all by ourselves."

"I expect Rexwell, Moss, and the Weeper would more 'n likely ride with us if we ask 'em. That'd give us five men 'n we'd outnumber them, even if you did count the Chinaman."

"What are we goin' to do with these cows even if we do get 'em?"

Jaco explained. "If we was to take all five hunnert of 'em, there ain't no doubt in my mind but what we could sell ever' one of 'em for thirty dollars apiece. That'd be fifteen thousand dollars."

"Woowee, I didn't know there was that much money in the whole world. You're good at cipherin'. What would that come out to for five of us?"

"That'd be three thousand dollars apiece," Jaco said. "You have to admit, that's pretty good money."

"Yeah, it is good money, if we could sell them."

"What do you mean, *if* we could sell them?"

Dawkins sighed. "When you are talking about that much money, you have to find someone who is stout enough to make the purchase, and yet don't have no problem with buying stoled cows. So, who do you think we could get to buy 'em?"

"I expect we could sell 'em to Dirk Kendrick. I hear tell he's buildin' hisself up a herd."

"You think Kendrick's got that much money?"

Jaco nodded. "I figure he has a lot more than that. And he's smart enough to know that he could take the cows to market 'n get near twice what he'd be payin' us for 'em."

"All right. It all sounds good to me." Dawkins rubbed his hands together in anticipation. Now, how do we go about it?"

"They ain't plannin' on movin' the cows till mornin'," Jaco said. "I say we go out there tonight and wait on 'em. We'll hit 'em tomorrow mornin', just before they cross

Cypress Creek."

"The Dunn Hotel would be a good place for us to spend the night," O'Leary said. "I don't know if they would let Mr. Wang stay there or not, but Ma Ling, who runs the Chinese restaurant, also has a boardin' house for Celestials out behind her restaurant. Mr. Bellefontaine will pay for it."

"That will be acceptable to me," Wang said.

"Are you sure, Wang?"

Wang laughed. "It will be good to see someone who does not have round eyes."

Duff laughed as well. "Aye, 'tis understandin' I am, for 'twould be good for me to hear the Scottish brogue spoken. Very well, Wang, go and spend some time with the heathens."

Half an hour later, Duff was standing in his hotel room, looking out onto the street below. It was a busy night in Merrill Town, with a full cacophony of sound floating in through the open window. From the Hog Pen and *Alabama* saloons, Duff could hear the two pianos competing with each other, the out-of-key piano winning the battle. The voices of scores of animated conversations spilled out through the open windows and

doors of the town's buildings and somewhere someone was singing. He heard a
gunshot, but knew, instinctively, that it
wasn't a shot fired in anger. The shot was
followed by a woman's high-pitched scream,
then a man's deep-voiced laughter.

Duff extinguished the lamp, then lay in
bed with his hands folded behind his head,
staring up into the darkness. It was at such
times that he sometimes thought about the
events in his life that had brought him to
the American West. He had been a soldier
in North Africa, and a landowner in Scotland, where he had every intention of marrying his sweetheart and settling down to
raise his bairn to follow him someday.

But his sweetheart was murdered before
the wedding, and it was his revenge of her
death that had brought him to this place
and this time. In America, he had started a
new life, and had made friends like Elmer
Gleason and Wang Chow, men whose loyalty
was without question.

Back in Chugwater he had a woman
friend, Megan Parker. She was more than a
friend. She was also a business partner.
Truth to tell, she was even more than that.
Not since Skye McGregor had Duff felt
about any woman as he felt about Megan.
And if he could get Skye out of his heart, it

would be Megan he would be marrying.

He wrestled with those thoughts. He didn't know if he was being unfair to Skye for having such feelings about Megan or if he was being unfair to Megan for holding on to such feelings for Skye. Finally, the thoughts settled, and he drifted off to sleep.

About two miles west of Merrill Town
Jaco, Dawkins, Rexwell, Moss, and the Weeper passed a bottle around a campfire.

"You know what we ought to do," Jaco said. "What we ought to do is join up with them Fence Busters."

"Why?" Dawkins asked. "Once we get our hands on these cows 'n sell 'em, we'll have more money than we'd make by ridin' with Dirk Kendrick."

"Yeah, but this is just one time. After this money is gone, what'll we do next? With the Fence Busters there's always money to be made. And there ain't no law that can touch 'em, neither."

"What do you mean the law can't touch 'em?" Moss asked. "Are you sayin' what they're a-doin' ain't against the law? You done said that Kendrick would be willin' to buy stoled cows. It's agin' the law to buy 'em if they was stole, same as if you had stole 'em yourself."

"Well, yeah, it's against the law to buy property that someone else has stoled. But the reason I say there ain't no law than can touch 'em, is on account of they's at least thirty of 'em, or maybe more. 'N Kendrick's got 'em organized like an army, so there ain't no sheriff that can go up ag'in 'em, 'n there ain't no posse that wants to run into 'em, either. Yes, sir, joinin' up with the Fence Busters is just exactly what we need to do."

"Yeah, but Kendrick won't take just anyone," Moss said.

"Oh, he'll take us," Jaco said. "After we pull this deal off, he'll take us. Especially if we trade these cattle to him for takin' us in."

"Trade the cattle?" Dawkins said. "What are you talkin' about? Jaco, you ain't sayin' give 'im the cattle for nothin', are you?"

"No. But I figure we could use the cattle to bargain. You know, sell 'em to 'im for a little less, in return for takin' us into his group."

"How much less?"

"Say, fifteen dollars a head. We'd still wind up with fifteen hunnert dollars apiece."

"That ain't the three thousand dollars you said," Dawkins complained.

"No, it ain't. But let me ask you this.

When's the last time you had fifteen hunnert dollars all at one time?" Jaco asked.

"I ain't never had that much money."

"Then think about it. More money 'n you ever had in your life, plus a way of makin' a lot more money."

"Yeah," Dawkins said. "Yeah, you're right. All right. You want to bargain to get us in, go ahead. I'm with you."

"Now you're bein' smart about it."

"What time you reckon someone'll get here?" Dawkins asked Jaco.

"I figure sometime 'round mid-mornin' tomorrow."

"How you plan to do it?" Moss asked.

"There's only four of 'em. We'll just wait until they get into rifle range, then we'll each one take a rider and shoot 'em," Jaco said. "Once all four of 'em are down, taking the cattle will be a piece of cake."

Merrill Town

"Well, Sky," Duff said to his horse the next morning, "sure 'n I bet you had a better night last night, than you did all those nights you were on the train."

Sky whinnied and shook his head as if he understood and was answering.

"But we'll be goin' for a wee bit of a walk now, so you'll be able to get all those kinks worked out."

When Sky and the other three horses were saddled, the four men rode from the stable to the holding pens where the cattle had spent the night. The bell was still hanging around Brother Ben's neck, and Elmer rode into the pen, found the big steer, and led him out. The others followed.

Fifteen minutes later, the small herd and Duff, Elmer, Wang, and O'Leary were riding down Bratton Road through the middle of town, the passage of the cattle being watched by dozens of onlookers on either side of the street. As the cattle were following behind Brother Ben, it was more of an orderly procession than it was a cattle drive. The dulcet clang of Brother Ben's bell echoed back from the buildings that lined both sides of the street.

"Hey, O'Leary! What's that bell that's a hangin' around that steer's neck? Is it a dinner bell?" someone shouted.

The remark got a few laughs.

"Only for them's that can afford it, Carl. I reckon you'll just have to keep eatin' bacon." O'Leary's response got even more laughs.

The cattle streamed on through town, then started toward the Slash Bell outfit.

After they were out of town, the cattle fell into a steady three-mile-per-hour walk, which meant they should reach the Slash Bell Ranch sometime around noon.

There was something about sitting in a saddle with the warm sun streaming down and the familiar smell of cattle filling his nostrils that Duff found comforting. He let his horse match the pace of the moving herd. Sky had moved cattle so many times Duff had no doubt that even if he wasn't in the saddle, his horse would be able to keep the herd moving.

Cypress Creek

Jaco, Dawkins, Moss, Rexwell, and the Weeper were waiting at the creek. They could hear the approaching herd before they could see it — a clanging bell, the lowing of the cattle, the shuffle of hooves, and an occasional whistle. They waited until the advancing cattle came into view, moving across the prairie like a low-lying, black cloud.

"Look there," Jaco said. "It's just like I said. They's only four of 'em."

"How are we goin' to do it?"

"As soon as the first ones of the men actual gets into the water, we'll commence to shootin'. That'll more 'n likely spook the cows, and the first thing those riders will do is try 'n stop 'em. While they're worryin'

102

about the cows, we'll be pickin' 'em off. Soon as we get all four of 'em kilt, we'll gather up the cattle."

"By that time, the cows will be stampedin', won't they?" Moss asked.

"They might turn 'n start runnin', but I don't know as I'd call it a stampede. All we have to do is catch up with them, then turn them back in on themselves, get them to runnin' in a circle 'til they get tired. After that, they'll be easy enough to handle."

"Somehow, I don't see this as easy as you do," Moss said.

"You want the money, don't you?"

"Well, yeah, I want the money."

"Then you just do what I tell you to do 'n you'll have fifteen hunnert dollars in your hand by nightfall."

"Hey, Moss," the Weeper said. "What you goin' to do with all that money?"

"I'm goin' to Austin, 'n I'm goin' to get me the best-lookin' saloon gal in the whole town."

"Ha! That would more 'n likely take up ever' cent you'd have," the Weeper replied.

"Quiet," Jaco said. "They're gettin' closer."

Wang rode up beside Duff.

"What is it, Wang?" Duff asked.

"I think there are men ahead," Wang said.

"What kind of men?"

"They are not men we wish to meet," Wang said. "I think they are trouble."

Duff and Wang rode to the front of the herd to share Wang's warning with O'Leary.

Elmer, seeing the three men congregate, rode up to join them. "What's up?"

"Wang says there are men waiting for us ahead," Duff said.

"How could Wang know? He was riding in the back." O'Leary stood in his stirrups and looked ahead. "I'm the one that's been up front and I don't see anyone."

"If Wang says there are men up ahead of us, you better believe there is someone there waitin' for us," Elmer said.

O'Leary gave in. "All right. Let's say Wang is right. What do we do?"

"Wang, you hold the cattle here. Elmer, would you be for coming with me now?"

"Ha. You just try 'n hold me back."

"Mr. O'Leary, I'm inviting you as well, but if you've nae wish to join us, I'll nae hold it against you."

"It'll be my pleasure to ride with you."

While Wang, who was carrying neither pistol nor rifle, kept the cattle behind, Duff, Elmer, and O'Leary went ahead.

"See anything?" Duff asked.

"No, but I can feel it," Elmer replied.

CHAPTER NINE

"What is it they's a-doin'?" Weeper asked. "How come the cattle's stopped back there?"

"What are them three comin' up like that for? You think maybe they know we're here?" the Weeper asked.

"There ain't nobody been dumb enough to stick their head up so's they can be seen, has there?" Jaco asked.

"There ain't no way they coulda saw none of us. Maybe they're checkin' to see if they can ford the creek here," Dawkins suggested.

"Well, hell. They know they can ford here. Maybe them others don't, but O'Leary knows. He's brought cows this way enough times before," Jaco pointed out.

"What if they get up here and see we're a-waitin' on 'em?" Moss raised the rifle to his shoulder. "I say let's kill 'em now."

"No, wait. They're out of range," Jaco

cautioned, but even as he was giving the warning, Moss fired his rifle.

They heard the sound of rifle fire and saw the bullet kick up dirt in front of them, but because of Wang's warning, neither Duff nor Elmer were really all that surprised.

"O'Leary, you go up that side!" Duff shouted, pointing to the left edge of the trail. "Elmer, you take the right!"

The three men split up, then started advancing toward the rustlers, with Duff moving up the center.

Dawkins, Jaco, and the others were caught off guard. They had been sure that, with the benefit of surprise, they would have the superior situation. But the surprise was lost, and while they were locked into the position they had chosen for themselves, which was without cover and only minimum concealment, the three men advancing toward them had the advantage of maneuverability.

"Shoot them!" Dawkins shouted. "Shoot them!"

For the next sixty seconds the sound of gunfire echoed back from a nearby ridge and frightened birds flew from the trees. A cloud of noxious gun smoke rose formed over the area.

Moss and the Weeper went down under the deadly accurate gunfire. What had started out a five-to-three advantage very quickly became a two-to-three disadvantage.

"Let's get out of here!" Jaco shouted as he ran toward his horse.

"What about Moss 'n the others?" Dawkins shouted.

"Leave 'em!" Jaco replied. "I expect they're dead, 'n even if they ain't, there's nothin' we can do about it."

Duff saw the two remaining men ride off and gave a fleeting thought to going after them. He dismissed the thought almost as quickly as it was born, however, because he knew he couldn't leave the herd.

He, Elmer, and O'Leary rode on up to where the bodies of three men lay on the ground and dismounted.

Duff ascertained, rather quickly, that all three were dead. "Do you know any of these men?" he asked O'Leary as they stood over the three downed men.

"That's Walt Moss," O'Leary said, pointing to one of the men. "He used to ride for the J Bar J, till Mr. Jenkins fired him. He never was worth a damn. If he hadn't got hisself kilt here, he woulda more 'n like wound up gettin' shot tryin' to hold up a mercantile or somethin'." He pointed to a second man. " 'N that's a fella ever'one calls the Weeper. I don't have no idea what his real name is. Last I heard of him, he was in prison. I can't tell you who this other feller is, on account of I ain't never seen 'im before. Leastwise, not that I recollect."

"What are we goin' to do with the bodies?" Elmer asked.

"I'd say leave 'em here for the time being," O'Leary suggested. "I'll tell Mr. Bellefontaine about 'em, 'n he'll more 'n likely send a wagon here to pick 'em up 'n carry 'em on back to town."

"Sounds like a solution to me," Duff said. "Let's get the cattle moving again and hope we aren't visited by any more rustlers before we get there."

"We're more 'n half way there now," O'Leary said. "I can't think of another place where any rustlers could set up an ambush for us. I'm damned ashamed I didn't think about it before, this place bein' 'bout the only place between Merrill Town and the ranch where such a thing could even be planned."

The three men rode back to rejoin the herd, and within five minutes they were under way again.

By the time they reached the ranch the sun was high overhead, a brilliant white orb fixed in the bright blue sky in such a position as to take away all the spots of shade where the cattle would normally congregate. With the shade denied them, the cows had all moved down to mill about in and along the banks of Wahite Creek, the stream of water that made the Slash Bell a ranch instead of a stretch of barren desert. Some of the cows had come to water, while others were there just to be nearer the band of green grass that followed the stream on its zigzagging path across the otherwise brown floor of the valley.

They were met by a group of riders.

"Hello, Sam," O'Leary said when the riders were close enough to speak. "Mr. Mac-Callister, this is Sam Post. He's the foreman."

"Mr. Post," Duff said with a nod.

"Mr. Bellefontaine said you should ride on up to the house," Post said. "Me 'n the boys will take the beeves on in."

"That's very nice of you," Duff said.

"O'Leary, you can go, too. You can show 'em the way."

O'Leary nodded, then making a motion toward Duff and the others, led the three

110

men on up to the house.

The large, two-story house was painted white with a green tile roof. There were cupolas, dormer windows, and a covered porch that went all across the front.

A gray-haired man came out to greet them.

"Hello, Mr. Bellefontaine," O'Leary said as they dismounted.

"Hello, Tim. Which of these gentlemen would be Mr. MacCallister?"

"That would be him," Elmer said, pointing to Wang Chow.

Bellefontaine's eyes widened, and Duff laughed.

"I'm afraid my friend is having a bit o' fun with you, Mr. Bellefontaine. I'm Duff MacCallister. The jokester is Elmer Gleason, and this is Wang Chow."

Bellefontaine laughed as well and extended his hand, first to Duff, and then to the other two. "How was your trip down?"

"We was set on by rustlers back at Cypress Creek," O'Leary said.

"Fence Busters?"

"No, sir, I don't think so. I think it was just rustlers. Walt Moss was one of 'em, 'n the Weeper was another 'n. Them two and one other of the rustlers got themselves kilt. I think they may have been two other 'n,

111

but they got away afore I could see 'em close enough to see if I knowed either of 'em."

"What about the cattle?"

"We didn't lose nary a one of 'em," O'Leary said proudly.

"And you're sure it wasn't the Fence Busters?"

"I'm not a hunnert percent sure, but I don't think it was them," O'Leary said. "I mean, as far as I know, neither Moss nor the Weeper was part of the Fence Busters. 'N none of 'em was wearin' a blue kerchief."

Bellefontaine nodded. "Then you're right. More 'n likely they weren't Fence Busters. The bodies are still there, are they?"

"Yes, sir, we left 'em there."

"All right. I'll have Sam send two men and a wagon back to pick up the bodies and take them on into town."

"Yes, sir, I figured you would. I'll tell Sam." O'Leary turned to Duff. "Mr. Mac-Callister, it was sure nice meetin' you boys."

Duff nodded as O'Leary left to attend to his task, then turned back to Bellefontaine. "Who or what are the Fence Busters?"

"There is a company in New York called the New York and Texas Land Company," Bellefontaine said. "They are making a lot of money by claiming and selling land that they say is public. More 'n likely the land *is* public, but a lot of ranchers are running their cattle on public land . . . something we've been doing from the time Texas belonged to Mexico. And, by a mutual understanding, we have been fencing off areas of public land so that our herds don't get mixed together.

"But now the New York and Texas Land Company has hired armed men to cut those fences. They call themselves Fence Busters."

"I can see how they come by their name," Duff said.

"It would be bad enough if all they did was cut fences. But I'm convinced they are also stealing cattle."

"You mean like those men tried today?"

"No, that's why I would have been surprised if the men you ran into today had been Fence Busters. Most of the cattle they steal come from those public land areas where they cut the fence. And of course, with the fences cut, the cattle tend to wander off, so there's no real way of proving that they're actually stealing the cattle."

"Have any of the cattle that wandered off ever returned or been found?" Duff asked.

"No. 'N that's why I'm sure that they've been stolen. Somewhere, I'm sure, the

Fence Busters have a ranch full of stolen cattle. Either that, or they are in cahoots with a rancher who is holding the stolen cattle for them."

"Has there been no effort to deal with these men?" Duff asked.

"Nothin' we can really point to. A couple cattlemen hired some gunmen to go against the Fence Busters for cutting fences, but it didn't work out."

"Let me guess. The Fence Busters furnished the gunmen themselves, didn't they?" Duff said.

"Well, yes. At least, that's what I think, though I don't believe I've been able to get a lot of people to agree with me. How did you know that?"

"It just seems like a natural thing," Duff replied. "This way they are making money from both sides of the issue. They are getting paid to cut fences, they are stealing cattle, and they are getting paid to furnish their own opposition."

"That's it exactly," Bellefontaine said. "I've told some of the other ranchers what is happening, but they are so insistent that something must be done to stop it that they don't believe me."

"Obviously there is a law against cattle rustling," Duff said. "Is there a law against

114

cutting the fences?"

"No, and that's what's giving them their cover. It's legal to cut fences on public land, even if there are cattle there. But they're also cuttin' fences on private land owned by the cattlemen, and that is illegal. So far they've been getting away with it. We've tried to get Governor Ireland to make it a felony even to cut fences on public land, but we haven't succeeded, and I'm not sure it would make that much difference even if the law was passed."

"Why do you say that?"

"Because the truth is, the Fence Busters are too many, too strong, and too well organized for any law. That means they can pretty much get away with doing anything they want, and there's very little that we can do about it. I think that's the reason John Ireland isn't trying to get the law through. He thinks it would just be a waste of time."

"John Ireland?" Elmer said. "That wouldn't be Colonel Ireland, would it?"

"Colonel Ireland? Yes, I believe he was a colonel in the Confederacy. Why do you ask?"

"If it's the same Colonel John Ireland I'm thinkin' about, I know him," Elmer said. "We was good friends, once."

115

"You were a good friend of the governor?" Bellefontaine asked.

"Well, he warn't the governor when I know'd him."

"I'm . . . impressed," Bellefontaine said.

Duff chuckled. "Mr. Bellefontaine, I've been around Elmer Gleason for some time now. His experiences never cease to amaze me."

Bellefontaine held an outdoor barbeque that evening, with long tables set up to accommodate all the cowboys on his ranch.

"I'm running thirty-five thousand head of cattle, mostly Longhorns," he said to Duff. "But I recently bought five hundred head of Herefords, and now the Black Angus. I intend to eventually get rid of all my Longhorns and start a herd of Herefords or Angus. I just haven't made up my mind yet which it will be. That's why I want to compare the two breeds."

"I'll admit to being a wee prejudiced," Duff said. "But 'tis sure I am that you'll be for settling on the Angus."

"It could be," Bellefontaine agreed. "I hate to see the Longhorn go, though. They are the hardiest animal you can imagine. They practically take care of themselves. But their beef doesn't begin to compare with Here-

116

ford or Angus. And beef is what we raise cows for."

"If you have thirty-five thousand head of cattle, your ranch must be what? Seventy thousand acres?" Duff asked.

"It's about a hundred thousand acres, though forty thousand of it is fenced public land."

"Aye, you told me about using public land. And 'tis fenced, you say?"

"Yes. We all do it, and it's not a problem as long as we keep the water open. That is, it wasn't a problem until the Fence Busters began cutting the fences."

"And rustlin' cows," Post added. "More 'n likely it's several thousand head with a dozen or more different brands."

"Speaking of branding, if you would like, Elmer, Wang and I will stay here for a week or so to help you with the branding of the Angus," Duff said. "It's nae like it is when they are calves. 'Tis full grown they are, and it'll take some doing."

"Are they already carrying your brand?" Bellefontaine asked.

"Aye."

"There'll be no need to blot out your brand. When we go into town for me to draw the draft for payment, we'll have a paper drawn up for you to sign, saying that you've transferred the cattle to Slash Bell, and that they'll be wearing two brands."

"How soon do you want to start on the branding?" Duff asked.

"I'd say tomorrow, if that's all right with you."

"Aye, then tomorrow it will be. 'Tis thinkin' I am, that we can get a hundred a day. We'll be done within a week."

CHAPTER TEN

Blowout

Ethan Quinn, a tall, slender man, was clean shaven, but he wore his blond hair hanging to his shoulders. He also wore a turquoise-studded silver band around a low-crowned black hat. He had arrived in Blowout two weeks earlier, but his reputation had preceded him. He was a gunfighter who had sold his gun to some of the warring factions in New Mexico. When Quinn learned about the Fence Busters, he decided that joining them would be an easier way of earning a living with his gun than his current status as a freelancer.

Quinn very much wanted to join the Fence Busters, but he didn't want to ask, he wanted to be asked. So far, the invitation had not been forthcoming. As he stood at the bar of the Pair of Kings Saloon, he decided that he needed to do something to get Kendrick's attention. Even as he was thinking about it, the opportunity presented itself when two young cowboys stepped into the saloon.

In their early twenties, both were wearing guns, and they were talking and laughing a little louder than usual, as if purposely calling attention to themselves.

"Barkeep," the taller of the two said as he put a dime on the bar. "How about putting a beer up here for me 'n my friend?"

"All right." The bartender picked up two empty mugs and stepped back to the beer barrel.

"Do you know who we are?" the talkative one asked.

"No, I can't say that I do," the bartender replied as he drew two mugs of beer and set them before the customers.

"Well, you'll hear of us soon enough, because" — the cowboy turned to his partner — "what is it that Gypsy woman said?"

"Destiny awaits us."

"Yeah, that's what she said, all right. Destiny awaits us. Someday you'll be able to say that you served beers to Titus Ford and Jake Adams, the very first day we come to Blowout."

"I'm sure I will," the bartender replied with a smile.

One of the bar girls approached the two young men and greeted them with an inviting smile. "Welcome to Blowout, fellas."

"Well now, ain't you a purty thing, though?" Titus said. "What's your name?"

"My name is Glitter."

"Glitter? Your mama named you Glitter?" Jake asked.

"Don't you like my name?"

"Yeah, I think it's a real nice name. I'll just bet you'd like for one of us to buy you a drink, wouldn't you?"

"Oh, that would be very nice," she replied.

"Tell you what, Glitter. Why don't you go get another girl for my friend here? You do that, 'n we'll pick us out a table and just drink 'n have a fine time together."

"I'll be glad to," Glitter said. "Now, don't you two handsome fellas go away while I'm gone."

"We ain't a-goin' nowhere," Titus said. "Not with a purty thing like you around. I can promise you that."

"Hey, Titus. Did you see how that feller near 'bout peed in his pants when I told 'im I was goin' to throw down on 'im?" Jake asked after Glitter left to find another girl to join them.

"What do you mean, near 'bout?" Titus replied. "I swear I seen the front of his pants

121

get wet. They warn't no near 'bout to it. Hell, he did let loose in his pants."

Both young men laughed.

From his end of the bar, Quinn had been watching and listening to the two loud young men. "Now, that wasn't very nice of you two boys," he said, speaking for the first time.

The two glanced at him for just a second, then turned their attention back to each other.

"What are you tellin' me? Are you tellin' me that feller really did pee in his pants?" Jake asked.

"If I'm lyin', I'm dyin'," Titus replied.

"Funny you would say somethin' like that," Quinn said. "Seein' as both you boys will prob'ly be dyin' just real soon."

Titus turned back toward Quinn with an angry expression on his face. "Mister, I don't know who the hell you are 'n I don't really care, but if I was you, I'd not be pokin' my nose into other people's business."

"Oh, but you ain't me," Quinn replied. "And I think you should apologize for makin' that poor man make water in his pants."

"What? Are you crazy? You don't even know the man."

Quinn's smile was little more than a sardonic smear across his face. "Oh, I don't have to know someone in order to know what's right. I'd say the way you two were treatin' the man you're a-talkin' about tells me you don't have no regard for your fellow man. Now, I'm goin' to have to ask the two of you again to apologize for what you done. But this is the last time I'm goin' to ask."

"Apologize?" Titus replied. "Apologize for what? In the first place, the feller we're talkin' about ain't nowhere aroun', so how 'n the hell are we supposed to apologize to him? Even if we was goin' to, which we ain't. In the second place, even if he was aroun', you can believe I wouldn't be doin' no apologizin' to 'im."

"Oh, you don't have to apologize to *him*. You have to apologize to *me*."

"What? Now, that don't make no sense at all. Why the hell should we apologize to you?"

"Because just listenin' to how you made that poor man suffer has upset me somethin' terrible. Now, I'll be takin' that apology from you."

"The hell you say. You'll play the devil gettin' an apology from either one of us."

"Then, like I said, you two are goin' to have to die."

"Mister, what's wrong with you? This here ain't none of your affair. 'N maybe you ain't noticed it, but they's two of us, 'n they's only one of you. You're takin' a bigger bite than you can chew, 'cause we're both pretty good with our guns."

"Are you now?"

"Yeah, we are. Now back off before it's too late," Jake said.

"What if I don't want to back off?"

"Bartender," Jake said. "I want you as the witness. You've heard me 'n Titus try 'n be nice to this feller. So if it comes down to us havin' to kill 'im, we'll be wantin' you to tell the sheriff we was pushed into it."

"Well now, boys, you see, that's a problem." The bartender shook his head. "We ain't got no sheriff nor town marshal, neither. We sorta make our own law, if you understand what I mean. So you 'n Mr. Quinn are goin' to have to work this out between you."

"Quinn?" Titus questioned. He turned back toward the man who had been harassing them. "Your name is Quinn?"

"That's right."

The confident smile on Titus's face faded. "Would that be, uh, Ethan Quinn?"

"You've heard of me, I see."

"Uh, Mr. Quinn, listen, there ain't no

need in this a-goin' no further," Titus said. "Me 'n Jake was just funnin' is all. 'N you're right, we didn't have no call in embarrassin' that feller like we done. So I reckon I will be apologizin' for what we done."

"What the hell are you doin'?" Jake asked. "Don't be apologizin' to anybody."

"Jake, that's Ethan Quinn. Don't you know who Ethan Quinn is?"

"No."

"Well I do, and believe me, we don't want to be a-messin' none with the likes of Ethan Quinn."

Jake nodded, then turned toward Quinn. "All right, Quinn, maybe we was gettin' a little out of line here. My friend's right. This don't need to go no further. Why don't you let us buy you a drink 'n we'll forget any words that was said."

"Sure," Quinn replied easily. "As soon as the two of you bow to me, and confess to ever'one in here that you are cowards."

"What?" Jake said. "Hell no, we ain't goin' to do that."

"Well, boys, if you don't do that, you're both goin' to die."

"Draw!" Jake shouted, reaching for his pistol even as he shouted the challenge.

Jake's reaction took Titus by surprise, but not Quinn. He had survived many gunfights by being able to anticipate what the other person was about to do, and a split second before Jake shouted his challenge, Quinn's hand was already dipping toward his gun. He had it out in lightning speed. Jake managed to get his pistol out of his holster, but when he shot, it was the final reflexive action before he died, and the bullet went into the floor. Although Titus went for his own gun, he wasn't even able to clear leather before the second shot from Quinn's gun punched through his heart.

Glitter and the girl with her screamed.

Quinn held the smoking pistol for a moment as he looked down at the bodies of the two men he had just killed. Both had left unfinished drinks on the bar.

"Weasel," Quinn said, addressing the bartender.

"Yeah?"

"No sense in lettin' their drinks go to waste. Bring 'em down here."

Weasel picked the two drinks up, and handed them to Quinn, who drank them one after the other.

"You . . . you killed them!" Glitter said.

"What's the matter, girly? You upset because you didn't get the drink they promised?" Quinn asked. "Don't worry about it. You come on up here, and I'll buy you a drink. I'll buy both of you a drink."

"No!" Glitter said. "Why would I want to drink with you?"

"Because I told you to," Quinn said, his voice low and menacing.

"Go on, Glitter," the other girl said. "I don't think he'll hurt you."

With fear and loathing, Glitter moved hesitantly to the bar.

Although the Fence Busters had a place on the Blanco River, many of them spent a lot of time in Blowout, and Kendrick kept a room in the Del Rey Hotel, where he often spent the night. He was in town and having dinner at the Rustic Rock Restaurant when Peabody came over to his table.

"Just thought you'd like to know that there was a killin' down at the Pair of Kings," Peabody said.

"The man killed. Was he one of ours?"

"No, it was a couple cowboys that was just comin' through. They said their names was Titus Ford and Jake Adams, but there warn't nobody that had heard of 'em. Quinn, he's the one that kilt 'em."

"Was the killing justified?"

"What do you mean?"

"Was Quinn defending himself? Did the two men draw on him?"

"Well, yeah, they did, sort of."

"What do you mean, sort of? Did they or did they not draw on him?"

"Yeah, they did. But to be honest now, Quinn, well, he kinda prodded 'em in to it. He just kept a-pokin' at 'em, if you know what I mean, 'n the next thing you know, why the two men draw'd on 'im, 'n he shot 'em both down. Quinn's fast with a gun, 'bout the fastest I ever seen."

"So I have heard," Kendrick said as he cut off a piece of steak.

"It might be good to have someone like Quinn in the Fence Busters."

"Are you saying that if you were in charge, you would ask him to become a member?" Kendrick asked.

"Well, yeah, I would."

"Then it is a good thing you aren't in charge," Kendrick replied. "Quinn strikes me as a person who is infused with a degree of self-importance. If I ask him to join us, he would always think, because he had been asked, that he would have the superior position. I'll not give him that opportunity."

"Yeah, maybe you're right," Peabody agreed. "I was just thinkin' when you run across somebody like Quinn, well, it's better to have 'im on your side, than to have 'im ag'in you."

"We will have him on our side," Kendrick said. "But only on our terms. And that means when *he* asks."

Kendrick wasn't a Texan, and unlike the others in the Fence Busters, he wasn't even a Westerner, having arrived no more than two years earlier. He was originally from New York, and from time to time he would look at his surroundings, and recall his past.

Behind Dirk Kendrick, a train roared by on the elevated railroad over Sixth Avenue, between 42nd and 43rd Streets in Manhattan.

He looked at Paddy O'Malley, his "enforcer." "Are you ready, Mr. O'Malley?"

"Yeah," O'Malley replied, pulling from his pocket specially made brass knuckles. They were different from most brass knuckles because a spike protruded between the middle and index fingers.

Kendrick pushed open the door to the bakery, and the little announcement bell attached to the door jingled. The owner, Gavriel Cohen, looked up to greet his customer with a smile. The smile left his face when he saw who it was.

"Hello, Mr. Cohen," Kendrick said.

"You!" Cohen said, pointing at him. "Coming here will do you no good. I have told you that I am not interested in your insurance. Not one penny will you get from me!"

"But Mr. Cohen, wouldn't you like to know that you, your store, and your family will be safe from anyone who wishes to do you harm?" Kendrick asked.

"Harm? The only harm will come from you and the thugs and crooks with you. You call yourselves a legal service and insurance agency, but are no such thing! You are all hoodlums."

"Why, Mr. Cohen, I greatly resent your implication," Kendrick said. "This is strictly a business proposition. I'm sure you are aware that I am a member of the bar and a practicing attorney. If you would sign up for our program, that would also entitle you to my legal services, should they be required."

"Bah! The only bar you are a member of is Tony's Bar down the street! You are the biggest gangster of them all. If it is bread or a bagel you wish to buy, you have come to the right place. But if it is to sell me your insurance, I tell you now to leave my bakery."

"Is that your last word on the subject?" Kendrick asked, his voice agonizingly calm.

"Yes, it is absolutely my last word."

"I'm sorry to hear you say that." Kendrick nodded at O'Malley, who, with one quick thrust, poked the spike into Cohen's eye. The baker cried out and covered his socket with his hand as blood spilled through his fingers.

"We control all of Manhattan," Kendrick said. "When I come back, you will buy the insurance or you will lose your other eye."

Sarah Cohen, who had been in the back of the bakery, came out front when she heard Gavriel cry out. When she saw blood running from her husband's eye, she began to scream.

CHAPTER ELEVEN

Since Blowout was without city government of any kind, people looked to Kendrick to act as mayor and sheriff. Acting in that capacity, as soon as he finished his lunch, he strolled down Stoddard Street to the Pair of Kings, where he saw two young men lying on the wooden porch in front of the saloon. He looked down at them for just a moment. There was a single bullet hole in each and flies were buzzing around the wounds.

He stepped inside.

"Hello, Mr. Kendrick," the bartender said.

"Hello, Weasel," Kendrick replied, addressing the bartender by the only name he had ever heard used. "I hear you had a little excitement down here."

"Yeah, I'm sure you seen them two boys lyin' out front," Weasel replied. "They got into an argument with Mr. Quinn."

Kendrick saw Quinn standing at the far

end of the counter with a smug expression on his face and his arm around Glitter. Her expression could only be described as one of perturbation.

"You killed them, did you, Quinn?" Kendrick asked.

"Yeah, I killed them."

"Glitter, find someplace else to be," Kendrick said with a nod of his head. "Mr. Quinn and I are in a discussion, and you're just in the way."

"Yes, sir!" Glitter replied, thankful that she was being ordered away.

"Not much for us to discuss," Quinn said with a confident smile. "Ask Weasel what happened, and he'll tell you that both of 'em went for their guns first."

"Oh, I believe it," Kendrick said.

The smile on Quinn's face grew broader. "Then me 'n you don't really have nothin' to talk about, do we? Unless, maybe, you're wantin' to ask me if I would be interested in somethin'."

"No, nothing," Kendrick replied. "As I'm sure you know, I am the de facto law in town and —"

"The fac what?"

"The de facto law," Kendrick repeated. "That means that I am the law."

"Yeah, well, why didn't you say so?"

"I was pretty sure you already knew that. Anyway, as the de facto law, anytime a citizen of this town is killed, it is my job to see that justice is served."

"Yeah, well, there you go, Kendrick," Quinn replied. "Them two draw'd on me, 'n I kilt 'em. That seems like justice enough to me."

"Are you saying you had no choice?"

"Yeah, that's what I'm sayin'. Leastwise, once the two started to draw their guns. Then there warn't nothin' I could do but draw back ag'in 'em."

"You are a loose cannon on deck, Quinn."

"A loose cannon? What does that mean?" Quinn asked, clearly not familiar with the term.

"It means that people like you quite frequently wind up in deep trouble. And the problem with that is, when you get into trouble, you more often than not get the people around you in trouble, as well. So do me a favor, will you? Try and stay out of trouble as long as you are here in my town."

"Yeah," Quinn replied, the expression on his face one of obvious disappointment over not being invited to join the Fence Busters. "Yeah," he repeated. "I'll just do that."

Kendrick nodded and left the saloon. For the rest of the day, he acted just as a real sheriff or mayor would. He "made the rounds," calling upon the merchants of the town, telling them that even though the town was without any official capacity, they could count on him, and they should report any shoplifting or outright robberies to him. He would find the thieves and administer whatever punishment fit the crime.

What he didn't say, but what everyone knew, was that if the perpetrator was a member of the Fence Busters, they would get off with a verbal reprimand unless their transgression was a particularly egregious one, and then, only if the offense affected Kendrick in some way.

Later, he and Peabody took their supper at Rosita's Cocina, after which, they each took a harlot to a crib behind the restaurant.

When Kendrick opened his eyes the next morning he knew he wasn't in his own hotel room and, for a moment, wondered where he was. Then he was aware of two things; one, he was in a crib behind Rosalita's, and two, he had a raging need to urinate. The prostitute was still asleep beside him. She had the bedcover askew, exposing one rather large, heavily blue-veined breast and one leg dangled over the edge of the bed. She was snoring loudly and a bit of spittle drooled from her vibrating lips. She didn't wake up when Kendrick crawled over her to get out of bed.

Outside, an outhouse stood twenty feet behind the little adobe crib, but he disdained its use, going against the wall of the crib instead.

"Peabody," he called through the wall as he relieved himself. "Peabody, are you still in there?"

A moment later, he heard a sound, then Peabody appeared in the doorway wearing his boots, hat, and long johns. He stepped up beside Kendrick and like him, began peeing on the wall.

"I want you to round up three good men." Kendrick shook himself, then put it away. "New men, I don't want anyone from the Fence Busters."

"Why not?"

"Let's just say that I'm recruiting new members. I'm goin' over to the saloon to have breakfast. Bring 'em there."

"Do you want Quinn as one of the men?"

"No, I most definitely do not want Quinn."

"Yeah, I remember. Where 'm I s'posed to get these men?"

"That's your problem." Kendrick looked back at the bed. The harlot had thrown all the covers off and was sprawled naked on the bed. Her mouth was open, she was snoring with each intake of breath, and her bottom lip was flapping like a reed as she exhaled.

"Damn," Kendrick said. "I can't believe I was blind enough to choose her last night."

Peabody chuckled. "You should see the one I got stuck with. Compared to her, this one is a real beauty."

Kendrick laughed as well, then the two men walked away as urine dribbled down the wall and formed a pool on the ground behind them.

In the Pair of Kings, Kendrick sopped up the yellow of a runny egg with a biscuit. He washed it down with a drink of coffee, then rolled and lit a cigarette as Peabody came over to his table, leading three men.

"Here they are, Kendrick. I got us three good men, just like you said."

Kendrick looked at the three, then he frowned.

"I said get good men. That one appears to be a Mexican."

The Mexican had obsidian eyes, a dark, brooding face, and a black mustache that curved down around either side of his mouth. He was wearing an oversized sombrero and registered no expression in response to Kendrick's disparaging remark.

"José *is* a good man," Peabody said.

"How do you know?"

"Before I joined up with the Fence Busters, me 'n him done a couple jobs together." Peabody chuckled. "Besides, you slept with his sister last night."

"I did?" Kendrick studied the Mexican. "Well, I have to tell you, José, the fact that I was with your sister last night doesn't say that much for you. She wasn't that good."

"I wouldn't know, Señor. I've never slept with her," José said, his face still expressionless.

Kendrick laughed out loud. "You're all right. You can come along." He looked at the other two men. "Who are these men?"

"I'm Pete Jaco, Mr. Kendrick," one of the men said.

"I'm Clem Dawkins."

"You two men know me?"

"Yes, sir, we know you," Jaco said. "Fact is, we come here to Blowout just hopin' we'd be able to join up with you."

Kendrick smiled. "Did you now?"

"Yes, sir."

"Why?"

"I beg your pardon?"

"Why do you want to join up with me?"

138

Kendrick repeated.

The two men looked at each other for a moment, then Jaco answered. "We figured we could make more money with the Fence Busters than we could on our own."

Again, Kendrick laughed. "All right. That's good enough. Peabody?"

"Yeah, boss?"

"Go round up five of our own men," Kendrick said.

"Mr. Kendrick," Jaco said after Peabody left. "What do you plan to do?"

"What do you mean, what do I plan to do?"

"The reason I asked is, when Peabody asked us if we'd like to come along, he said you was plannin' on a job. I was just wonderin' what job you was plannin' on doin'."

"Why? Are you saying that if it doesn't meet with your approval, that you won't come along?"

"No, sir, I ain't sayin' that at all. It's just that, if you ain't got nothin' particular in mind, me 'n Dawkins might have us a suggestion for you."

"Do you? And what suggestion would that be?"

"The Slash Bell."

Kendrick frowned. "The Slash Bell? That's Bellefontaine's outfit, isn't it?"

"Yeah, it is."

"Well, as it so happens, we have just recently paid Mr. Bellefontaine a visit, and I don't like to return to the scene of any previous operation without a pressing reason to do so."

"Yes, sir, but what did you get? Long-horns?"

"Herefords."

"Herefords is good, but Black Angus is even better. Me 'n Dawkins happen to know that the Slash Bell just got five hunnert new Angus from some outfit up north," Jaco said.

"Oh? And how did you come by that information?"

Jaco started to say that he had tried to rustle the herd, but he decided that since he'd failed, it would only hurt his chances, so he said nothing about the unsuccessful attempt. "I was at the railroad depot when they brought the cows in and loaded them into the pens."

"Are they still at the pens?"

"No, sir. By now, they done all been took out to Bellefontaine's spread."

"Angus, huh?"

"Yes, sir, Black Angus, all purebred quality stock. I'll bet you ain't got none o' them yet."

140

"As a matter of fact, I haven't. All right, Jaco," Kendrick agreed, with a nod of his head. "Perhaps we shall revisit Mr. Bellefontaine, seeing as he made such a generous contribution to us the last time." He laughed at his own joke. "That is, if I can ascertain that the information you have given me is correct."

Kendrick put out the word he needed to know whether or not Jaco was telling the truth about the transfer of cattle.

One of his riders approached him in the saloon a half hour later. "Yes, Bellefontaine did just get five hundred head of Angus." Dooley said.

"How do you know that for a fact?"

"I was in Merrill Town, 'n I heard Heckemeyer talkin' about it. He kept 'em in his pen overnight. They were brung to him by a feller named MacCallister."

"MacCallister?" Jaco asked, reacting quickly to the name. "Would that be Duff MacCallister?"

"I don't know. I never heard his first name mentioned," Dooley said. "All I know is he brung the cows down from Wyoming. Oh, 'n he's a —"

"Scotsman," Jaco said, completing Dooley's sentence.

"Yes. At least that's what Heckemeyer said."

"I'll be damned," Jaco said.

"Jaco, do you know this man, MacCallister?" Kendrick asked.

"Yeah. Well, no. That is, I ain't never seen 'im. But I know who he is."

"How is it that you know?"

"I've just heard of 'im, is all," Jaco said. "I sure didn't have no idea that he was down here, though."

"Well, you heard Dooley. He's down here to deliver some cattle." Kendrick smiled. "Our cattle, as it will turn out."

Peabody had rounded up the men who would be making the raid, and they were all mounted and gathered in the street in front of the Pair of Kings. He walked into the saloon. "We're all ready to go, Boss."

Kendrick nodded, then followed Peabody back outside.

"I wonder what they're fixin' to do," Glitter said to her closest friend Penny. They were sitting at a table against the far wall.

Because so many of the Fence Busters were about to ride out, no one was left in the saloon. Quinn wasn't a member of the Fence Busters, but fortunately, he wasn't there, either.

"Probably goin' out to cut some more fence." Penny was also the girl Glitter had summoned to drink with her and the two young cowboys Quinn had killed.

"Do you think they do anything more than just cut fence?" Glitter asked.

"What do you mean?"

"I've heard stories," Glitter said. "Some people say that they don't just cut fences, but they also rustle cattle."

"Shhh," Penny said, laying her finger across her lips. "Don't talk like that, Glitter. Don't even think like that. I don't want to get Kendrick mad at me, and I don't think you want him mad at you, either."

"No, I don't."

"Whatever it is that they do, let them do it, 'n let's stay out of it."

"I agree."

"Glitter, do you ever think about leaving?"

"You mean, leaving Blowout?"

"Yes. That, and leaving the line. Do you ever think about it?"

"Yes, but I'm afraid. I don't know where I would go or what I would do." Glitter smiled. "I didn't exactly choose this life, my mama chose it. She brought me up in the business. I was only sixteen when she got kilt by a drunken cowboy, 'n because I didn't have any other way of makin' a livin', well, I came on the line."

"But you don't really have to. You've got Mr. Tadlock."

Glitter smiled. "Yes, I do."

"What do you see in that old man, anyway?"

"He is very nice to me."

"But he's an old man."

"You can be old and still be nice."

Penny shuddered. "It's just that I can't see climbing into bed with an old man like Tadlock. I don't think Weasel likes it, that you go out to visit him so often. I think Weasel is jealous."

Glitter smiled. "Maybe it's good for Weasel to be jealous."

"If Weasel asked you to marry him, would you?" Penny asked.

"What makes you think Weasel would ever ask me?"

Penny ignored the question and asked another. "But if he did, would you marry him?"

"He's not ever goin' to ask, so there's no need for me to answer that question."

Penny laughed. "I think he would like to. And I think you would say yes, if he does."

"You think so, do you?"

"Yes, I do."

"Well, you just keep thinking that." Glitter

looked over at the grandfather clock that stood against the wall near the piano. "Heavens, I need to go. I promised Mr. Tadlock I would visit him today."

Ed Tadlock was seventy-eight years old and looked his age. His hair was snow-white, and he had a bushy, snow-white beard. He liked to tell people that he had earned every white hair and every wrinkle during his long and often hard life. He had been with Sam Houston at San Jacinto, with Winfield Scott at Veracruz, and with John B. Hood at Franklin.

He smiled a greeting as Glitter drove up in the buckboard. "Hi, darlin'. I got a chicken in the pot. Thought I would make us some dumplin's."

"That sounds good, Mr. Tadlock," Glitter said.

"Your change of clothes is laid out inside."

Glitter nodded, then went inside to change from the revealing dress that was the apparel of her trade into a much more modest dress that she kept there for her visits. What nobody in town knew was that her visits to Tadlock were not of a sexual nature, nor had they ever been.

Tadlock paid her for her visits because, as he'd said, "I just appreciate the company of a nice young lady, and if she is also pretty, that's even better."

Over time, Glitter had come to look forward to the visits as much as Tadlock. He always prepared a meal for her, then they would sit on the porch or on the bank of the river, and he would tell her stories of his past.

It was the closest thing to a family she had ever experienced.

CHAPTER TWELVE

Slash Bell Ranch

Mid-morning the day after the last of the Angus had been branded, Duff, Elmer, and Wang were ready to go into town, where Bellefontaine would write a bank draft to pay for the cattle and Duff would sign the bill of sale, transferring ownership. They had just saddled their horses when Sam Post came riding in at a gallop.

"Sam, what is it?" Bellefontaine asked.

"Fence Busters, Mr. Bellefontaine! They're cuttin' the fences out at the field where we put the Black Angus!"

"Damn! Who have we got out there?"

"Nobody right now. Most all our men are up north."

"Gather up who you can!" Bellefontaine said. "I'm goin' out there!" He started off at a gallop.

Without giving it a second thought, Duff, Elmer, and Wang followed.

They hadn't gone far when they heard gunfire ahead of them. As they swept over a hill they saw several riders wearing blue kerchiefs herding off the cattle.

Duff saw one of the shooters chasing after a heifer trying to escape. He snaked his rifle and lifted it to his shoulder.

"He's too far away," Bellefontaine shouted. "You'll never get him from here."

Duff squeezed the trigger. A finger of fire spurted from the muzzle as the rifle roared, and the man pursuing the fleeing heifer was knocked from his saddle.

Another Fence Buster popped up nearby, and Wang started after him.

"Where's he going?" Bellefontaine shouted. "Wang isn't armed! He'll get killed!"

"He'll be all right," Duff replied as he put the rifle away and started after the remaining riders.

The exchange of gunfire between the rustlers and Duff, Elmer, and Bellefontaine left two more rustlers dead. Five of the remaining outlaws gave up trying to herd the cattle and started shooting into the cattle. Some of the herd went down under the fire before the outlaws managed to get away.

While Wang chased the only Fence Buster

rider left, Duff and the others went in pursuit of the fleeing cattle.

The outlaw was twisted around in his saddle, firing at Wang. When he saw that Wang wasn't returning fire, he stopped and turned to face his pursuer. "Damn, you ain't even got no gun, have you?" With an evil smile he lifted the pistol and took aim. "Good-bye, Chinaman."

Wang lifted his arm from his side and whipped it down over his head. A small object whirled forth from his throw. Before the Fence Buster rider even realized he was in danger, one of the three blades of the throwing star stabbed into him, penetrating his heart.

He died with a look of surprise on his face.

Running at a full gallop, Bellefontaine, Duff, and Elmer managed to get to the head of the running herd and skillfully turned them. Under the supervision of the riders, the cattle soon tired of running and were brought under control. Less than half an hour after it had all started, the remaining cattle were pushed back through the cut wire and into the pen.

"Sam, get Tim and some of the boys out here to repair that fence," Bellefontaine said.

"Yes, sir," Post replied.

The brief battle had left six of the Angus

lying dead out on the open plain. In addition to the dead cattle, four of the would-be rustlers were also dead.

"What I don't understand is why they shot the cattle," Duff said when they returned to the house.

"They steal cattle when they can," Bellefontaine said. "And when they can't steal them, they kill them."

"Why would they kill them?"

"They'll do anything they can to disrupt the cattlemen," Bellefontaine said. "The more of us they can drive out of business, the more public land they can get their hands on."

"Can't the governor do anything about it?" Duff asked.

"I don't know. He's aware of the problem, but the Fence Busters claim the only thing they are doing is cutting fences on public land. We're the ones that's on shaky ground here," Bellefontaine replied. "Remember, this isn't our land we are fencing; it is public land. If anyone is violating the law, it might be us."

"Aye, but the blaggards we were just chasing did more than cut a fence. 'Twas cattle they were stealing. And as you've not yet paid me, 'twas my cattle."

"The cattle rustling is just an aside for

them," Bellefontaine said. "The New York and Texas Land Company is a legitimate organization, chartered in New York and in Texas. It would almost be political suicide for the governor to go up against them."

"I just wonder if this here governor is the same John Ireland I used to know," Elmer said.

"Would you like to find out?" Duff asked.

"What do you mean?"

"Austin is the capital of Texas, and it's not very far from here. Why don't we see if the governor would be for receiving us?"

"Oh, the governor is a very busy man," Bellefontaine said. "I don't think anyone could get in to see him without an appointment. And that would take several days, if not weeks."

"If it is the same feller I know, he'll see me," Elmer said.

"You're sure of that, Elmer?"

"Damn right I'm sure. If it is the Colonel Ireland that I know, he will see me. And we won't have to wait no several days or weeks, neither."

"Then I suggest that we go see him at the soonest."

"Before you go to Austin, might I suggest that we call a meeting of the cattlemen's association and discuss this?" Bellefontaine

151

asked. "If you do get in to see the governor, and you've got the backing of the association, it might help your position."

"Good idea," Duff said. "All right. Call your meeting."

Blowout

Kendrick had gone to the Slash Bell Ranch with nine other men. He returned to Blowout with five men and no cattle. Tying up in front of Pair of Kings, he went into the saloon, pushing aside a customer who was just coming out. "Weasel! Bring a bottle!"

He went straight to "his" table at the back of the saloon, expecting the others to follow.

He grabbed a chair and turned to them. "Who the hell were those men with Bellefontaine?" he asked angrily. "They aren't his riders, are they?" He sat down, nodding to the others to do the same.

"I ain't never seen any of 'em a-fore," Beans said as he and the others grabbed chairs and sat around Kendrick's table.

"MacCallister was one of 'em," Dooley said. "He's the feller that brung them Angus cows down from Wyoming. They was three of 'em actually, but MacCallister was the only name I heard. Don't know who the other two was."

"Elmer Gleason was one, and the Chinaman's name is Wang," Jaco said.

"How is it that you know the names of the other two?" Kendrick asked suspiciously.

"I've heard of 'em. MacCallister is sort of a —" Jaco stopped in mid-sentence.

"Sort of a what?" Kendrick asked.

"He's some sort of a hero, or so people say. He was in the British Army 'n he won some medals fightin' overseas. And he was the one that broke up the Kingdom Come Gang right here in Texas, some time back."

"The Kingdom Come Gang? I've never heard of 'em."

"That's 'cause you ain't from here," Jaco said. "But they was somethin' while they was operatin'. Only MacCallister 'n Gleason 'n the Chinaman broke up the gang, 'n MacCallister is the one that kilt the head of the gang."

Kendrick frowned. "How do you know all of that?"

"Because the head of that gang was A. M. Jaco."

"Jaco?"

"Yeah. He was my brother."

Kendrick leaned back. "Is that a fact? So you've run across MacCallister before, have you?"

Jaco thought about the aborted attempt

153

he and Dawkins had made to steal the Angus cattle before they even got to the Slash Bell, but decided against telling it. "I ain't never run acrosst him a-fore this mornin'. I wasn't a part of my brother's gang. Iffen I had been, I'd more 'n likely be dead now, since ever'one that was in his gang was kilt."

"This MacCallister . . . how good is he?"

"He's the one that shot Dewey Hensen out of his saddle. And that shot had to come from at least four hunnert yards away."

"Interesting," Kendrick said. "Since he's already delivered his cows, I doubt that he will stay here."

"If he does, I want to be the one to kill 'im," Jaco said.

"That's a pretty tall order, isn't it? You just told me how good he is. Are you sure this is a task you wish to undertake?"

"I didn't say nothin' 'bout goin' up ag'in 'im. I said I wanted to kill 'im. A.M. ain't the only one o' my brothers he kilt. He also kilt my brother Deke."

"Deke Jaco was also in this Kingdom Come Gang?"

"Nah, and his name warn't Jaco. It was Pollard, Deekus Pollard. We had the same ma, but not the same pa. Deke tried to kill MacCallister before he left Wyoming. I got a telegram from one o' Deke's friends, tel-

154

lin' me about it. So now, I got me two reasons I want to kill 'im."

"You do seem to be well motivated toward seeking Mr. MacCallister's demise. If, perchance, he does remain in the area, our operation would benefit greatly from the gentleman's untimely death. Therefore, I shall assign you the task of taking care of MacCallister, if you truly think you are capable."

"I'm capable, all right," Jaco replied.

"And, apparently, motivated," Kendrick added. "That is a good thing, for sufficient motivation will often compensate for diminished capability."

"He is an evil man," Glitter said to Tadlock that afternoon. She was speaking of Kendrick. "He is real educated, and when I first met him, I thought he was nice. I mean, he does have nice manners."

"Some of the most evil men you can imagine had good manners," Tadlock replied. "They say that Santa Anna had good manners, but look what a damn dictator he was. Excuse the language."

Glitter laughed. "Mr. Tadlock, you don't have to apologize for swearing. My word, you should hear the language the men use in the Pair of Kings. Why, sometimes, it positively makes your ears burn."

"You don't have to stay there, darlin'."

"Sure I do. Where else would I go? Consider what I do, Mr. Tadlock. I know I never done nothing with you, but if I left Pair of Kings, all I could do is the same thing, just in some other saloon. And what if I didn't find someone else as nice as Weasel?"

"Does Weasel know how you feel about him?"

"No, and you dasn't ever tell him," Glitter said.

"Now, darlin', I haven't been in a saloon of any kind in more 'n twenty years. When would I tell 'im?"

"I guess you're right. If you don't ever go there, you won't be able to tell him."

"You're wrong about not havin' anyplace to go, though," Tadlock said.

Glitter frowned. "What do you mean?"

"You could always come here 'n live with me."

"Ha. Don't think there haven't been times when I've thought of that very thing."

Merrill Town

The arrival of Duff, Elmer, Wang, Bellefontaine, and Post generated a lot of attention. The reason for the interest was the four bodies in the wagon driven by Post. They

156

headed straight for the sheriff's office, their progress followed by several citizens of the town.

Deputy Seth Bullock stepped out of the sheriff's office, put his hand on the post that was supporting the porch roof, then spit a stream of tobacco juice into the watering trough. "What you got there?"

"It seems fairly obvious, doesn't it?" Bellefontaine asked. "We have four bodies."

"Who kilt 'em?"

"We did."

"What did you kill 'em for?"

"We killed them because they were rustling my cattle," Bellefontaine replied.

"But there warn't really none of your cows that got stoled, was they? So, that means they ain't really rustlers, don't it?"

Bellefontaine's eyes narrowed. "How do you know they didn't get away with any? We just got here. Who, besides us, could have told you?"

Bullock flinched at Bellefontaine's words, then he took another chew of tobacco as he tried to formulate the answer. "Didn't nobody tell me. I just sort of figured that."

"Well, you figured right. They didn't get away with any of my cattle."

"If they didn't get away with any of your cows, then you didn't actual have no right in shootin' 'em. You know what I think?"

"I'd love to hear what you think, Bullock," Bellefontaine said. "In fact, I'm surprised that you think at all."

Bullock pointed to the four bodies. "All four o' them boys is wearin' blue kerchiefs. I think they're Fence Busters."

"You think they are Fence Busters, do you?"

"Yeah, that's what I think."

"Maybe you aren't as dumb as I thought you were. Yes, it is obvious they are Fence Busters."

"You know what else I'm thinkin'? I'm thinkin' they warn't stealin' your cows a-tall. I'm a-thinkin' they was just cuttin' fence on public land, 'n you shot 'em for that. 'N that would be murder, seein' as there ain't no law agin' cuttin' fence on public land."

"Where is Sheriff Wallace?"

"He ain't here," Bullock said.

"Well, you tell him that I'll be leaving these bodies at Ponder's Mortuary."

Bullock squirted out another stream of tobacco, then he looked over at Wang as if noticing him for the first time. "Who's the Chinaman?"

"He's my priest," Duff said, speaking for the first time.

"A priest? I ain't never heard of no Chinaman priest."

"Give him a blessing, Father Wang," Duff said.

"I don't want no blessin' from no damn Chinaman." Bullock turned and walked back into the office.

Duff and the others laughed.

"Who's going to pay for burying them?" Ponder asked when he came from his office to look at the bodies.

"Give them the cheapest burial you can," Bellefontaine said. "I expect the county will pay for them. If they don't, I will."

"They're Fence Busters, aren't they?"

"Yes."

"I don't want any trouble with the Fence Busters," Ponder said.

Bellefontaine frowned. "How are you going to have any trouble with them, just by burying some of their men?"

"I guess you're right. All right. I'll bury them. You wouldn't happen to know any of them, would you?"

"No."

"Then, if you don't mind, after I get them ready, I'll stand them up in front of my place for a few hours. Maybe someone will recognize them. I like to know who it is I bury, just in case some of them have relatives that want to know what happened to them."

The rancher nodded. "That's probably a pretty good idea."

CHAPTER THIRTEEN

Bellefontaine, Sam Post, Duff, Elmer, and Wang stepped into the Texas Hill Country Cattleman's Association office next door to the CSS *Alabama* Saloon.

They were greeted by Jack Porter, who had been hired by the association to manage the business and run the office. "Jason, what brings you here? We aren't scheduled to have another meeting for a week, yet."

"I want you to call a special meeting," Bellefontaine said.

"What for?"

"The Slash Bell was hit by the Fence Busters this morning."

Porter frowned. "Cutting your fences?"

"Yes, but it wasn't just a fence-cutting raid. They also tried to rustle cattle, some of the new Black Angus I just acquired."

"The Black Angus you've been telling us all about? That's too bad; I know how you've been looking forward to getting them. How many did they get away with, do you know?"

"They didn't get away with any cattle," Bellefontaine said. "As a matter of fact, we killed four of them."

Porter's eyes grew wide. "You killed four Fence Busters?"

"Yes. They're down at Ponder's Mortuary right now."

"Damn, that's never happened before. That could be trouble."

"It's not just 'could be.' It *is* trouble. And it has been trouble for some time now. That's why I want you to call a meeting of the association. We need to talk about this."

"Jason, we've talked about the problem with the Fence Busters before, and we've never gotten anywhere with it. What makes you think we could accomplish anything now?"

"Like you said, we've never killed any of them before. I think this is going to come to a head soon. I want to go talk to the governor, but when I go, I want the association behind me."

"We've tried to get the governor to act before, but he won't even meet with us. What makes you think he'll talk to you now?"

Bellefontaine looked over at Elmer, inviting him to talk.

"Me 'n John was good friends oncet. I'm pretty sure I can at least get him to talk to us."

"You?" Porter examined Elmer for a long moment. "Are you trying to tell us that you and the governor are friends?"

"I'm not *tryin'* to tell you nothin', sonny," Elmer said. "I *am* tellin' you that me 'n the governor is good friends. And if I go to the capital to talk to John, he *will* see me."

"All right. I'll call the meeting. It'll probably be one o'clock this afternoon before I can get everyone gathered, though."

"We'll spend some time in town until then," Bellefontaine said.

Leaving the Cattlemen's Association, Elmer, Wang, and Post stepped next door to the CSS *Alabama* Saloon. Duff and Bellefontaine went on to the bank.

"I believe the agreed-upon price was twenty-two thousand, five hundred dollars," Bellefontaine said.

"That was for five hundred head," Duff said. "There are only four hundred ninety-four head now. That will be two hundred seventy dollars less."

"That's no fault of yours, Mr. MacCallister. You delivered five hundred head as agreed. I'll pay the entire amount."

163

Duff smiled and nodded. "Aye, 'n 'tis a good man you be."

"Very good," the banker said. "Will you be wanting cash or a draft for the money, Mr. MacCallister?"

"I would like twenty-five hundred dollars in cash 'n could you be for doing a wire transfer to the Bank of Chugwater in Chugwater, Wyoming for the remainder?" Duff replied.

"Yes, sir, we would be glad to do that for you." The banker counted out the cash, handed it to Duff, and took care of the wire transfer.

Duff signed a notarized bill of sale for the cattle, annotating that the cows bore two brands.

With the business in the bank taken care of, Duff and Bellefontaine started back toward the Alabama Saloon, passing by the undertaker's on the way. As he said he would, Ponder had the four bodies in pine coffins, standing up in front of his place of business. A hand-lettered sign was pinned to the wall above the row of coffins.

DO YOU KNOW THESE MEN?

In another part of the town, three of the men who had ridden with the Fence Busters during their aborted attempt at rustling cattle from the Slash Bell Ranch had come into Merrill Town and were drinking at the Hog Pen Saloon.

"Did you see what they got standing out front down of the undertaker's shop?" one of the men asked. "They got Smitty, Hensen, Miller, 'n Perkins standin' up out front. That ain't right."

"Hell, Logan, 'stead of worryin' 'bout whether it's right or not, you should just be glad that you ain't one of 'em. I sure as hell know I'm glad I ain't one of 'em," Martell said. "Whoever expected a bunch o' cowboys to be able to shoot like that?"

"It wasn't cowboys. Leastwise, it wasn't none of Bellefontaine's cowboys, exceptin' for Sam Post. I don't know who them others was," Logan said.

"One of 'em was a Chinaman," Clay said.

"Yeah, it was the Chinaman that kilt Perkins," Martell said.

"Yeah," Clay said. " 'N I seen 'im do it, but the Chinaman didn't shoot 'im. What he done was throwed somethin' at 'im. Warn't a knife, though. I don't rightly know what it was."

"What I want to know is why they got 'em standin' up like that for, anyhow?" Logan asked.

"They're wantin' someone to identify 'em," Clay said.

"Well, they should be identified. It ain't right for 'em to be buried without nobody knows who they are," Logan said.

"You want to go down there and identify 'em, Logan?"

"Somebody ought to."

"If you identify 'em, then ever'one will know that you was with them when they tried to steal them cattle," Martell pointed out.

"Yeah, I guess you're right. All right. I won't say nothin' 'bout who they are."

The Double D Ranch

"I don't know how many more head of your cattle I can handle. Too many more, and people might get to wondering where all the cattle are coming from." The speaker was a large man with a protruding brow and chin whiskers.

"The reason I chose you in the first place is because you already have a big enough herd that ours can blend in without the increase in herd size being noticed right away. In addition to the ten thousand I already got with you, I plan to put at least another twenty thousand with you," Kendrick said.

"That would more than double the herd I have now. That's too dangerous."

"But then you would have thirty thousand head of my cows. And since you are getting five dollars a head to keep them, that's a hundred and fifty thousand dollars."

"Yeah," the rancher said, smiling broadly. "Yeah, that's right."

"Besides, once a herd is as large as yours is now, you could easily double the size without arousing too much suspicion," Kendrick added. "You don't actually expect people to come around counting how many cows you have, do you?"

The rancher laughed. "No, I don't expect anything like that."

"Then just sit back and watch the money pour in. Besides, I expect by this time next year to have the cattle sold and gone. You'll have your hundred and fifty thousand dollars, and we'll be out of your hair."

"Yes, well, there is still one problem," the rancher said.

"What problem is that?"

"There's been a special meeting called of the Hill Country Cattlemen's Association."

"Why is that a problem?" Kendrick asked.

"You know damn well they are going to talk about you. You did say that you hit Jason Bellefontaine's place, didn't you?"

167

Kendrick gave a nod. "Yeah, but we didn't get away with any of his cattle. And that's a shame because I really would like to get my hands on some Angus."

"I'm just as glad you didn't."

"Why do you say that?"

"Where would you put them?"

Kendrick smiled. "Why, I would put them with you, of course."

"You may be a smart lawyer and all, but you aren't thinking straight about this. Bellefontaine is the only rancher in the entire three-county area who has any Black Angus cattle. Not only that, he's been talkin' about it for at least three months."

"So?"

"A Black Angus cow in with my herd would stand out like a pumpkin in a turnip patch. Seeing as Bellefontaine is the only one with Black Angus, it wouldn't take much for someone to figure out how I got them."

"I see," Kendrick said. "Yes, now that you mention it, they would be difficult to hide, wouldn't they?"

"Not difficult. Impossible."

"Then we shall have to leave the Angus alone for a while. When is the association meeting?"

"Porter sent a messenger by just before

168

you got here. He said the meeting is this afternoon."

"You will tell me what transpires during the meeting."

The rancher agreed. "Yes, of course I will. By the way, the messenger also told me that four bodies were brought into town, Fence Busters who tried to rustle some of Bellefontaine's cattle."

"Yeah."

"That was a pretty expensive raid, wasn't it? Losing four men like that?"

"Yes, it was. As it turns out the man who delivered the Angus to Bellefontaine is a most dangerous adversary. I wasn't aware of him, and I paid the price for my ignorance of that fact. However, with the cattle delivered, I've no doubt but that he will return to Wyoming, and I don't expect any future encounters with him."

Merrill Town

Duff, Elmer, Wang, Prescott, Bellefontaine, and Sam Post were having lunch in the CSS *Alabama* Saloon. Prescott had sent someone down to Ma Ling's to get a carry-out meal so Wang could have lunch with his friends.

"Do you think the association will support our going to see the governor?" Duff asked.

"I can't say for sure," Bellefontaine admitted. "I think they might, but there are a couple on the board who seem to be against anything anyone suggests. To tell the truth, I wouldn't be surprised if they were hooked up with the Fence Busters in some way."

"Why would that be? Don't all the cattlemen have problems with them?"

"You would think so," Bellefontaine said. "But some seem to have less trouble than others, if you know what I mean."

"Do you have any suspicion as to who, in the association, might be connected with Kendrick?"

"I do have my suspicions, but I'd rather not say," Bellefontaine replied. "I'd rather let you watch and see if you suspect anyone, without any input from me. If you choose the same person I have, it would go a long way toward validating my suspicion."

"Aye, it would," Duff agreed.

"It's coming up on one o'clock. I think we should be a little early, just to make certain Porter calls the meeting like he promised," Bellefontaine suggested.

CHAPTER FOURTEEN

Duff and the others walked back to the office of the Texas Hill Country Cattlemen's Association. A couple surreys and a buckboard were already parked out front. Bill Lewis and Bull Blackwell were on foot, approaching the office from the opposite direction.

"Hello, Lewis, hello, Blackwell," Bellefontaine said. "Glad you men could make it to the meeting."

"What's this meeting about, Jason?" Lewis asked. "We aren't supposed to have another meeting until next month."

"I asked Porter to call a special meeting," Bellefontaine replied.

"Did you, now? Well, I hope it's important. I'm puttin' a new roof on the barn," Blackwell said.

"Hell, Bull, what do you mean you was putting a new roof on the barn? When I rode by, you wasn't doin' nothin' but watchin'," Lewis said with a chuckle.

"Well, someone has to watch, don't they?" Blackwell replied, eliciting a laugh from all.

Once inside, the members of the board took their usual seats around the long conference table. Don Webb, in his position as the association's president, sat at the head of the table. Duff, Elmer, Wang, and Post sat in chairs away from the table, lined up along the wall.

As the office had been closed up for most of the day, it was quite hot and stuffy. One of the men raised a window to let in some air, and with the air came the odor of horse droppings from the street. To most of the townspeople the street odors were as un-noticeable as the other odors of the town — the rotting garbage, the stale beer and whiskey from behind the saloons, the several dozen outhouses that reeked in the midday sun. But most of the men gathered were cattlemen, used to the wide-open spaces, and to them, the smells of civilization were overpowering.

Porter took out a handkerchief and wiped his face as the others looked at him, not only because he was the business manager of the association, but because he was the one who had called the special meeting.

"All right, Webb, you got us all here," one

of the men said. "What's this all about?"

"Gentlemen, I didn't call the meeting," Webb replied. "Well, as president, I authorized the meeting, that is true. But it was Mr. Porter who called it. Mr. Porter, I'll turn the meeting over to you."

Porter drummed his fingers on the table for a moment. "I was asked by Mr. Bellefontaine to call the meeting, so I'm going to turn it over to him." He looked at the Slash Bell owner. "You have the floor."

"What's this all about, Jason?" asked one of the other ranchers.

"I wonder if any of you happened to pass by Ponder's place on the way here?" Bellefontaine said.

"The undertaker? Yeah, I came by. Say, I saw four bodies were standing up in front of his place. Does this meeting have anything to do with that?"

"You might say so," Bellefontaine said.

"I noticed that they were all wearing blue kerchiefs. Are they Fence Busters?" Blackwell asked.

"I believe they are."

"Did you have anything to do with them being killed?" one of the other cattlemen asked.

"You might say that," Bellefontaine answered. "They were killed while they were trying to rustle some of my cattle."

"Are you sure they were tryin' to rustle cattle? Or were they just cuttin' fence?" someone asked. His chin whiskers bobbed as he spoke.

"What are you saying, Dobbins? Are you saying you don't think they were stealin' cattle?" Bellefontaine asked.

"I'm just saying this. There's no law against cuttin' fence on public land. I know that we all wish there was such a law, but there isn't. If someone would happen to catch some fence cutters in the act, and got so riled up that he shot 'em, seems to me like the easiest way to justify killin' them would be to say they were stealin' cattle."

"Shooting someone just for cutting fence, when it's legal to cut fence, would be murder," Bellefontaine said. "Are you accusing me of murder, Dobbins?"

"No, no, nothin' like that," Dobbins said quickly. "It's just I wonder if they were actually stealin' cattle, or did, perhaps, a few cows sort of wander out through the cut in the fence?"

"They were stealing cattle," Duff said, speaking for the first time since the meeting started.

"Who are you?"

"The name is Duff MacCallister."

174

"How do you know they were stealin' cattle?" Dobbins asked.

"Because I was there, and I saw them. And, since the transaction had not yet been completed, technically the cattle that were being rustled were still mine."

"The cows that were being stolen were yours? What are you talkin' about?" Dobbins asked now.

"Mr. MacCallister had only recently brought five hundred head of Black Angus down from Wyoming," Bellefontaine said. "He was at the Slash Bell when the rustlers hit us. At the time of the attack on my ranch, I had not yet paid him for the cattle. Therefore, he is correct in saying that the cattle being rustled belonged to him."

"So you killed the fence cutters?" Dobbins asked.

"Yes."

"And you have no compunctions about that?"

"None whatsoever. At the time, it seemed to be the thing to do," Duff said.

"What about these men? Were they in on the killing as well?" Dobbins pointed toward Elmer, Wang, and Sam Post along the wall.

"Dobbins, for cryin' out loud, what are you getting at here?" Lewis asked. "Are you tellin' us that if you caught these men rustlin' your cattle, you wouldn't shoot 'em?"

"Yeah," Blackwell asked. "What is the problem?"

"I'll tell you the problem. We've already had one meeting to discuss the situation with the Fence Busters. Sure, they are cutting fence line on public land, and that's aggravating to all of us, but it don't rise to the level of killing someone. Most especial' since fence cuttin' on public land isn't against the law. We're either going to have to put up with it, or we'll become outlaws ourselves. And, to kill them just because they might be cuttin' fence line, well, gentlemen, you know as well as I do that that would be murder."

"We didn't kill anyone who wasn't trying to kill us," Bellefontaine pointed out. "And despite what you think, those men standing up down there in front of Ponder's were rustling my cattle."

"So, what are you tryin' to tell us? That the Fence Busters, who have no history of cattle rustling, have suddenly decided to become rustlers?" Dobbins asked.

"Damn, Dobbins, what do you mean they have no history of cattle rustlin'? No more 'n a week or so ago they took a bunch of Herefords. You don't think they was plannin' on just borrowin' Mr. Bellefontaine's cattle, do you? Because if that is what they was doin', well, they ain't brought 'em back yet," Sam Post said, speaking up for the first time.

Some of the other cattlemen around the table laughed, and Dobbins glared at them for a moment before he turned his attention back to Sam Post. "You're one of Bellefontaine's hands, aren't you?"

"You know Sam Post, Dobbins. And you know that Mr. Post is my foreman," Bellefontaine said.

"Yes, I know who he is. Bellefontaine, please remind your . . . hired hand" — Dobbins set the words *hired hand* apart, so he could slur them — "that this is a private organization with its membership restricted to cattlemen only. And since Mr. Post isn't a cattleman, he has no business talking in here at all, unless he has been specifically invited to talk."

"Oh, for heaven's sake, Dobbins," Webb said. "He was obviously a witness to it. That makes his information valuable, and as president of this organization, I welcome any contribution he might make to this discussion."

"I know, I know," Dobbins said, waving it off. "I ask you all to forgive me if I'm just a little upset. But I know two of those boys

177

that Ponder's got standin' up down there. Dewey Hensen and Monk Perkins used to work for me, and as far as I'm concerned, they was good boys, both of them. Neither one of them ever gave me a lick of trouble."

"How is it that they wound up ridin' with the Fence Busters?" Bellefontaine asked.

"I don't know. Maybe Kendrick was payin' 'em more. I just know that they aren't" — he paused then looked around Duff — "that is, they *wasn't* bad boys. And I don't believe for a minute that they was rustlin' cattle."

"Well then, Dobbins, since I have testified here that I, personally, saw them rustling cattle, that can only mean that you are calling me a liar," Bellefontaine challenged.

"What? No, uh, no. I didn't mean that. I mean, what if they cut the fence, and your cattle just went through the fence on their own? It could've been that, and I could see how you might think they were being stolen."

Bellefontaine was quiet for a long moment before he replied. "Yeah," he finally said in a gruff voice. "I suppose it could have been that."

"Let's get on with the meeting, shall we?" President Webb asked.

"Yeah, what is the purpose of the meet-

178

ing?" Lewis wanted to know.

"If you people will let Mr. Bellefontaine continue, I'm sure you'll find out," Webb said. "All right, Bellefontaine. Let's hear it."

"I want the endorsement of the Texas Hill Country Cattlemen's Association to send someone to meet with the governor, and ask that he get behind making it a felony to cut fences."

"It's already a felony to cut fences on private land," Dobbins said.

"I'm talking about public land."

Dobbins shook his head. "That would be a foolish mission. There is absolutely no way you're goin' to get a law like that. Public land is public land."

"Yes, but the cattle grazing on public land is private. And we came to an agreement a long time ago to put fences up to keep our stock from getting mixed up," Price said. "If you cut those fences, it exposes the cattle, which are private. I think we could use that as justification for a law that would make it a felony to expose private cattle in such a way. And the only you can protect those cattle is to make it a felony to cut fences, even on public land."

"I agree, that might work," Webb said. "But you might remember that we sent Reynolds and Spencer to see the governor once before. Tell us what happened, Ron."

Reynolds ran his hand through his thinning hair before he spoke. "Well, we didn't have an idea of maybe protectin' penned-in cattle, which I think is a good idea, but it didn't matter 'cause we didn't even get to see the governor."

"There you go, Jason," Webb said. "What makes you think you'll even get in to see the governor?"

Bellefontaine looked over toward Elmer. "Mr. Gleason, would you care to comment?"

"I'll go talk to the governor for you fellers," Elmer said.

"You? You are going to talk to the governor?" Dobbins asked, his voice dripping with derision.

"Yes."

"What makes you think the governor would even agree to see you, let alone listen to someone like you?"

Elmer stared at Dobbins for a moment, then he smiled. "I'll ask him just real nice."

"What's that supposed to mean?"

"I'd try to explain it to you, sonny, but you've already shown that you don't have any idea what it means to be nice."

"Why you wrinkled-up old — !" Dobbins sputtered in anger. Getting up from the conference table, he walked over to stand in front of Elmer. "I'm goin' to teach you some manners." He drew his fist back.

From the time Dobbins left the table, Elmer made no move to defend himself. Suddenly, Wang shot his hand out so that his extended fingers struck the thigh of Dobbin's right leg. The rancher let out a sharp yell of pain, then jumped back, barely able to stay on his feet.

The cause of his pain was a mystery. Elmer hadn't made a move, and Wang had done it so quickly and with such little effort of motion that neither Dobbins nor anyone else in the room saw what happened.

"What the hell's wrong with you, Dobbins?" Reynolds asked.

Dobbins didn't answer, but with his hand over the aching part of his thigh, he staggered back to his seat.

"I know that you men are wondering why I would suggest that Mr. Gleason be the one to petition the governor on our behalf," Bellefontaine said. "But he has assured me, and I believe him, that he and the governor are friends of long standing. Since we have not been able to carry our grievances to the governor by any conventional route, I see no reason why we should not approach him on the basis of an old friendship."

181

"Jason is right," Lewis said. "The governor will either agree to listen to him or he won't. And if he doesn't listen to him, we are no worse off than we are now. I say we send Mr. Gleason to Austin."

"Gentlemen, the proposal has been made that we authorize Mr. Gleason. Is there a second?" Webb asked.

"I second," Reynolds responded.

"The question has been called. All in favor, raise your right hand."

When the vote was taken, there were nine in favor and one opposed. Dobbins was the one who was in opposition.

As a result of the vote, the association gave its official endorsement of Elmer's approach to the governor on their behalf.

After the meeting broke up, the men from the Slash Bell rode back out to the ranch. Duff, Elmer, and Wang would spend another night before getting an early start to Austin the next day.

At his ranch, Dobbins was met by Ned Tolson, his foreman. "We got another twenty cows to look after."

"Did you get paid for 'em?"

"Yeah, a hunnert dollars. What was the cattleman's association meeting about?"

"Some foolish idea to ask the governor to

outlaw cutting fences on public land," Dobbins replied.

"He ain't goin' to do that, is he?"

Dobbins shook his head. "I am absolutely convinced that he will not do it. It's been tried before, you know. I would be very surprised if the governor even agreed to meet with them. I consider the whole thing too foolish to even make the attempt, so I voted against it."

"Yeah, well, Mr. Dobbins, you do realize that we have a lot of public land fenced in ourselves."

"I'm quite aware of that, Tolson."

"And it's where we're runnin' them cows that we're boarding."

"So?"

"So, what if them fences gets cut, and all them cows get out?"

"Think about it, Tolson. Do you really think those fences will be cut?"

"No, under the circumstances, I reckon not."

CHAPTER FIFTEEN

Blowout

"It is of no consequence," Dirk Kendrick said to Martell, who'd brought him the news that the association had authorized someone to approach the governor. Sitting at "his" table in the Pair of Kings Saloon, Kendrick didn't interrupt his game of solitaire during the subsequent discussion. He laid a red ten upon a black jack. "There have been others who went to the capital to try and talk to Ireland, but he's never agreed to see anyone, and he won't see these people, either."

"Well, it's Bellefontaine that's pushin' it, and this MacCallister feller that Jaco was talkin' about is the one that put 'im up to it, I think."

"I don't think the governor makes a habit out of meeting with just anyone who comes in off the street. What makes MacCallister think the governor will see him?" He put a black seven on a red eight.

"Well it ain't MacCallister as much as it is that other feller that's with 'im all the time. Gleason, his name is, 'n the word I got is that this Gleason feller is a personal friend of the governor's."

"Gleason? That white-haired old man is a personal friend of the governor's?"

"Yeah. It turns out they fought together durin' the war."

Kendrick laid down three more cards. Turning up an ace of hearts, he put it at the top of the board.

"What you are telling me, then, is that MacCallister and Gleason are the ones who will be carrying the petition to the governor."

Martell nodded. "That's what I've found out."

"When do they plan to see the governor?"

"From what I was told, they're stayin' at the Slash Bell tonight, and they're plannin' on leavin' for Austin first thing in the morning."

Kendrick stopped playing cards for a moment so that he might contemplate how to react to the news. He stroked his chin. "Hmm. As I recall, there's only one road that goes from the Slash Bell to Austin, isn't there?"

"Yeah, the Salcedo Road."

"Good, that's what I thought. I plan to have a little surprise waiting for them on Salcedo Road."

"What kind of a surprise?"

"The kind of surprise they won't appreciate. Where is Jaco right now? Have you seen him recently?"

"Last I seen 'im, he was out at the cabin, playin' poker."

"Bring him to me," Kendrick ordered.

An hour later, Jaco showed up at Kendrick's table in the Pair of Kings. "What did you want to see me about?"

"How would you like to earn five hundred dollars?"

"Damn! I'd like that a lot!" Jaco said.

"Were you serious when you said you wanted to kill MacCallister?" Kendrick asked.

"Yeah, I was serious. Why do you ask?"

Kendrick smiled. "I'm glad you were serious. I will pay you five hundred dollars to do it. The opportunity is about to present itself."

The next morning Jaco and Dawkins were out on Salcedo Road at just after daybreak.

"Where do you want to do this?" Dawkins asked.

"I don't know yet, but I'll know just the place when I see it."

They continued their ride down Salcedo Road.

Slash Bell Ranch

After breakfast Bellefontaine and Wang accompanied Duff and Elmer out to the barn and stood there talking to them as the two men saddled their horses.

"Tell the governor we are well aware that he'll be taking a political risk," Bellefontaine said. "But tell him also, if we don't get something done about this, the cattle industry in Texas could wind up just about destroyed."

"Mr. Bellefontaine, if this here is the same Colonel Ireland I know, he ain't goin' to let somethin' like a little political risk stop 'im from doin' the right thing," Elmer said.

"Yes, well, that is the question, isn't it? Is this the right thing for him to do? I sincerely believe that it would be the right thing for the Texas cattle business for him to outlaw fence cutting on public land. But the problem is, I'm not sure it is legal for him to do that. And there is no doubt in my mind that if he does get a law passed, it's goin' to be

187

challenged in court. Believe me, the New York and Texas Land Company has more than enough money to prosecute this case."

"I wouldn't worry about that," Duff said. "Elmer tells me that your governor is a good man. It has always been my observation that among good men, what is right to do takes precedence over what is legal to do. I think he will listen to our cause."

Swinging in to the saddle, Duff and Elmer tossed a wave toward Wang and Bellefontaine, then rode out.

Along the Salcedo Road

Jaco and Dawson were more than halfway to Austin when Jaco saw two boulders, each of them large enough to offer concealment for a person. What made it better was that the rocks would also provide cover from any return fire . . . and the best part of all was the fact that the rocks were on opposite sides of the road and separated by some thirty yards. It was an ideal situation for getting his quarry in cross fire without any danger of being in each other's field of fire. It could not have been a better place for an ambush if Jaco had set about building it himself.

He pointed to one of the rocks. "I'll be waiting at this rock" — he pointed at one across the road — "and you'll be waiting at that one. When they get between us, we'll have 'em in a cross fire. You'll be behind and I'll be in front."

"What will be the signal to shoot?" Dawkins asked.

Jaco chuckled. "The signal to shoot will be me shooting. I'll open fire. Since you'll be behind them they can't turn and run away from us. Make sure when you're shooting, though, that you are shooting in a direction that's away from me."

"You goin' to shoot at MacCallister first?"

"Damn right I am. He kilt two of my brothers. I'm goin' to take a lot of pleasure in killin' him."

Just about halfway to Austin, a pistol cracked and a bullet whizzed by Duff, removing his hat and coming so close to the top of his head that it fluffed his hair. "Elmer, get down!"

The shout wasn't necessary. Elmer had leaped from his horse as quickly as Duff.

Duff pulled his rifle from the saddle sheath and slapped Sky on the flank to get him out of the line of fire. Elmer did the same thing, and the two men darted across the road, seeking out the protection of a shallow drainage ditch rimmed with a low-lying line of rocks that ran parallel with the road. A second shot chased them, hitting the rocks, then careening off with a loud scream.

"Do you see the shooter?" Elmer asked.

"I've nae yet seen him." Duff wriggled his body to the end of the little bank of rocks, then peered around cautiously. Though he couldn't see anybody, he did see a little puff of smoke drifting north on a hot breath of air, and realized that the shooter must be somewhat to the south.

Moving his eyes in that direction, he saw the tip of a hat rising slowly above the rocks. He watched as the hat began to move up. Jacking a round into the chamber of the Winchester, he waited. When enough of the hat was visible to provide a good target, he aimed and fired. The hat sailed away.

"Ha! That's the oldest trick in the book," a voice called. "I had my hat on the end of a stick."

At the sound of the voice, Duff fired again. His bullet sent chips of rock flying and he was rewarded with a yelp of pain.

"Damn it! You sprayed rock into my face!" the shooter said.

"Did I now? And here 'twas my intention to shoot you between the eyes," Duff replied.

"Hold it!" a voice suddenly yelled from behind Duff.

He turned quickly and saw someone standing behind Elmer, holding a gun on him.

"Jaco, I've got 'em!" the man yelled. "You can come on over."

"Good job, Dawkins." Jaco stood up from his position behind a rock about thirty yards away from Duff. Both Jaco and Dawkins were wearing blue kerchiefs.

"Get up, you two," Dawkins said.

Duff and Elmer got up, then stepped out into the middle of the road. Duff still clutched his rifle, but he was holding it with one hand down by his side.

"Did I hear him call you Jaco?" Duff asked.

Jaco smiled, showing yellowed teeth. "Yeah. You remember the name, I see."

"A. M. Jaco," Duff said. "He was with the Kingdom Come Gang."

"That's right. A.M. was my brother."

"And here you are with the Fence Busters."

"Yeah," Jaco said with a chuckle. "What gived you the notion?"

"I would say 'twas the blue bandana that gave me the clue."

Jaco smirked. "Ain't you the smart one,

though?"

"Your brother was with the Kingdom Come Gang and you are with the Fence Busters. Seems neither one of you have enough intestinal fortitude to stand on your own," Duff said.

"Intestinal fortitude? What does that mean?" Jaco asked.

"You have to get used to Duff. Him bein' a foreigner 'n all, he sometimes talks just real fancy like that," Elmer said. "But what it means is, you are a yeller-bellied coward."

"We'll see who the coward is," Jaco said. "I was just goin' to shoot you down from behind that rock, but as it turns out, this is better. I want you to know that I'm a-killin' you on account of you kilt my two brothers."

Duff frowned. "Your two brothers? I am aware of having killed only one person named Jaco."

"Yeah? Well, what about a feller by the name of Pollard?"

"Pollard?"

"Yes, Deekus Pollard. I got a telegram from a friend of my brother, a man by the name of Abe Tremble, 'n he told me that you are the one that kilt Deke. So that makes two of my brothers you kilt."

"Yes, Deekus Pollard, the philosopher,"

Duff said easily.

"The what?"

"Never mind. You wouldn't understand. By the way, in case you are interested, I also killed your brother's friend, Tremble."

"I don't care none about Tremble. I never actual met him. Just got the telegram from him. When you get to hell, you can tell A.M. that you was kilt by his brother, Pete. I think that'll give him some comfort, for all that he's burnin' in hell and ever'thing now." Jaco chuckled. "It's likely to make Deke jealous, though, that it was me that kilt you 'n not him."

Because Dawkins had his gun pointed at Elmer, Jaco relaxed his vigilance to the point that his pistol was hanging loosely by his side as he started toward the men from Sky Meadow.

From behind him, Duff heard a strange grunt and knew without being told that Elmer had just gained advantage over Dawkins.

It took Jaco a split second to realize that he no longer held the advantage. He tried to bring his pistol up to firing position, but he was too late. With a shell already in the chamber of the rifle, and the rifle still cocked, Duff didn't even have to bring it up. He fired it from the waist, putting the bullet exactly where he had intended to put the first one . . . right between Jaco's eyes.

Jacking another round into the chamber even as he spun around, he saw that a second shot wasn't needed. Elmer had smashed his elbow into Dawkins's face, then, grabbing him, broke his neck with one, quick jerk. Dawkins lay on the ground as dead as Jaco.

"You all right?" Duff asked.

"Right as rain," Elmer replied with a smile.

" 'Twould appear that someone learned that we were going to see the governor, and they dinnae approve of the idea," Duff said.

"I wonder how they found out." Elmer said.

"My guess is that they had a spy in the meeting yesterday," Duff said.

"Yeah, that would be my guess, as well. And I'd bet a dollar to a nickel that I know who it was."

"Aye, 'tis thinkin' I am that you would be right, too."

"What do you think we should do with the bodies?" Elmer asked.

"I'd say just leave them here. I want to get on in to see the governor, and I've nae wish to waste time dealing with the brigands."

A whistle called Sky and Elmer's horses back. The two men swung into the saddles and continued their trip.

Behind them, the buzzards were just beginning to circle.

Austin

Reaching the town, Duff and Elmer went straight to the capitol building, and finding the reception room of the governor's office, they approached the appointment secretary. The rather small man with a pencil-thin mustache and slicked-back hair was wearing rimless glasses.

"Yes, how may I help you gentlemen?"

"We're here to see the governor," Duff said.

"And you are?"

"Duff MacCallister and Elmer Gleason."

The governor's secretary made a show of checking a book. "Oh, my. I don't seem to see either name in the appointments book."

"I wouldn't think you would see it, seein' as how we don't have no appointment," Elmer said.

"Oh, well, gentlemen, surely you understand that the governor is much too busy a man to see just anyone off the street. Leave your names with me, and I will submit them for consideration."

"That won't do. We need to see him now. Tell him that Elmer Gleason is here and wants to see him. Tell him that he might remember me from Jenkins' Ferry."

The secretary laughed a rather condescending laugh. "Sir, just because you may have met the governor while on a ferry, I hardly think that would justify interrupting his busy day to meet with you. After all, he is recognized everywhere he goes. I've no doubt but that he exchanged some pleasantries with you. But really, I must ask you to go now."

"We ain't leavin' till we see the governor," Elmer said.

"If you gentlemen don't leave immediately, I will call security, and you will be forced to leave."

Elmer pulled his pistol, pointed it at the supercilious official, then pulled back the hammer. The secretary's eyes opened wide in fear as he heard the ominous metallic click of the pistol being cocked.

"Tell him that Elmer Gleason from Jenkins' Ferry wants to talk to him."

"J-J-Jenkins' Ferry," the clerk repeated nervously.

CHAPTER SIXTEEN

When the frightened secretary stepped into the inner office, the governor looked up from behind his desk.

"Yes, Mr. Fitzhugh, what is — Good heavens, man, you look as if you have seen a ghost. What is wrong?"

"There are two men here, demanding to see you," the secretary said. "When I told them that you saw no one without an appointment, one of them pulled a gun and pointed it at me."

"What? Who are they? What do they want?"

"I don't know what they want, sir, but one of them gave me his name. I believe he said it was Elmer Jamison. He said you would remember him."

Governor Ireland shook his head. "No, the name means nothing to me."

"He said I should tell you about Jenkins' Ferry. I told him that just because there

197

might have been a casual meeting on a ferry that —"

Suddenly and inexplicably, the governor laughed out loud. "Wait just a minute. You said Jamison, but could his name have been Elmer Gleason?"

"Gleason, yes, sir. Now that I think about it, I believe Gleason *is* the name he gave me. What shall I tell him, sir?"

"You don't have to tell him anything," the governor said. "I'll tell him myself."

"Yes, sir," Fitzhugh replied. "I think perhaps it should come from you."

Governor Ireland opened the door and looked into the outer office. When he saw Elmer, a wide smile spread across his face. "Lieutenant Gleason, you old horse thief! Get in here!"

"Hello, Colonel. I was beginnin' to think you might not remember me," Elmer replied.

"Now how am I going to forget the man that saved my life?"

"This man saved your life?" the secretary asked in surprise.

"Yes, Mr. Fitzhugh, at Jenkins' Ferry. My horse had been killed, and when I looked up, I saw that there were three Yankees coming toward me, thinking, perhaps, that they had a rebel colonel all set up for the slaughter. All my men were in full retreat. I don't think any of them knew what had happened to me.

"Then Lieutenant Gleason showed up, spouting off a string of cusswords, most of which I had never even heard before." The governor paused. "Though I think, somewhere in there, I did hear the words *damn no-good Yankees.*"

"That ain't words, Colonel," Elmer said. "That's only one word. *Damnnogoodyankees.*"

The governor laughed. "Fortunately, Elmer did more than just curse the Yankees. He also began shooting at them. After he took two of them down, the third one turned and ran. Elmer scooped me up onto the back of his horse and, well . . . as you can see, I'm here today.

"Elmer, come on in here and bring your friend with you," the governor said with a wave of his arm.

The governor's secretary cleared his throat. "Governor, you have a meeting with the head of the university board at two o'clock."

"Cancel it. I'll see him tomorrow."

"But Governor —"

"I said cancel it, Mr. Fitzhugh."

"Yes, sir."

"Who is your friend, Elmer?" The governor led them over to a seating area with a leather sofa and two leather chairs on one side of his office.

"This is Duff MacCallister," Elmer replied. "He's a Scotsman so he don't talk real good English. I mean, what with his accent 'n all. Now, me, I don't have no trouble understandin' 'im on account of 'cause I'm used to it by now. Some folks might have a problem, but iffen you listen real close you can near 'bout always make out what it is he's a-tryin' to say."

"Governor, 'tis pleased I am to make your acquaintance," Duff said, speaking in a heavier brogue than normal. "Aye, 'n 'tis a fact that any man who calls himself a friend of Elmer's can count himself my friend as well."

"See what I mean, Colonel? He calls that a brogue. I say it's a foreign accent that you have to work at to understand."

The governor laughed. "I shall make a concerted effort. Now, what brings you here, my friend? What can I do for you?"

"Colonel, are you aware of a group of no-account polecats that call themselves the Fence Busters?" Elmer asked.

"Yes, unfortunately, I am quite aware of them." The governor's smile left his face.

"Have you had a confrontation with them?"

"Yes, sir, we truly have." Elmer told about the incident at Slash Bell. He made no mention of the incident that had occurred on the road en route to Austin.

"The reason we're here, Governor," Duff said, "is to ask you to make it a felony to cut the fences."

"It's already a felony to cut the fences on private land," Governor Ireland said. "It's only the public land where it's not against the law, and I'm not sure how we could get around that."

"But would you be for considering this?" Duff asked. "The cattlemen have all made agreements with each other to erect fences so their stock doesn't all get intermingled. When the fences are cut the cattle, which are private property, can wander off. Or, what's more likely, can be stolen by the same people who have cut the fence. Then, of course, it would be a felony. But even if the cattle aren't stolen, they could wander off as a result of the fence having been cut. Couldn't you classify that as reckless disregard of private property?"

"Whew, I don't know," Governor Ireland replied. "It seems to me that might be a bit of a stretch. If such a law is passed and is challenged, I'm not sure that it would hold up in court."

"Aye, but there's a good chance that it would hold up in court. And even if the court overturns the law, the cattlemen will have bought enough time to, perhaps, stop the Fence Busters from stealing any more of their cows."

"Colonel, what can we tell the cattlemen back in Merrill Town?" Elmer asked. "Can we tell 'em that you're goin' to help 'em out, that you will give 'em a law that says it's illegal to cut the fences, even on public land?"

"Do you really think that would help?" Governor Ireland asked.

"Aye, sir, I believe it would," Duff said. "As it is now, the cattlemen cannae protect their cattle until after the fence is cut and the rustlers start running off their cattle. Only then is it legal to oppose them for cattle rustling, but by that time 'tis often too late.

"On the other hand, if you would make the cutting o' the fence illegal in the first place, the cattlemen could defend their cattle before they were put at risk."

"You do present a good argument." Governor Ireland chuckled. "Perhaps if the bill is challenged, you can present the state's argument before the court. All right. I'll

202

introduce a bill before the legislature making the cutting of all fences a felony. That will be a political risk but" — he looked at Elmer and smiled again — "a political risk doesn't compare with the risk this old varmint took when he came galloping in to scoop me up from the ground and save my hide. Consider it done."

"Thank you, Colonel," Elmer said, reaching out to shake the governor's hand.

During Duff and Elmer's conversation with the governor a young woman entered the office unannounced. She was quite pretty, of medium height, slender, and with hair the color of burnished copper. Duff had noticed her when she came in, but because she stood silently, he gave no indication that he had seen her.

"Daddy?" the young woman called out once there was a lag in the conversation.

"Hello, darlin'. I didn't see you come in," Governor Ireland said.

Duff and Elmer stood when the young woman approached.

"I wasn't sure you would be here since Mr. Fitzhugh isn't at his desk."

"I sent him on an errand. Oh, let me introduce these two gentlemen to you. The young, handsome man is Duff MacCallister, and the old, ugly-looking reprobate is Elmer Gleason. Gentlemen, this is my daughter, Rosalie."

"Gleason? Daddy isn't he . . . ?"

"Yes, darlin', this is the very man who saved my life during the war."

"Mr. Gleason," Rosalie said, smiling broadly and extending her hand. "I'm very glad to meet you. And I thank you for saving my daddy's life."

"I'm pleased to meet you, too, Miss Ireland."

She turned to Duff. "And you are Mr. MacCallister?"

"Aye, lass. Duff MacCallister. 'Tis most pleased I am to make your acquaintance."

"Oh, I love the way you talk," Rosalie said.

"He does talk funny, don't he?" Elmer said. "Of course, I'm so used to it, that I don't hardly take no notice a-tall anymore."

"Oh, I don't think it is funny at all. I think it is quite sophisticated."

"Rosalie, what do you want? What's so important that you have to come to my office when I'm in conference?"

"I'm sorry, Daddy. I didn't mean to interrupt. But there is a dress for sale in The Elite Shop that I simply must have for the ball Saturday night, and I'm two dollars short."

"You *must* have it, huh?"

"Yes, Daddy, but it's not for me, you understand. It's for you."

Governor Ireland chuckled. "Darlin', you are going to explain how you buying a dress for the ball Saturday night is for me, aren't you?"

"Of course I am. You know me, Daddy. Why, I would be satisfied wearing just any old rag of a dress. But how would that look for you? I mean, you wouldn't want the governor's daughter to go the ball in a dress that wasn't suited to your position, would you?"

Governor laughed again, and shook his head as he took out his billfold. "No, I certainly wouldn't want my daughter to be caught going to the ball wearing a dress that wasn't appropriate for the occasion." He gave her a twenty-dollar bill. "Find something real pretty."

"Oh, I will, Daddy, I will! And thank you! Thank you so much!" She took the money, then looked back at Duff and Elmer. "It was so nice meeting you gentlemen."

"Be on your way, darlin'. As you can see, I am busy."

"Yes, Daddy," Rosalie said, then tossing a smile at the visiting men, she stepped back out of the office.

"Your daughter is as nice as she is pretty," Duff said.

"She has me wrapped around her little finger, and she knows it," Governor Ireland said.

Duff turned the conversation back to the more serious situation. "Governor, I think you should be for knowing that on the way here this morning, we were set upon by two men, both of whom were wearing the blue kerchiefs of the Fence Busters."

"Set upon? What do you mean, set upon?"

"He means that two no-'count, lowdown fellers ambushed us on the road 'n tried to kill us," Elmer said.

"Good heavens, you mean they shot at you?"

"They sure as hell did." Elmer laughed. "They shot at us, 'n that was their big mistake. Their last mistake, as it turned out, " 'cause we kilt both of 'em."

"Where are these men now?" the governor asked.

"Unless someone has picked them up and brought them into town, they are still lying out there," Duff said. "I tell you this because I don't want someone to find them and have it be a mystery as to who they are and why they are there."

"All right," the governor said. "Come with

206

me. We'll go see Captain Brooks of the Texas Rangers. He'll send some men out to pick them up."

The governor led Duff and Elmer down one of the long corridors of the capitol building until they reached a door that designated the room behind it as the office of the Texas Rangers.

A young man sitting at a desk stood quickly when the governor stepped inside. "Governor Ireland, sir."

"Is Captain Brooks in?" the governor asked.

"Yes, sir. I'll tell him you're here."

"You say these two men jumped you on the road as you were coming to see the governor?" Captain Brooks asked after Duff and Elmer shared their story with him.

"That's what they done, all right," Elmer replied.

"What was their purpose? Were they trying to rob you?"

"I believe that, somehow, they came by the intelligence that we were going to see the governor to put in a request, and they intended to stop us," Duff said.

"You see," Elmer put in, "both of 'em was wearin' blue kerchiefs."

"Fence Busters," Captain Brook replied.

207

Duff nodded. "Aye, Fence Busters they were."

Captain Brooks shook his head. "The Fence Busters are beginning to be quite a problem. They have a small army, and they operate at will. I hate to say this, Governor, but there's no doubt in my mind but that they may have a sheriff or two helping them out."

"You may be correct, Captain, but I'm about to introduce a law that may help us with the situation. At least, it will give us more tools to use in dealing with the situation."

"I hope your bill works, Governor."

"I do, too, Captain. I do, too."

CHAPTER SEVENTEEN

Slash Bell Ranch

By the time Duff and Elmer rode back to the ranch two days later, the bill had already been introduced and signed. Duff was carrying a copy of the *Austin Gazette*. He had brought the newspaper with him so he could share one particular article.

GOVERNOR IRELAND SIGNS EXECUTIVE ORDER

A new act, signed into law by executive order of the governor, will henceforth prohibit anyone from cutting fences behind which cattle are being protected.

Such a law is already in existence for fences around private property, but this law will cover fences that surround public land, as well. No doubt there will be some objection to this as the public land belongs, in fact, to all the people of Texas, and not just to the rancher who has erected the fence. Despite the objection, it is believed that the law enjoys enough support from the ranchers to enable it to stand.

"Congratulations. This bill will certainly make all the cattlemen happy. And," Bellefontaine added with a wide smile, "make the other members of the Hill Country Cattlemen's Association eat their words when they doubted that Mr. Gleason would have access to the governor."

"Did Mr. Wang behave himself while we were gone?" Duff asked.

"I'll say. Why didn't you tell me he could cook? I don't think I've ever eaten as delicious a meal as the one he prepared." Bellefontaine chuckled. "I even tried to hire him away from you, but, apparently, he is well satisfied in his current position."

"Loyalty is a matter of honor with Wang, and I believe he would die before bringing dishonor to himself."

"Tell Kendrick there is a way of getting the governor to get the legislature to cancel the law that was just passed with regard to the fence-cutting bill."

"How?"

"I've written it all out for Kendrick, including the schedules."

"What schedules?"

"It will be clear to him when he reads the letter I have written."

"You know, when you first started givin' us information, I didn't think we could really trust you. But Kendrick said he had dealt with people like you before, and he said that we could. He said that people like you were driven more by avarice than by altruism. I'm not sure what them words mean, but he said that was why we could trust you."

"Ha! Yes, Kendrick is quite accurate in his appraisal. I suppose you could say that I am driven more by avarice than by altruism, though I would prefer to say that I am motivated by practicality and self-preservation. Now, please get this letter to him right away. If it is to be of any benefit to him, he must get it right away."

Fence Busters' cabin on the Blanco River
The cabin sat back from the creek, tucked up under the overhang of Bat Cave Mountain. The overhang had been created by the guano explosion that had occurred some forty years earlier. The back wall was protected, not only from the weather but from any attack launched from that direction.

The cabin could be approached from

either side, though that would have been difficult. The easiest approach was by following the creek bed. And because that was the easiest approach, it was always very well guarded.

Disappointed to learn that Kendrick wasn't in Blowout, where it would have been much easier to give him the letter, the messenger rode out to the cabin. He wasn't actually a member of the Fence Busters, but because he had a working relationship with Kendrick, he knew where the cabin was, and how to approach it. He was always uneasy about going to the cabin, though, because he would be in sight of the guards who were posted. Since he was just a messenger, and not one of them, he always feared that one of them might get nervous someday and shoot at him. But the pay was worth it . . . so he took a deep breath and rode on ahead.

He stopped at the dome, which was how Kendrick referred to a large rounded rock, where the creek made a hard turn to the left. From there, the cabin couldn't be seen. From the other side of the dome, just after the curve in the creek, the cabin could be seen, but if anyone got that far before giving the secret signal, they would be shot.

The messenger took off his hat, hooked it

onto the stock of his rifle, and, holding the rifle by the end of the barrel, held it and the hat as high as he could. He stayed riveted in that position until his arm began to hurt, but he knew better than to lower it before he was told he could do so.

"Higgins?" an unseen voice called from the other side of the rock.

"Yeah."

"Come ahead."

"Can I lower my arm?"

"Yeah. Put your rifle back in the sheath." Higgins did as he was instructed, then, rounding the rock, recognized Martell. "Is Mr. Kendrick here?"

"Yeah. You got somethin' for 'im?"

"I do." Higgins followed Martell on up to the cabin, then dismounted and went inside.

Kendrick was drinking a cup of coffee. "Grab a cup," he invited, reaching for the letter Higgins had brought.

The governor's daughter, Rosalie, takes frequent rides, unaccompanied. This Friday she will be going to Manor to visit her grandmother. She normally leaves at about one o'clock in the afternoon for the one-hour ride. She stays about two hours, then leaves at four p.m. to return.

While Kendrick read, Martell and several others sat at a table a short distance away.

"Jaco and Dawkins are dead," Martell said. "I thought Jaco was so all-fired set on killin' MacCallister. How come, you reckon, he couldn't get the job done?"

"Who is this MacCallister anyway?" Logan asked. "What the hell is he doin' gettin' in our way like he's a-doin'?"

"You remember that outfit folks called the Kingdom Come Gang?" Rand asked.

Logan nodded. "Yeah, I remember 'em."

"Well, it was MacCallister and that feller that's with him, Elmer Gleason, what brought that gang down."

"I'll be damned. They was runnin' high, too. I remember them. And you say that it was MacCallister and this Gleason person that brought 'em down?" Martell asked.

Rand leaned back in his chair. "Yeah, it was them, all right. And the thing is, Jaco's brother was in that Kingdom Come Gang. And MacCallister bringin' 'em down like he done is the reason why Jaco wanted to be the one to kill him. It was real personal with him. Only it didn't work out, 'n he wound up gettin' hisself kilt instead."

"Yeah, and not only that, the governor's gone and got a law passed agin' cuttin' fences on public land."

"We'll get around that," Kendrick said, looking up from the letter.

"How?" Rand asked. "How we goin' to get around that?"

"I'll give it some thought. I'm sure I can come up with a way."

"Supper's ready," Finn said. While in the cabin on the Blanco River, the men rotated cooking duties.

The men picked up a plate from the stack of ten plates on the sideboard, then stepped up to the stove to be served.

"What do you mean, supper? This ain't nothin' but beans," Felker growled as they were spooned onto his plate. "Is that all we ever have around here?"

"Beans is all I got to work with," Finn said. "They's some pork with 'em."

"Pork? No beef? This is a hell of a note, ain't it?" Felker complained as he walked over to sit at the rough-hewn table with half a dozen other men. "I mean we've rustled enough beef to start a full-sized stampede, but we ain't got so much as a mouthful to lay alongside our beans."

"Quit your complaining, Felker," Kendrick said as he held his own plate out. "If you want beef for every meal, you can always go back to doing whatever it is that you . . . cowboys . . . do for low wages and food. We're cutting fences and rustling cattle because it pays more, not because it's an easy life."

"Perhaps you ain't noticed it, Kendrick, but we ain't exactly been rustlin' a hell of a lot of cows lately, neither," Felker said. "In fact, it's been quite a while since we've so much as took one steer and got away with it."

"Felker's right," one of the other men said. "You said it'd be a piece of cake to go out to Bellefontaine's place and take his herd. Well, we went out there. And we lost four men. They was good men, too, ever' one of 'em. All that and for what? We didn't get so much as one cow."

"Tell me, Conroy, since when were you such good friends with Smitty, Hensen, Miller, 'n Perkins?" Kendrick asked. "Besides, who knew that MacCallister, Gleason, and the Chinaman would stay 'n fight with Bellefontaine?"

"And now the governor's got a law passed sayin' we can't cut fences," Conroy said. "How the hell did them cowmen get him talked into doin' that, anyway?"

"It turns out that Gleason is an old friend of the governor," Kendrick said.

Conroy frowned. "He is? How can somebody like that be friends with the governor?"

"Apparently, Gleason saved the governor's life during the war," Kendrick said.

"Now, how the hell would you know somethin' like that?" Woodson asked, surprised by Kendrick's comment.

"I'm an attorney, and by definition, attorneys must learn everything they can about any project they undertake." Kendrick held up the letter. "I've come up with a way of dealing with the situation and I intend to get that law repealed."

"Oh yeah? Just how are you goin' to do that?" Woodson asked.

"You'll see this afternoon," Kendrick replied. "I'll take you with me."

The Capitol Building, Austin
"Hello, Mr. Fitzhugh," Rosalie said to the governor's secretary. "Is Daddy in his office?"

"He is indeed, Miss Ireland."

"Is he alone? I don't want to disturb him if he is in a meeting."

"He's quite alone, and I'm sure he'll be happy to receive you. You're wearing your riding clothes, I see. Riding up to see your grandmother again?"

"Yes, I am."

"Every Wednesday afternoon, as regular as clockwork," Fitzhugh said. "I'm sure your

217

grandmother looks forward to it. If you missed a week, I believe she would be very upset."

"I would as well. I so enjoy my Wednesday rides." With a smile and a wave, Rosalie pushed open the door to her father's office and stepped inside. "Daddy?" she called.

"Yes, dear, come on in," Governor Ireland called out. "All ready for your ride, I see."

"Yes, I am. Any message for Grandma?"

"No, just give her my regards. And be careful on your ride."

"Now why would you say that? Daddy, you know that I'm a very good rider."

"I know," the governor said. "But just be careful, is all I'm asking."

CHAPTER EIGHTEEN

Outside Austin

On Friday afternoon, armed with the information that had been in the letter, Kendrick, Conroy, Felker, Woodson, and Martell were waiting on the Manor Pike, about five miles northeast of the capital.

"Kendrick, there's a rider comin'," Conroy said.

"All right. Everyone get in position. Martell, when she passes by, you and Woodson come out behind her. Conroy, you and Felker come out in front of her. That way, she'll have no way to get away from us. But remember, don't hurt her. She'll only be useful to us if she is alive and unhurt."

Rosalie was enjoying her ride. A few moments ago, she had seen a mama fox and three kits, and she knew her grandmother would enjoy hearing about them. From a nearby thicket of trees, she heard the staccato tap of a woodpecker, and on the side of the road, colorful butterflies were flitting about. It was such a beautiful day for a ride. Then, suddenly, her ride was rudely interrupted by an unexpected sound.

"Now!" she heard someone shout.

Her curiosity as to the meaning of the sound was quickly answered when two mounted men suddenly appeared in front of her.

Startled, Rosalie turned her horse around quickly. She didn't know who they were or what they wanted, but she was a good rider and well mounted, and had no doubt that she could get away from them.

As soon as she turned her horse around, though, she saw two more men blocking her path. One of the men rode up to her and grabbed the halter of her horse, while the other jerked the reins from her hand.

"Who are you? What do you want? Do you have any idea who my father is?"

"Yes indeed, Miss Rosalie Ireland. We know exactly who your father is," a fifth man said, riding up to her. He had dark, obsidian eyes and a purple scar on his left cheek that he rubbed with the tip of his finger. "You are the governor's daughter and are on your way to see your grandmother, but I'm afraid your grandmother is going to be disappointed today."

His speech wasn't with the soft drawl of Texas or anywhere else in the South or West. His rather cultured accent totally belied his appearance. "Tie her up, men, but don't hurt her," he ordered.

"Who are you?" Rosalie asked again.

"The name is Dirk Kendrick, Miss Ireland. And I'm pleased to make your acquaintance."

"Kendrick? You are the head of the Fence Busters, aren't you?"

"I am indeed. And I must say, I'm flattered that you have heard of me," Kendrick said with a smile.

"I don't see why you are flattered. I've heard nothing good about you. Why have you stopped me? Do you want me to give my father a message or something? If so, this is no way to go about it."

"Oh, your father *will* get the message, all right," Kendrick said as one of the men was tying her hands.

"Why are you tying my hands? What do you plan to do with me?"

"Nothing, if you behave yourself," Kendrick said. A second man dropped a rope around her neck, then tightened the noose so that she could feel it quite easily. Her eyes grew wide in near panic.

"Don't worry about the rope," Kendrick said. "It's just to keep you from trying to run away from us. Because if you do, you'll be jerked off your horse, and, well, I'm certain you can anticipate the results of such an unfortunate event." He blindfolded her.

"How am I going to see to ride?" Rosalie asked.

"You won't have to see. All you have to do is hold on to the saddle horn. We will lead your horse where we want you to go."

They had been riding for some time, and Rosalie had no idea where they were taking her, but she was aware that they were going up and down some rather sizeable hills. They crossed a railroad, but she didn't know if it was the Houston and Texas Central or the Austin and Northwestern Railroad. They crossed water. She didn't think it was the Colorado. The stream wasn't wide enough. *Walnut Creek? Decker Creek? Blanco River?* She had no idea, because she didn't know what direction they were traveling.

After a ride of at least two hours, they came to a stop.

"Get down," someone ordered.

The voice was beside and beneath her, so she knew that the man who gave the order was dismounted.

"I'm afraid to," Rosalie said. "My hands are tied, and I have a rope around my neck. What if I fall?"

"Take the noose off her, Felker," the voice said.

"And the blindfold?" Rosalie asked. "Please?"

"And the blindfold."

"Hold still, girl," said another voice right beside her.

"I'm not going anywhere." Rosalie felt the rope being taken from around her neck, then the blindfold was removed. Looking around, she saw that they were in a canyon, though the canyon was so small that it could actually be called a draw. "What is this place?"

"It's where you're going to be for a while. Now, get down," Kendrick ordered.

"Mr. Kendrick, I've never heard that you were a kidnapper before."

"Well, I've never had a reason to kidnap anyone before."

"Why have you kidnapped me? My dad is the governor, but he isn't rich. If you ask for too much ransom, he won't be able to pay it."

"He can do what I want." Kendrick made a motion toward the cabin. "Inside."

"I, uh, need to . . ." She didn't finish her sentence.

"Felker?"

"Yeah, boss?"

"Go with her."

A huge grin spread across Felker's face. "Yeah, I'll go with her."

"What?" Rosalie gasped. "You aren't going to tell me I can't have some privacy, are you? Are you afraid I would run away? Where would I go?"

"Put the noose back around her neck," Kendrick said. "Take her over to those rocks, but you stay on this side."

"Yeah, all right," Felker said, obviously disappointed.

Rosalie attended to her business without incident, then was taken back to the cabin. It had one window and one door.

Inside was a stone fireplace, a rough-hewn table, and four "chairs" that weren't chairs at all, but logs that had been split. With the flat side up, each was supported by four legs. There were no bunks.

"Here?" Rosalie asked. "How long do you expect me to stay in a place like this?"

"How long you stay here is up to your father," Kendrick said. "If he cares enough about you to want you to come home, he'll do our bidding and repeal that law."

Governor Ireland looked up when Fitzhugh walked in. "Yes, Mr. Fitzhugh, what is it?"

"I just received this by messenger, sir," Fitzhugh said, handing the governor a folded sheet of paper.

Curious, the governor read it.

We have your daughter, Rosalie. If you want to see her alive again, you will repeal the fence-cutting law. Do not go to the sheriff or the Texas Rangers, for if you do, the girl will be killed.

"My God! When did you get this?" Governor Ireland asked, his voice laced with horror and concern.

"Just now. Why, is there something wrong?" Fitzhugh replied.

"Where is the messenger?"

"He's gone,"

"He's gone? You mean you just let him go?"

"Governor, I saw no reason to hold him just because he was delivering a message. What does the message say?"

"You mean you didn't read it?"

"No, sir, why should I? It was addressed to you."

Governor Ireland handed the message to

225

Fitzhugh.

"Oh, my!" Fitzhugh put his hand to his head. "Oh, my. This is awful!"

Slash Bell Ranch

Music spilled from the large music box, the resonant tones filling the parlor. Duff and Wang were enjoying the music. Elmer was enjoying pictures through the stereopticon. He reached his hand out as if trying to grasp something.

"What are you doing, Elmer?" Duff asked.

"I'm tryin' to grab ahold of that cup that's just sittin' on the table there," Elmer replied.

Duff laughed. "There is no cup . . . there is no table. You're looking at a picture."

Elmer lowered the stereopticon, then blinked. "I'll be damned. You're right, there ain't no cup. It sure looks real in this picture, though. I ain't never seen no picture that looks this real."

"That's because you are seeing the photo in three dimensions," Bellefontaine explained.

"In what?"

"Three dimensions. You are seeing not only up and down and side to side, you are also seeing the pictures in depth. That's what makes them seem so real to you."

"Well now, whoever thought up such a thing?"

There was a loud knock on the front door, and Bellefontaine excused himself.

When Bellefontaine opened the door, he saw a tall man with a walrus mustache holding a high-crowned white hat in his hand.

"Captain Brooks," Bellefontaine said, greeting the head of the Texas Rangers. "What brings you here?"

"Do you still have as your guests Mr. Duff MacCallister and Mr. Elmer Gleason?" Brooks asked.

Bellefontaine's smile disappeared. "What is it? J.A., are you accusing them of something? Because whatever it is, I'm prepared to defend them."

"You think that much of them, do you?"

"I do indeed."

Brooks nodded. "It's good to hear that the governor's trust isn't misplaced."

"The governor's trust? What do you mean, the governor's trust? What's this about?"

"I'd rather tell all of you at the same time," Brooks said.

"Look, I'm not —"

Brooks stopped him with a wave of his hand. "Jason, the governor is in trouble, and he thinks that Mr. MacCallister and Mr. Gleason might be able to help him."

"Oh, well, why didn't you say so in the first place? Of course, come on in," Bellefontaine said. "They're in the parlor."

When the two men stepped into the parlor, Duff, Elmer, and Wang stood to greet the guest of their host.

"Gentlemen, this is Captain J. A. Brooks of the Texas Rangers. J.A., this is Mr. Duff MacCallister, Mr. Elmer Gleason, and Mr. Wang Chow."

"It is good to meet you gentlemen," Brooks said, extending his hand.

"Captain Brooks was sent here by the governor, specifically to talk to you three," Bellefontaine.

"How can we help you, Captain?" Duff asked.

"Specifically, it was to talk to Mr. Gleason," Brooks said, "though I'm sure that anything that involves him would also involve you, Mr. MacCallister."

"And Wang," Duff added.

Brooks nodded in acceptance that Wang would be included in the discussion. "Gentlemen, Governor Ireland has a daughter, a young woman named Rosalie."

"Aye, we met the lass," Duff said. "A pretty and well-mannered young lady, as I recall."

"That's her," Captain Brooks said. "She's

as nice a young lady as you'd ever want to meet. No conceit at all, for all that she is the governor's daughter."

"What about Miss Rosalie?" Elmer asked.

"She's been kidnapped."

"What?" Duff asked.

"Kidnapped," Captain Brooks repeated. "And the governor received this note from the kidnappers." He handed the note to Duff.

Duff read it, then passed it to Elmer, who then passed it to Bellefontaine.

"Oh, my Lord," Bellefontaine said, pressing the heel of his hand against his forehead. "This is all my fault."

"How can you say that?" Brooks asked.

"I'm the one who wanted the governor to pass a law against cutting fences on public land."

"That may be so, Mr. Bellefontaine, but I'm the one who talked the governor into doing it. If it's anybody's fault, it's mine," Elmer said.

"The governor isn't looking to find fault with anyone," Captain Brooks said. "What he is looking for is help."

"Help? Help how?" Duff asked. "Whatever he wants, if 'tis in our power to do it, we'll do it."

"He wants you to see if you can find his

daughter and bring her back safely," Brooks said.

"Of course, we'll do what we can," Duff said. "But I'm curious. You are a captain of the Texas Rangers, and John Ireland is the governor. I assume he has the authority to order the Texas Rangers onto the case, doesn't he? Why aren't you on the case?"

"Oh, indeed he does, sir, indeed he does, and believe me, I would like nothing better than to take my men out in search for the girl."

"Then I don't understand. Why don't you do so?"

"We could scarcely get involved without the outlaws finding out about it. I'm sure you saw, in their note, that the governor is not to go to the law. The governor is afraid that if we get involved, they will kill his daughter."

Duff nodded. "Aye, I can see how he might fear that. But his daughter is only worth something to the outlaws as long as she is alive. Were they to kill her, they would nae have an advantage."

"I believe so as well," Captain Brooks said. "But the governor is too concerned over the fate of his daughter to take the chance on getting the Rangers involved. He thinks that perhaps you could look for his daughter in such a way as to not raise any suspicion."

"Aye, 'n he may be right," Duff said. "We'll do what we can to find the young lass and bring her home safely."

Captain Brooks smiled. "I was hoping you would say that. Now, if you would please, would you come back to Austin with me? The governor wants to meet with you before you get started."

"Mr. Bellefontaine, it has been a pleasure doing business with you," Duff said. "But, we'll be taking leave of you now."

"I understand. And I wish you the best of luck in finding the girl."

CHAPTER NINETEEN

Austin

"Elmer, thank God you came," Governor Ireland said. When he saw Wang, he got a surprised expression on his face.

"Wang is with us, and he is a good man," Elmer said. "Believe me, Colonel, if we are going to be able to find your daughter 'n bring her back home to you, Wang will be a big help."

The governor nodded.

"I read the note, Governor. It wasn't signed, but I assume it was the Fence Busters?" Duff asked.

"I'm sure of it," the governor replied.

"I know that the law was just recently passed making it against the law to cut fence on public land. But my own experience with these brigands has proven that, even before making all fence cutting a felony, they were breaking the law. I dinnae mean this as a criticism, Governor, but how is it that you have nae gone after them before now?"

"I've known about them for some time, but they are so well organized and there are so many of them that no county sheriff departments have been able to stop them. Cutting fences on public land wasn't against the law until recently, and I'm not sure that law would stand up now, if it was challenged in the federal court."

"As I understand it, all you have to do to get your daughter back is repeal the law," Duff said.

"Yes."

"Have you considered that?"

"I've considered it, but I just got the legislature to pass the law. I can't very well go back to them now and ask them to repeal it. To be honest with you, I'm not sure the legislature would be willing to do so, even if they knew the reason for my request."

"I think you are doing the right thing, Governor. 'Tis a courageous decision on your part not to give in to them," Duff said.

"Yes, well, I don't know if it is courageous or foolish," Governor Ireland said. "But I do know this. If I do what they ask, and they return Rosalie unharmed, she'll always be a hostage, even if she is at home. They will know that all they have to do is threaten her, and they can bend me to their will. She would always be in danger."

"Governor, you said there are many Fence Busters. Do you know how many there are?" Duff asked.

"I don't have an exact count, for the number varies as new members join, while some back out or are killed. The best estimate we have is that there are between thirty and forty. Their leader, as I'm sure you have already heard, is Dirk Kendrick."

"Do you know anything about Kendrick?" Duff asked.

"Oh, I know a great deal about him, and none of it is good," the governor replied. "He is originally from New York, where he practiced law. According to the information I have been given, he was a very good lawyer, successfully defending some of the most disreputable people in the city.

"He was, for a long time, the counselor for a gang of hoodlums known as the Whyos."

"The what?" Elmer asked.

"The Whyos," Governor Ireland repeated. He shook his head. "Don't ask me what that means. According to what I learned from the New York Police, the Whyos are an Irish gang that started out as a loose collection of petty thugs, pickpockets, and murderers, but were brought together as a gang by a man named Googie Corcoran. They controlled all of Manhattan. The petty criminals either joined the gang or they were put out of business for not joining. Kendrick was his chief counselor.

"One of their most effective ploys was to sell 'insurance' " — he raised his hands and made quotation marks above his head — "to business owners, to prevent their businesses from being attacked by criminal elements. The criminal element, of course, was the Whyos themselves. Kendrick, as a lawyer, would visit the businesses and write up the contracts between the businesses and the 'insurance' company.

"When the New York and Texas Land Company needed someone to do their bidding down here, they recruited Kendrick."

"Ha! He's from New York then and not a Westerner?" Elmer asked.

"Yes, and that makes him all the more dangerous," Governor Ireland said. "He doesn't seem to have the same sense of honor that even our criminals have out here."

"How is it that the New York and Texas Land Company was able to recruit Kendrick?" Duff asked.

"Apparently, the police cracked down on the Whyos and most of them wound up in jail. Kendrick took advantage of that opportunity to leave New York before the police began their raid."

"Have the New York police asked you to arrest Kendrick?" Duff asked.

"No, they haven't, and I don't think they will," the governor replied. "Don't underestimate Kendrick's intelligence. The same skills he used to negotiate the contracts with the victims of the Whyos kept his name free of any association with them beyond that of being their lawyer. And of course, there is no crime in defending criminals, since the constitution guarantees everyone the right to counsel."

"So now he is here, with an army of what could be as many as forty men, and he is holding your daughter in captivity," Duff said.

"Yes. Please tell me you'll do what you can."

"You are aware, Governor, that there are but three of us."

Governor Ireland hung his head for a moment. "Yes, I am quite aware of that," he said quietly.

"What makes you think that three of us could best a force of some forty men?"

"I . . . I don't know," the governor admitted. "I suppose I was just clutching at

236

straws. Of course, if you don't wish to undertake this task, I can certainly understand why."

"I haven't said that we won't help, but we do have to have some sort of workable plan. Let the three of us have lunch, so we can discuss this among ourselves. We'll come up with some idea, then we'll get back to you this afternoon," Duff said.

"I would like for you to be my guest at the Capitol Restaurant," the governor said. He took a sheet of monogrammed paper from his desk and scrawled out a quick note. "Show this to the maître d'."

"Governor, my friend, Wang?"

"There will be no problem," Governor Ireland said.

Five minutes later Duff, Elmer, and Wang were sitting at a table in the Capitol Restaurant discussing the governor's request as they waited to be served.

"We've got to do something for the wee lass," Duff said. "For 'tis our fault she was taken."

"Accordin' to the colonel, they's an awful lot of 'em," Elmer said.

"Aye, 'tis true that the odds are against us."

"I figure it's goin' to take about ten guns,

just to even up the odds some," Elmer said. "But, where are we going to get ten guns?"

"You need but three more men to have ten guns," Wang said.

"Damn, Wang, didn't they teach you no cipherin' over there in China?"

"You have a pistol and a rifle, yes?" Wang said, pointing to Elmer.

"Yeah."

"MacCallister *Xian shen* has a pistol and a rifle. I have no pistol, I have no rifle." Wang used the Chinese word, *Xian shen,* which was an address of respect reserved for teachers and others who occupied an honorable position.

"What are you gettin' at?" Elmer asked.

Duff chuckled. "Think about what Wang is saying, Elmer. Three more men, each with a pistol and a rifle, would be six more guns. Their six with our four would be ten guns."

Elmer laughed. "Yeah, I see what he's a-gettin' at. I reckon you did take cipherin' back in China. You're right, all we need is three more men."

"They must be good men," Wang said.

"If we had time to get my cousin Falcon and my friends Smoke and Matt Jensen down here, we would have three more good men," Duff said.

"Yeah, 'n if a frog had wings, he wouldn't

bump his ass ever' time he jumps, neither," Elmer said.

"Well, now, Elmer, I must say, that is quite an astute observation," Duff said.

"Perhaps it is a saying of Confucius," Wang suggested.

"The hell it is. My own pappy said that," Elmer replied.

Duff and Wang laughed.

"Say, Duff, I've got me an idee as to where we might get us them three more men, but if I tell you what I'm thinkin' about, why you're more 'n likely goin' to think I'm crazy. I'd like you to hear me out before you decide to throw me into the madhouse, though."

"Elmer, almost every idea you've ever had has been daft. But almost all of them have worked out. What is the idea?"

"Do you 'member readin' that newspaper story sayin' that Roy Kelly got throwed into prison for ridin' with Bill Anderson?"

"Aye, I remember. I believe you said that you knew him."

"That's a fact. I do know 'im. Me 'n him rode through some pretty rough times back durin' the war, 'n I could always count on Roy to pull my bacon out of the fire. What I'm gettin' around to is this. He's a man you can ride to the river with."

"You are suggesting that the governor pardon him?" Duff asked.

"Yeah. He could pardon 'im if Kelly agrees to come with us. I know Kelly would do that."

"Do you think Mr. Kelly can find two more men that we could . . . as you have put it, 'ride to the river with'?" Duff asked.

"Yeah, Roy's just real good about makin' friends, 'n what's even better is, he knows what kind of folks he should be makin' friends with. He can get us two more men, 'n most likely, it'll be men that he's met while he's been locked up in prison."

"Let me see if I understand this," Governor Ireland said when the three men returned to his office. "You want me to pardon three men that we now have in prison, but you don't know who the three are."

"Yes, sir, Colonel, that's pretty much it," Elmer said.

"Lieutenant Gleason, don't you think it would be a good idea to know the names of the men I'm going to pardon?"

"Well, I know one of 'em," Elmer said. "And I'm figurin' he can give me the names of the other two we'll need."

"All right. Who do you want me to pardon?"

"Roy Kelly."

"Roy Kelly? Seems to me that I've heard that name before," the governor said.

"Yes, sir, I expect you have. Me 'n him rode some with Quantrill 'n Bloody Bill Anderson. Only time he warn't with me was when I was ridin' with Asa Briggs."

"What is Mr. Kelly in prison for?" the governor asked. "If it's for murder, I don't think I could pardon him."

"It ain't murder," Elmer said. "It ain't nothin' more 'n the fact that he rode with Bloody Bill Anderson. They was some Yankee judge that throwed him in jail for that."

Governor Ireland stroked his beard for a moment as he stared at Elmer. "You know, Elmer, you've got me over a barrel here. I want my daughter back, and you're saying the only way I can get her back is by freeing three convicted criminals, two of whom I don't even know."

"Yes, sir, well, two of 'em I don't know, neither," Elmer said.

"Governor, I promise you, we are going to do whatever it takes to get your daughter back," Duff said. "But if Elmer believes this is the way that offers the most chance for success, then I think we should go with it. I've been around him long enough that I've learned to listen to him."

The governor nodded. "Yes, I seem to recall that he was most sagacious. If he has come up with this plan, I am more than willing to allow it to be put into place."

He called out for his secretary. "Mr. Fitzhugh?"

"Yes, sir?" Fitzhugh stepped into the room.

"Don't we have some printed forms for pardon?"

"Yes, sir, we do."

"Bring three of them to me."

"Three, sir? You are going to grant three pardons to incarcerated prisoners? Don't you think that might be a bit impolitic?"

"Impolitic, Fitzhugh? Impolitic? Dammit, man, my daughter is being held by a bunch of heathens, and you are telling me that granting a pardon to some men who might help me get her back is impolitic? Just do it."

"Yes, sir," Fitzhugh replied.

CHAPTER TWENTY

Texas State Penitentiary, Huntsville

Duff, Elmer, and Wang, each of them leading a saddled horse, were challenged by the guard when they arrived at the main gate of the prison.

"You'll have to go back," the guard said. "This isn't visiting hours."

"We're nae here to visit a prisoner," Duff replied. "We're here to visit with the warden."

"You got an appointment with the warden?"

"We got somethin' better," Elmer said. "We got a letter from the governor, tellin' the warden to meet with us." He showed the letter to the guard.

The sentry looked at it, then called out to one of the others in the blockhouse. "Barnes, you want to go get Cap'n Phillips? This is for him."

As Barnes left the blockhouse, the guard

stood in place. "What are the three extra horses for?"

"Well now, if we're goin' to break three men outta here, you don't expect 'em to walk while we're ridin', do you?" Elmer asked.

"What?"

Elmer laughed. "I'm funnin' with you."

"We do hope to be leaving with three of your current residents," Duff said, "but we'll nae do it without permission of the warden."

A moment later, Barnes returned with an older man who was also wearing a guard's uniform.

"What's this about, Blake?" he asked the guard who had detained the three.

"This here letter's from the governor, 'n it's for you," Blake said.

To: Captain Emory Phillips

The three gentlemen bearing this letter, Duff MacCallister, Elmer Gleason, and Wang Chow, are on a special mission authorized by me. Please allow them entry into the prison and arrange for them an audience with the warden.

John Ireland
Governor

"What is this about?" Phillips asked.

"We'll be stating our mission to the warden," Duff said. "I expect it will involve you, so I'll have nae problem with you listening to the request as we make it. But I'll nae be asking you first."

It was obvious that Duff's refusal to clear his mission with the captain of the guards didn't fit well with Phillips, but with a grunt, he led them to the warden's office and ushered them inside.

"The governor has granted a pardon for Roy Kelly?" the warden asked incredulously after he read the pardon form presented to him by Duff.

"Aye, Roy Kelly and two more," Duff said.

"Who are the other two?"

"We'll tell you after we have spoken to Mr. Kelly."

The warden shook his head. "There's something fishy about this."

"Warden, might I suggest that you send a telegram to the Governor to verify what I am saying? We'll wait here until you have received your reply."

It took less than thirty minutes before the warden came back in, holding the telegram in his hand. There was a look of total confusion on his face. "I don't know what's going on here."

"Did you get a reply from the governor?"

Duff asked.

Wordlessly, the warden held the telegram out for Duff to read.

I JOHN IRELAND GOVERNOR OF THE STATE OF TEXAS ORDER YOU TO EXTEND FULL AND COMPLETE CO-OPERATION WITH DUFF MACCALISTER AND ELMER GLEASON STOP

"Do you have a place where we can visit with Mr. Kelly?" Duff asked.

The warden nodded. "Yes, there is a room where prisoners can receive visitors."

"Will there be guards present?"

"Well, yes, of course."

"We would prefer to meet with him in a private room with no guards present."

"That would be against the law," Captain Phillips put in. "We cannot let our prisoners visit with anyone without a guard present."

"Aye, that might be so," Duff said, "but Mr. Kelly is nae longer a prisoner."

"What do you mean, he's no longer a prisoner?" Captain Phillips asked.

"Warden, would you please be for showing Captain Phillips the pardon I just gave you?" Duff asked.

The warden showed the pardon to Captain Phillips.

"You man Kelly is bein' set free?" Phillips asked.

"Yes," the warden replied.

"And we'd like to meet with him in a private room, if you please," Duff said.

The warden nodded toward Captain Phillips. "Please arrange for their meeting and bring him to the hearing room."

The glaring expression on Captain Phillips's face showed his displeasure, but he nodded and left the office to carry out the warden's order.

"What's going on here?" Kelly asked when he stepped into the room a few minutes later. He looked at Elmer with a curious expression on his face. "Gleason? Elmer Gleason, is that you?"

Elmer nodded. "It is."

Kelly smiled broadly and extended his hand. "I'll be damned! What are you doing here?"

"I came to get you," Elmer said.

"Get me? Get me for what?"

"For a job I want you to help us with."

Kelly chuckled. "Uh, maybe you ain't noticed, but I'm a little tied up at the moment."

"No you ain't. Not no more, you ain't.

The governor's givin' you a pardon, if you agree to help us with this job."

"Hell yes, I'll help you with the job!" Kelly said excitedly.

"You ain't asked what it is."

"I don't care what it is as long as it'll get me out of here."

"It'll get you out, all right. It could also get you kilt," Elmer said.

"Well, hell, Gleason, it ain't like I've never been in a situation like that before. With you, in fact. Now, what kind of job is it?"

"Before we tell you that, we need for you to recommend two more in here that might help us," Duff said.

"Who are you?" Kelly asked.

"This here is my friend, Duff MacCallister," Elmer said.

Kelly looked at Duff for a moment, then he looked back toward Elmer. "Who's the Chinaman?"

"His name is Wang Chow, and he'll also be with us. Duff will be in charge of the job."

"Which you ain't goin' to tell me what it is until I give you two more names of somebody that's likely to take on a job that might get 'em kilt?"

"Yeah. Do you know two more men like that?"

Kelly smiled. "Yeah. Yeah, as a matter of fact, I do."

"These here two men are Al Simmons and Hugh Decker," Kelly said when the two men came into the room. "Decker, Simmons, this here is an old friend of mine, Elmer Gleason. This is Duff MacCallister, and the Chinaman is . . . what was your name again?"

"I am Wang Chow."

"Yeah, Wang Chow."

"What's this all about, Kelly?" Decker asked. "And how come it is that the warden let us come in here without no guards?"

"Truth to tell, I don't know nothin' about it yet, neither," Kelly said. "Exceptin' this. The governor is goin' to give us a full pardon iffen we will agree to do a job for him."

"A full pardon? You mean he's goin' to let us out of prison?"

"Yeah, but, like I say, he's only goin' to do that if we agree to do a job for 'im."

Decker frowned. "What kind of job?"

"A job that could get us all kilt."

"Do you plan to take 'im up on it?" Simmons asked.

"You're damn right I do. I'd rather get kilt tryin' to do somethin' that will get me out

of here than spend the rest of my life rottin'
in here," Kelly said.

"What about them two and the Chinaman? Are they the ones that's goin' to sit
back and send us out on this job?"

"The Chinaman has a name," Elmer said.
"His name is Wang Chow."

"Where's he come in?" Decker asked.

"Wang is with us," Duff said. "And he will
take orders from me, as will you."

"You don't say." Decker said.

"We'll all be goin' on the job together,"
Elmer pointed out. "We're as likely to get
kilt as you are."

"That is, unless you choose to stay in
prison. And if you choose to stay, I'm sure
Mr. Kelly can find two other men who are
willing to take a chance for a full pardon,"
Duff said.

"No, no. We'll do it!" Simmons said.
"Leastwise, I'll do it."

"What about you, Mr. Decker. Are you
willing to come with us?" Duff asked.

"I'd like to hear what this is all about
before I say as to whether or not I'm willin'
to go along with it," Decker said.

"Mr. Kelly, would you call the guard to
come get Mr. Decker?" Duff asked. "I'm
sure you can come up with another name
for us."

"I sort of hate losin' Decker," Kelly said. "I've always figured he was a pretty good man."

"Wait, wait!" Decker said. "I never said I wouldn't do it. I just wanted to know a little somethin' about what we was goin' to do, is all."

Duff nodded. "I can see how you might be curious about it. But in order for this to work, we cannae let anyone know what we have planned. The longer we can keep the secret, the safer we'll all be. Once you commit to working with us, we'll fill you in on everything you need to know. Now, it's your choice. Do you go with us or do we call the guards to return you to your cell?"

"All right," Decker said. "Whatever you've got in mind, I'll go along with it. I'm like Kelly. Even if I get kilt, I'd rather die a free man than a prisoner."

Duff smiled. "It takes a good man to make that decision, the kind of man we need in order for this to work."

"We'll need a name," Elmer said.

"A name?" Kelly asked. "What do you mean, we'll need a name?"

"Ever' good outfit has got to have themselves a name," Elmer said. "There was Quantrill's Raiders, Bloody Bill Anderson's Bushwhackers, 'n Asa Brigg's Ghost Riders.

I figure we can call ourselves the Ten Guns from Texas."

"You plannin' on gettin' four more men?" Simmons asked.

"No, they's five of us. We'll carry two guns apiece. That'll make ten," Elmer explained.

"They's six of us," Decker said.

"Wang won't be carryin' no guns," Elmer said.

"If he ain't carryin' no gun, what's he comin' with us for? He'll just be in the way, won't he?"

"Oh, I think he can keep out of our way," Duff said with a little chuckle.

Two hours later, Kelly, Decker, and Simmons were wearing new clothes and each of them was equipped with a Colt .44, a Winchester .44-40 carbine, and four boxes of ammunition. They were also well-mounted.

"Hey! How come you boys is gettin' out of here?" one of the prisoners in the yard yelled. "I know damn well your time ain't up."

"Ain't you heard?" Kelly shouted back. "Today's the governor's birthday, 'n he's invited us to his house for a birthday party."

"What the hell? How come he invited you all 'n none of us?"

" 'Cause we sent 'im a letter tellin' 'im Happy Birthday," Decker added with a chuckle as the guards opened the front gate for them.

So far, none of them had any idea as to the nature of the job for which they had been recruited, but none of them asked, satisfied that they were out of prison.

CHAPTER TWENTY-ONE

Shortly after they reached the area where they were to camp for the night, Wang began walking around, examining the various wild plants, gathering some, passing on others.

"What's the Chinaman a-doin'?" Kelly asked.

"He's fixin' to cook our supper," Elmer replied.

"Supper? Damn, he's cuttin' weeds! He don't expect us to eat weeds, does he?"

"Whether or nae you eat what he prepares, will be your choice," Duff said. "Aye, 'n 'twill be your loss if you decide you dinnae wish to partake of the fare."

"How come you talk like that?" Simmons asked.

Elmer chuckled. "He does talk funny, don't he? He's from Scotland."

"Scotland? Where's that? Somewhere in New York?"

"Damn, he's still cuttin' weeds," Decker

254

said. "I'll tell you right now, I ain't a-goin' to eat no weeds."

Kelly, Decker, and Simmons watched curiously as Wang wandered along the bank of the creek, then moved out to gather plants from beneath the trees and farther out in open prairie.

Half an hour later, gleaming orange sparks rode a column of heated air to add their brilliance to the stars, lighting the darkness. The night was perfumed with the aroma of fried bacon. Into the bacon grease, Wang dropped cattail, fireweed, field pennycress, wild onion stems, and wild mushrooms. As that concoction was cooking, he made a dough of flour and water, and rolled it out into one large circle. Laying the cooked vegetable ingredients, as well as crumbled bacon bits, into a single line all the way across the circle of dough, he folded it up into one long roll, then cut it into several smaller pieces. Using chopsticks, he dropped them into the hot bacon grease.

Kelly, Decker and Simmons watched in curiosity as Wang worked.

"What the hell are you a-makin' there, Chinaman?" Decker asked.

"Do not worry, *Laowai,* If you do not wish to eat, I think Gleason *Xian shen* will eat it."

Elmer laughed. "You're damn right, I'll eat it."

"What's that you called me, Chinaman? Loywee? That ain't my name."

"Indeed," Wang said. "And Chinaman is not my name."

"*Laowai* is Chinese for anyone who ain't Chinese," Elmer said. "And it ain't all that good of a thing to be called."

"Wait a minute. You mean he insulted me?"

"Yeah, you might say that," Elmer said. "But then, you insulted him, so you could call it even."

"I'll be damned if I'm goin' to stand here 'n let some Chinaman insult me. Why don't I just knock him on his scrawny little ass. Then we'll call it even." Decker suggested.

"Go ahead. Be my guest," Duff said.

"I hate to do this, Chinaman," Decker said, "but you need to learn how to deal with your betters."

Wang, who was using his chopsticks to move the cooking rolls around in the grease, was seemingly paying no attention to Decker.

"Look at me when I'm talkin' to you, Chinaman!" Decker said angrily.

Wang continued to tend to the cooking rolls.

"Don't say I didn't warn you!" Decker said loudly as he sent his right hand toward Wang.

Wang didn't look up from the skillet, but he caught Decker's fist in his left hand, then jerked it down. The momentum supplied by the punch caused Decker to tumble head over heels. He rolled down the hill, stopping just short of landing in the creek.

The others laughed.

When Decker stood up, he saw that Wang was still paying no attention to him. "How the hell did you do that?" he asked as he climbed back up the hill.

Wang didn't answer, but he picked up one of the rolls with his chopsticks and held it out. "Decker taste first. If you do not like, you do not have to eat."

Warily, Decker took the proffered fried roll. It was hot, and he tossed it from hand to hand for a moment, then he took a bite. "Damn!" he said as a broad smile spread across his face. "Damn, this is good!"

Wang nodded.

"Wang, you're all right by me. You're a man I'd be willin' to ride to the river with."

"I will ride to the river with you, Decker *Xian shen.*"

"What is this shinshang?"

"Don't worry about it, Decker, it's the

257

same thing as *mister,* only maybe just a little bit more," Elmer said. "He only uses that word for people that he respects."

"Yeah, now that I think about it, he called you that, too, didn't he? Hey, Gleason, how come you know his lingo? Did he teach it to you?"

"No, I learned some of it while I was in China."

"You was in China?"

"Yeah."

"I'll be damned. You're the first person I've ever knowed who was ever actual in China."

Kelly laughed. "Decker, you don't reckon this here feller, Wang, come from St. Louis, do you?"

The others laughed as well.

"Hey, MacCallister," Kelly said. "Don't you think now might be a good time for you to tell us what this here job is all about?"

"I'll tell you as we are eating our supper," Duff replied.

"Yeah, let's eat," Decker said. "This is damn good. What do you call these things?"

"They are called egg rolls, but they are without eggs because we have none," Wang said.

As the six men sat around the fire, enjoying the meal Wang had prepared for them,

Duff told them about their mission to rescue the governor's daughter.

"Wow, the governor's daughter?" Simmons asked. "That'd be kinda like them stories I've heard about where a knight rescues the princess."

"This here ain't no princess," Decker said.

"Sure she is. What is a princess?" Simmons asked. "A princess is the daughter of a king, ain't she? Well, when you think about it, a governor is kind of like a king, ain't he? So that makes this here girl . . . what did you say her name was?"

"Miss Ireland," Elmer said.

"Yeah, but don't she have another name besides Miss?"

"Rosalie," Duff said.

"Yeah, well, her bein' the governor's daughter 'n all, that sorta makes her a princess. Princess Rosalie." Simmons smiled broadly at his analogy.

Slash Bell Ranch
Duff and the others reached the big house and were greeted by Bellefontaine and Sam Post.

"Have you located the governor's daughter?" the rancher asked.

"No, not yet. If you would nae mind, Mr. Bellefontaine, could I be for parking my

259

men with you for a short while? I plan to go into Merrill Town and do a bit o' recon- noitering," Duff said. "Perhaps I can pick up some intelligence on the young lass."

"Sure. I'd be happy to put them up," Bellefontaine said.

"MacCallister *Xian shen,* I will come as well if you will have me," Wang said. "I can be invisible."

"What the hell? Wang, are you telling me a Chinamen can really be invisible?" Kelly asked.

"Shi," Wang replied.

"She? She who?"

"I do not mean lady. *Shi* means *yes.* I can be invisible."

"Now I know you are just foolin' me. Hell, they can't nobody make hisself invisible."

"What Wang means is, people pay no at- tention to a Chinaman who doesn't draw attention to himself," Duff said. "Most people think that they either can't under- stand what is being said or they are so detached that it doesn't matter to a China- man what anyone is saying. It makes such a person a very valuable tool for gathering information."

"Huh. I ain't never thought of that, but it's most likely true, ain't it? It's like talkin' aroun' Injuns when you know they don't know our lingo," Kelly said.

"Mr. MacCallister," Post said. "If you're wantin' to find out somethin', you're more likely to hear it at the Hog Pen than you would at the *Alabama*. They don't never wear them blue kerchiefs when they come to town, but I know damn well they's Fence Busters that come into Merrill Town pretty often, 'n when they do, they most of the time hang out in the Hog Pen."

"Thank you, Mr. Post. That is the establishment I shall visit."

Merrill Town

Jug Bitters was in Walker's Grocery when he saw Muley Ledbetter with a sack of beans, a side of bacon, flour, and coffee on the counter in front of him.

"Damn, Muley. You hungry?" Jug teased.

"This ain't all for me."

"I thought you boys done all your shoppin' in Blowout."

"Yeah, well, that ain't the cabin I'm a-goin' to. Some of us is stayin' up at Miller Creek Draw."

"What are you doin' up there?"

"We got . . . uh . . . some business up there," Muley said. "I ain't s'posed to talk about it."

Jug looked around to make certain there

was no one close enough to overhear their conversation.

"I heard the governor's daughter got took. Is that where you're keepin' 'er?"

"Who told you that?" Muley snapped. "There ain't nobody except Fence Busters that's s'posed to know that's where at we're a-keepin' 'er."

"You can trust me, Muley. I used to be in the Fence Busters, remember?"

"Yeah, but you ain't no more, so I can't tell you nothin' 'bout anything. Beside which, if Kendrick even know'd I was talkin' to you 'bout this, he'd be on me like a duck on a june bug."

Jug held both his hands up. "You don't have to worry none. I won't say a word to Kendrick."

Duff had been to the CSS *Alabama* Saloon several times since he first arrived in town, but it was his first visit to the Hog Pen Saloon. As soon as he was inside, he stepped away from the door, then pressed his back against the wall, thus providing a target to no one that he couldn't see. He had been taught the maneuver by his cousin, Falcon, shortly after arriving in America, and it had served him well ever since.

Although the Hog Pen was just as large

and just as busy as the CSS *Alabama,* the similarity in the two saloons stopped there. In the CSS *Alabama,* shining, cut-glass chandeliers hung from the ceiling, and the lights were brightly burning gas flames.

The "chandeliers" of the Hog Pen were wagon wheels, from which hung kerosene lanterns. The bar was filled with patrons who hooked a boot onto the foot rail, which was wood, unlike the brass rail at the CSS *Alabama.* They leaned across their drinks protectively. A dozen or more painted women drifted through the room, working the patrons for drinks.

"What can I get ya?"

"Tell me, barkeep, and would you have a decent Scotch now?"

"What kinda accent is that you got?" the bartender asked.

"Ah, 'tis nae an accent, lad. 'Tis the music of Scotland, m' homeland."

"Only kind of whiskey we got is Old Overholt."

"Then I'll be troublin' you for a beer."

Woodson and Jenkins were standing at the other end of the bar when Duff ordered his drink.

"Lou, you know who that is?" Woodson asked.

"You think that's the Scotsman that's been causin' all the trouble?"

"Yeah. I'd be willin' to bet that's MacCallister."

"Let's get out of here," Jenkins replied.

Woodson frowned. "Why leave?"

"So we can tell Kendrick where he is."

"I got a better idea. How much do you think Kendrick would pay us to make his trouble go away?"

Jenkins answered quickly. "Quite a bit, I would say."

"Yeah, I'm thinkin' maybe as much as five hunnert dollars apiece."

"All right. What do you have in mind?"

"You're a better shot than I am, but I'm a bit faster 'n you, so this is how we'll do it. You go upstairs, have your gun out, and keep an eye open. I'm goin' to prod this feller into drawin' his gun, but you'll already have your gun out, so as soon as you see him start to draw, shoot 'im. I'll be shootin' 'bout the same time, 'n ever'one will be watchin' me 'n him. Nobody will even see you. Once he goes down, you put your gun away and just come down the stairs real casual like. Ever'one will think I'm the one that done it."

"So you'll get all the credit," Jenkins said.

"What difference does it make who gets

264

all the credit? We'll both get the money." Woodson said.

"Yeah." Jenkins smiled. "Yeah, we will."

CHAPTER TWENTY-TWO

Duff had been watching the two men at the other end of the bar from the moment he came in. He was almost positive that they had been with the rustlers who had cut the fence and tried to run off the cattle after they were delivered to the Slash Bell. He was observing them surreptitiously, watching in the mirror as they were engaged in some sort of intense conversation.

His curiosity deepened when one of them walked away, leaving half a mug of beer and going upstairs. That, in itself, wouldn't have aroused much suspicion had he gone up with a woman. But he went upstairs alone. The suspicion changed to absolute certainty when Duff saw the man draw his pistol once he reached the top of the stairs. Not realizing he was being watched, the man held his pistol down by his side so that it wasn't noticeable, then he stepped up to the railing to study the floor below.

Slowly and unobtrusively, Duff drew his pistol, then mimicking the man at the top of the stairs, he held the pistol down by his leg. He moved closer to the bar so that the gun was hidden between the bar and his leg. Not even the person standing closest to him had any idea what he had done.

He didn't have to wait long to see what the next step would be.

"Hey, you!" shouted the man who had stayed at the far end of the bar.

A few others in the saloon, alerted by the harshness and challenge of the voice, looked around to see what was going on.

"And would you be addressing me now?" Duff asked.

"No, I ain't dressin' you, you idjit. I'm talkin' to you."

"Indeed," Duff replied. "And what would be the subject of your interest in me?"

"Is your name MacCallister?"

"Aye, MacCallister is my name. How is it that you know me? Have we met?"

"No, we ain't met. You're a damn ferriner, ain't ya?"

"Oh I dinnae think I have been condemned to eternal perdition, so I wouldn't say that I'm damned. But since I came to this country from Scotland, aye, you could call me a foreigner."

Woodson blinked, not sure that he understood what Duff had said. "Yeah, well, here's the thing, mister. We don't like ferriners in this town, so you got two choices. You can either leave town now with your tail between your legs or you can stay here and get yourself kilt."

"And would you be for killing a person just because he is a foreigner?" Duff asked.

"Yeah," Woodson said. "Yeah, I would. What do you think about that?"

"Oh, I dinnae think I would like to be killed," Duff said. "I think if it came right down to it, I would have to kill you."

"You think you can beat me to the draw, do you?" Woodson challenged.

"Probably not," Duff said. "I have never really had to develop the proficiency of a rapid extraction of my weapon from its holster."

"Mister, why the hell don't you speak English? You're in Texas now."

"Well now, feller, just what lingo is that you are a-wantin' me to speak, anyhow? Do you want me to speak Texan, slow enough so that even a dumb sumbitch like you can understand me? Or do you want me speak English?" Sounding no different from any cowboy in Texas, Duff asked the question in

268

the same flat drawl that Woodson was using.

"What the hell? Are you a-funnin' me?" Woodson asked in exasperation.

"Well, now that you mention it, pardner, I reckon I just might be a-funnin' you at that," Duff said, continuing with the Texas drawl.

"Now, that's just the kinda thing that can get a feller like you kilt," Woodson said.

"Is it now? 'N here I thought you said it was bein' a ferriner that was a-gonna get me kilt."

"Whether it's 'cause you are a ferriner or you got yourself a smart mouth, it don't matter which. The thing is, I'm about to kill you, right where you stand," Woodson said.

"Oh, I dinnae think so," Duff said, dropping back into the Scottish brogue. "You see, as it turns out, I am quite an excellent marksman and will have nae trouble in shooting your friend, who even now is waiting on the balcony for the opportunity to shoot me. Of course, as you are much closer, shooting you will be even easier."

"What the hell, Woodson? He knows what you got planned!" Jenkins shouted from the balcony, raising his pistol and punctuating his shout by squeezing the trigger. In his shock and haste, his bullet broke the beer

269

mug from which Duff had been drinking, missing Duff by several inches.

Duff raised the pistol already in his hand and returned Jenkins's fire. He didn't miss. Jenkins, with a black hole right in the middle of his forehead, tumbled over the railing, then came crashing through a table right below. Cards and poker chips scattered as the players, startled by the sudden turn of events, just managed to get out of the way of the falling body.

Taking advantage of the distraction, Woodson started for his gun, but because he hadn't been able to call the move, he was a beat slower than he would have been.

Duff, who already had the pistol in his hand, turned his gun on Woodson. Both men fired at the same time, but the bullet from Woodson's gun whizzed by Duff's ear and smashed through the window behind him. Duff returned fire and Woodson dropped his gun to slap his hands over the middle of his chest. He looked down in disbelief as blood oozed through his fingers.

"You . . . you. . . ." Woodson never got beyond the repeated word. Whatever he was going to say remained unspoken as he collapsed on the floor.

"Damn, Slim!" someone said. "Did you see that?"

"Hell yeah, I seen it," Slim replied. "We all seen it. We're here, too."

"Mister, I ain't never seen no one as fast as you," the first man said. "I never even seen you draw."

Duff kept a bit of information to himself — that he hadn't drawn because it wasn't necessary and that he had been holding the pistol in his hand from the moment he saw the first man climb the stairs to the overlook.

With the still smoking pistol in his hand, Duff looked around the saloon to see if there was any further threat. Ascertaining none, he put his pistol away, then turned back to the bar. He looked toward what was left of his beer. "Barkeep, I think perhaps I will have a whiskey after all."

"I believe you said you like Scotch," the bartender replied.

"Aye, but you said you dinnae have any."

The bartender smiled, then reached under the bar and pulled out a bottle of Haig. "Don't always believe everything a bartender tells you."

"Well now, 'tis m' thanks I give you."

Duff had just finished his drink when Sheriff Wallace and Deputy Bullock came running into the saloon with guns drawn.

"Hog Jaw, what the hell's goin' on here?"

Wallace asked authoritatively.

"There ain't nothin' goin' on," the bartender replied. "It's done gone on, 'n it's all over now."

Wallace held his pistol for a moment longer, then, seeing that nobody else was holding a gun in their hand, he holstered his. Bullock, seeing the sheriff put his gun away, did the same thing.

"What the hell?" Wallace asked. "Is that Woodson?"

"Yeah." Slim pointed toward the back of the room. "And you'll find Jenkins back there, a-lyin' in the middle of that busted table."

"Who shot 'em?"

"I shot them," Duff said, turning to face the sheriff and his deputy.

"You," Sheriff Wallace said. "You're the one that kilt all them men for doin' no more 'n cuttin' a fence on public land, out near the Slash Bell, ain't you? What was your name? MacCallister, was it?"

"Aye, 'twas and still is my name. Duff MacCallister."

"What'd you shoot these two men for, MacCallister? Was they tryin' to rustle cows, too?" Wallace asked with a humorless laugh.

"I shot them because they were shooting at me."

"Who shot first?"

"The first shot came from the deceased gentleman lying on the broken table back there. The second shot came from him." Duff pointed to Woodson, who was lying on his back, the pistol still in his hand. "I shot just a split second later than both of them."

"How do you know that you didn't shoot just a second before he did?" Wallace asked.

"Because if I had, he would have nae got his shot off," Duff explained.

"So, let me get this straight. You're a-sayin' that they was both of 'em a-shootin' at you, 'n they started out a-shootin' a-fore you, but you still kilt 'em both?"

"Aye," Duff said with a nod of his head. "That's the way it happened."

"I don't believe you, mister," Sheriff Wallace said.

"If you will notice, Constable, the beer glass from which I was drinking is smashed, and there is a bullet hole in the window. Both missiles came from the guns of the deceased."

"He's tellin' you the truth, Sheriff," the bartender said. "He come in here 'n didn't do no more 'n order hisself a beer when Woodson started tryin' to pick a fight with him."

Wallace frowned. "What for? What did he

do to get Woodson all angered up?"

"He didn't do nothin' atall. It's like I said, all he done was order hisself a beer."

"Where does Jenkins fit into all this? Did Jenkins try an' pick a fight with him, too?"

"No, 'n that's the hell of it," the bartender said. "Jenkins was standin' up on the balcony up there, 'n he's actual the one who shot first. Then this fella shot back at him, then him and Woodson shot at each other, 'n, well . . . you see what happened."

The sheriff looked at Duff. "Did you know Woodson and Jenkins?"

"No," Duff replied.

"Then why in the hell did they just commence a-shootin' at you for no reason atall?"

"As near as I can gather, it's because I'm a Scotsman."

"That don't seem like reason enough to me," Sheriff Wallace said.

"Well now, I tend to agree with you, Constable," Duff replied. "Sure 'n nobody else has tried to shoot me just because I'm a Scotsman. At least, not since I arrived in the United States. So 'tis my thinking that 'twas for some other reason."

"Now we're getting somewhere," the sheriff said. "And what reason would that be?"

"Do you remember the attempt the Fence

274

Busters made on Mr. Bellefontaine's cattle the other day?"

"I remember his fence gettin' cut. Seems to me like there warn't no cattle stoled."

"None were taken, 'tis true. But it isn't because they didn't try. These two men" — Duff nodded at the bodies — "were riding with the rustlers. It could be that they feared I might recognize them and tell the law that they were there."

"I thought Bellefontaine said it was the Fence Busters that done it."

"Yes."

"Well, I happen to know that neither of these men belonged to the Fence Busters," the sheriff said.

"You know the identity of all the Fence Busters, do you, Constable?"

"What? No, why should I?"

"Exactly. Why should you? That means that these men could very well be members of the Fence Busters, and you would nae know about it."

"Yeah. Yeah, iffen you put it that way, I reckon you might be right." Wallace turned to his deputy. "Bullock, you'd better go get Ponder 'n tell 'im he has a couple customers."

"All right, Sheriff," Bullock said, turning toward the door

The sheriff turned back to Duff. "Let me ask you somethin', MacCallister. Are you getting some sort of payoff from Ponder?"

"Why would you ask that?"

"Because he's had more business from you in the last few days than he's had in the previous month."

Hog Jaw chuckled. "Damn if you ain't got that right, Sheriff. Damned if you don't."

Near Miller Creek Draw

Rosalie had been in the cabin for two days, and though she no longer had a rope around her neck, her hands and feet were still tied. Blankets and quilts were spread on the floor, and though it was not as comfortable as a bed would have been, it was better than sleeping on the dirt floor.

"Hey, Peabody, how long did Muley say he would be gone?" Morris asked.

"Why do you care?"

"I give 'im some money to buy a bottle of whiskey."

Peabody shook his head. "He didn't go to town to buy whiskey. He went to buy vittles. You know that Kendrick don't want nobody drinkin' out here. Especially since we're keepin' watch on the governor's daughter."

"Yeah? Well Kendrick ain't here now, is he?"

"It don't matter none whether Kendrick is here or not. I'm here, 'n as long as Kendrick says there ain't goin' to be no drinkin', then there ain't goin' to be no drinkin'."

"It don't seem right, spending all this time out here without so much as a single drink." Morris looked over at Rosalie.

She was leaning against the wall, sitting on the blankets with her knees drawn up in front of her.

"You know what else don't seem right? It don't seem right to have a good-lookin' woman like that, 'n not be able to enjoy it none." A satanic smile spread across his lips, and he reached down to grab himself. "You a virgin, little girl? 'Cause if you are, I'll break you in just real gentle. I ain't never had me a virgin before."

"You touch that girl, 'n Kendrick would more 'n likely kill you," Peabody said.

Peabody's words eased Rosalie's immediate fear, but what he said next brought another stab of fear.

"He'll prob'ly want her first, seein' as he's the boss. Then I expect he'll pass her around."

"Yeah," Morris said. "I still won't be gettin' me no virgin, but that won't bother me none. She'll just be broke in good by the time I get her."

CHAPTER TWENTY-THREE

Merrill Town

Jug and his friend Poke were having dinner at Ma Ling's Chinese Restaurant.

"How long are they a-plannin' on keepin' her in the Miller Creek Draw cabin?" Poke asked.

"I don't know. Muley didn't say."

"I can't believe Muley actually told you where they was keepin' the girl."

"He didn't exactly come out 'n say it. I sorta had to trick 'im. What I said was, 'You're a-holdin' that girl there, ain't you?' 'N then he got all nervous, wanted to know how I knew 'n all. Then he wanted me to swear that I wouldn't tell Kendrick."

Poke laughed. "Muley never was the smartest in the bunch, but we ought not to be talkin' about such things out in the open like this, Jug. You never can tell who might be listenin'."

"What are you worried about? You think

any o' these Chinamen might hear us? Hell, if they heard us and could understand what we was sayin', which most of 'em can't, it wouldn't make no difference to 'em. You think a Chinaman's goin' to give a tinker's damn 'bout the governor's daughter?"

Poke and Jug were speaking in conversational voices, with absolutely no concern over the fact that Wang Chow was sitting at the table next to them, eating with chopsticks.

"Do you think you know where they are a-keepin' 'er?" Poke asked.

"Yeah, I got me a damn good idea."

Poke put up a hand. "Well, don't tell me, 'cause I don't want to know. 'N if you ask me, I'm just as glad we ain't with the Fence Busters no more, neither. It seems to me like takin' the governor's daughter was just about the dumbest damn thing they coulda possible done. What the hell was they thinkin' about, anyway? They don't really think they're goin' to get away with it, do they?"

"To be honest with you, I don't have no idea what the hell they was thinkin' when they took her like they done."

A young and very attractive Chinese woman approached Wang's table. She smiled, and nodded her head in a quick bow. "Wang *Xian shen,* would you like more rice?" she asked in Mandarin.

"*Shi, xie xie,*" Wang replied in the same language, cupping his rice bowl in both hands and holding it out to her.

As the girl walked away, Jug spoke to Wang. "Hey, Chinaman. I think that girl likes you."

"*Wo ting bu dong,*" Wang said.

"What the hell did you just say?"

The attractive young Chinese girl translated Wang's response for them. "He said that he does not understand."

"You mean he don't speak English?"

"He does not understand," the girl said again.

"What the hell? If he don't speak English, what'd he come over here for?" Jug asked.

The girl shrugged, then went on toward the kitchen.

Jug smiled, then turned his attention away from Wang and back toward Poke. "I told you we could talk in here. Now, I've got a question for you. Just how much do you think the governor would be willin' to pay to find out where at they are a-holdin' his daughter?"

"Why are you askin' me a question like that? You ain't a-plannin' on tryin' to rescue her, are you, 'n maybe see if you can't get a reward from the governor? 'Cause if that's what you are a-thinkin' about, well, you can damn sure do it by yourself. I'm tellin' you right now that I ain't a-goin' up against Kendrick," Poke said, speaking emphatically.

"We wouldn't have to go up against him," Jug replied. "Leastwise, not so's anyone would know anythin' about it. But what iffen we was to tell the governor where the girl is, and he was to send someone else to rescue her? Why, don't you think he'd be a mite thankful for that?"

"Yeah," Poke said with a broad smile. "Yeah, I would go along with somethin' like that, iffen we don't have to be actual involved none. Only thing is, we got to be just real careful that it don't get out to Kendrick nor any of them Fence Buster boys that we was the ones that told where she is."

"I don't think we got to worry none about that," Jug said. "Only one we're goin' to tell is the governor, 'n you know damn well that he sure as hell ain't goin' to tell nobody."

"Yeah. Yeah, I reckon you're right," Poke agreed.

"What do you say we take a ride on up to Austin 'n start doin' some business with the governor?" Jug asked.

At that moment, the young Chinese girl returned with the rice, put it on Wang's table, then stepped back and made a very obvious bow. "We are humbled that you have chosen our place to take your meal, *Zongshi*."

"Why do you address me as a master?" Wang asked.

"My father says that you are a Shaolin priest. Is that so?"

"Here, I am as all others," Wang replied.

Their conversation was entirely in Mandarin.

"Did you see that?" Poke asked after the young woman left. "Why do you think she bowed to that Chinaman?"

"Who knows why the Chinese do anything?" Jug replied. "Come on. Let's go see the governor."

"You didn't hear the location of the cabin?" Duff asked when Wang reported on what he had overheard at Ma Ling's Chinese Restaurant.

"No, they did not say."

"But they are going to tell the governor."

"Shi."

"All right. Why don't we grab Elmer and just take a ride up to Austin?" Duff suggested. "By the time we get there, those two men will have already told him where Rosalie is being held. All we have to do then is gather up the others and go get her."

Austin

"I'm sorry, gentlemen, but the governor doesn't see just anyone who walks in off the street. You must have an appointment," Fitzhugh said.

"Yeah, well, here's the thing," Jug said. "Me 'n Poke here, we know where the governor's kid has been took, 'n we thought he might like to know that."

" 'N maybe he'd even like it enough to give us a reward for tellin' 'im," Poke added.

"You say you know where she is?"

"Yeah, we know where she is," Jug said.

"Tell me where she is being kept," Fitzhugh said. "You tell me, and I'll give the governor the information. And if your information proves to be accurate, I will see to it that you are adequately rewarded."

Jug shook his head. "No, sir. The only way the governor's ever goin' to find out where his kid is, is if we tell 'im our ownselves."

"And your names are?"

"We done tole' you. I'm Jug and this here is Poke."

"I will need your whole names if I am to announce you to the governor."

"Oh. Well that would be Jug Bitters and Poke Connelly."

"Very well, Mr. Bitters and Mr. Connelly, if you two gentlemen will just wait here for a moment, I'll see if the governor will receive you."

"He sure is sorta sissified, ain't he?" Poke commented as Fitzhugh stepped into the governor's office.

"Yeah, well people that works in offices most often is kinda like that," Jug replied.

A moment later, Fitzhugh returned. "The governor will see you now."

The governor was standing as the two men stepped into his office.

"Are you really the governor?" Poke asked.

"Yes. I understand you have news of my daughter."

"I ain't never actually seen a governor before," Poke said.

"Mr. Connelly, you said you had news of the governor's daughter," Fitzhugh encouraged.

"Oh, yeah. Well, it's actually Jug that knows."

The governor turned to Jug. "You would be Mr. Bitters?"

"Yeah."

"Where is my daughter, Mr. Bitters?"

"Don't tell 'im nothin', Jug, till he tells us how much money he's goin' to give us."

"Gentlemen, if you have actual information, I want to hear it now," Governor Ireland said. "Otherwise, I will put both of you in jail for attempted extortion."

"Attemptin' what?"

"Mr. Fitzhugh, would you get Captain Brooks in here? Tell him I am charging these two men with extortion, and I want them transported immediately to prison."

"No. Now, there ain't no need in you a-doin' that," Jug said. "They're a-keepin' 'er in a cabin that sits in Miller Creek Draw."

"Thank you very much, gentlemen. I am most appreciative," the governor said.

"How much?" Jug asked.

"I beg your pardon?"

"How much is it that you appreciate us a-tellin' you this?"

"If I find that my daughter is there, I will be most appreciative."

"Yeah, that's what you said. What I want to know is how much money are you going to give us?"

"If, indeed, my daughter is there and we are able to get her back, I'll give you one hundred dollars each."

"Yeah, but what about givin' us somethin' now?" Jug asked.

"I'll give you ten dollars apiece now, and the rest once Rosalie is safely back."

"All right," Jug said, holding out his hand. "Give us the money."

"Mr. Connelly and Mr. Bitters, if we don't find my daughter there, you will be arrested for extortion."

"I ain't a-worried none about that, 'cause she's there, all right," Poke said.

Governor Ireland took out his billfold and gave each of them a ten-dollar bill.

With huge smiles, the two men took the money, then left the office.

"Do you think they were telling the truth?" Fitzhugh asked.

"I don't know, but I think we will have to follow up on it. I want my daughter back, and I plan to leave no stone unturned until she is safe. I want you to ask Captain Brooks to come see me."

"But didn't the note caution you against using the Texas Rangers?" Fitzhugh asked.

"Please, Mr. Fitzhugh, just do as I say."

"Yes, sir."

Wang, Duff, and Elmer were dismounting in front of the capitol building just as Jug and Poke were coming out the front door.

"Those are the two men I heard talking," Wang said.

"Good," Duff said. "That means they have already spoken with the governor. Let's go

287

see what they told him."

"Mr. MacCallister!" the governor greeted them effusively when they stepped into his office.

"Pardon us for just barging in like that, Governor," Duff said, "but your man wasn't at his desk."

"Yes, I sent him after Captain Brooks. You two have chosen a most propitious time to visit me. I have just learned where Rosalie is being kept."

"We thought you might have heard," Duff said.

"Oh?" Governor Ireland was surprised by Duff's pronouncement.

"The two men who just left your office? Wang overheard them talking, but they didn't say where your daughter was. Did they tell you?"

"Yes. They said that she is being kept in a cabin that sits in Miller Creek Draw. Here, I'll show you where that is." Governor Ireland stepped up to a large map of Texas, which was attached to the wall behind his desk, then he pointed out the creek and the canyon. "I was going to send Captain Brooks and some of the Texas Rangers, but I think it might be best if you go."

"You're damn right, it'd be better to send us," Elmer said. "They'll be suspicious as soon as they see a Texas Ranger, but they won't even recognize the Ten Guns from Texas."

"Ten Guns from Texas?" Governor Ireland replied.

Duff chuckled. "Don't ask, Governor. I'll gather my men, and we'll ride out to the draw tonight. We'll sneak up on them and minimize the possibility of your daughter being hurt."

"All right. I am going to appoint both of you as special deputies to the governor's office, with authority that supersedes that of any sheriff in the state. That will also authorize you to deputize the men I pardoned. Elmer, Duff, Wang. Please bring my daughter back home safely," the governor pleaded.

"Colonel, if she is there, I guarantee you, we will bring her back to you," Elmer promised.

"Yes, if she is there," the governor said.

Duff put his hand on Governor Ireland's shoulder. "And if she isn't there, we'll find where she is. We'll do all we can to bring the lass back home safely."

Governor Ireland nodded. "Thank you." He said the words barely louder than a mumble.

The cabin near Miller Creek Draw

Rosalie was lying on a pad on the blankets, staring up at the bare rafters on the underside of the roof. Kendrick had left the first day after she had arrived, and she'd been frightened to see him go. He'd seemed to go out of his way to see that she was treated well, perhaps because he knew it would give him a better bargaining position with her father. So far, none of the others had actually mistreated her, but the way Morris looked at her all the time did make her nervous.

Besides, being held against her will was mistreatment enough.

She was very concerned about her father. She knew he was worried to death about her, unsure whether she was alive or dead. In a way, her captivity was easier on her than it was on him. At least she knew what her condition was.

She heard some horses approaching from outside and wondered who it was and why they were arriving. She didn't have to worry long.

Shortly after the horses arrived, a couple men came inside.

"Come on, girl," Peabody said. "We're goin' for a ride."

"Oh! Am I being released?" she asked, her

heart soaring with hope.

"Naw, you ain't bein' turned a-loose. We're just a-movin' you to someplace else, is all."

"Why am I being moved?"

"You're bein' moved on account a couple turncoats told the governor where you are at." Peabody began tying her hands.

"Oh, must you do that?" Rosalie complained. Although they had kept her tied for a while after they first brought her there, for the last twenty-four hours, she had been allowed freedom to walk around the cabin and also outside. They were confident that she wouldn't be able to get away from them, and their confidence was not misplaced.

"Yeah, I'm goin' to have to blindfold you, too."

A moment later, blindfolded and with her hands tied in front of her, Rosalie was led out of the cabin, then helped onto her horse.

"Dooley, you are in charge here," Peabody said. "Get the ambush set up and kill 'em as soon as they come into range."

Rosalie realized then that someone was coming to rescue her, and Peabody was arranging to have the men killed. She felt remorse, knowing that if they were killed, it would be because of her.

"Come on, girl, you've been through this

before," Peabody said as he hoisted her into the saddle, then slipped a noose around her neck.

She grabbed the saddle horn.

"Let's ride."

She had no idea how long they had been riding, but she knew it had been for several hours. She was blindfolded, so she tried to gauge her location from the ambient sounds, at one time hearing a babbling brook, and another time the sound of wind through some trees. She even tried to get clues from the sound of her horse's hoofbeats, sometime the dull thuds of footfalls on dirt, sometimes the soft brush of grass or vegetation, and sometimes the dry click of horseshoes on rock.

After a ride of another hour or more, she realized they were no longer riding through the countryside. She could hear the roll of wagon wheels, the sound of a hammer, and a woman's laughter. She felt a quick sense of elation as she realized they were in a town. Her first thought was that they wouldn't bring her into a town unless they were about to release her. Would they?

Finally they stopped, the noose was taken from her neck, and she felt her hands being untied.

"You can take off your blindfold," someone said.

With great relief, she did so. The first
thing she did was look around the town,
twisting in her saddle to observe everything
that she could.

Peabody chuckled. "You ain't goin' to find
one."

"I'm not going to find what?"

"You ain't a-goin' to find a sheriff or a
marshal's office, 'cause we ain't got one."

"Nonsense. Who enforces the law if you
don't have a sheriff or a marshal?" Rosalie
said.

"Well that's just it, missy. There ain't no
one to enforce the law, on account of we
ain't got no law in Blowout."

"Blowout? We're in a town called Blowout?"

Peabody nodded. "That we are," Peabody
said.

"Have we left Texas?"

"No, we're still in Texas."

"But I've never heard of a town named
Blowout. And my father has a map of Texas
on the wall behind his desk. Surely if there
were such a town, I would have heard of it."

"Well, you see, missy, you might say that
we are a town that don't want nobody to
know anythin' about us. We're what you

might call an outlaw town."

"You can't mean that everyone in this entire town is an outlaw?" Rosalie asked incredulously.

"No, I wouldn't say that at all," Kendrick said, coming out of the building in front of them. "On the contrary, the good citizens of this town are quite law-abiding. It's just that the laws they abide are laws that I have established."

Rosalie was confused. "What do you mean, laws you have established?"

"When we arrived here several months ago, the sheriff and the deputy met with a rather unfortunate . . . oh, shall we say . . . accident? Because of that tragic circumstance, the town of Blowout found itself without law. Therefore, as the preamble to our constitution says, in order to establish justice, ensure domestic tranquility, and promote the general welfare of the community of Blowout, I assumed leadership, acting as mayor and as the sheriff.

"And now, as a result of my providing peace, everyone in town works for me. *Everyone,*" Kendrick said, emphasizing the word. "So, even though I'm going to give you the freedom to walk around, it's not going to do you any good to go to anyone to ask for help, because nobody is going to help you. And if you manage, somehow, to escape, you'll wind up wandering around on your own and we'll find you. When we bring you back, your stay with us won't be so pleasant."

CHAPTER TWENTY-FOUR

Along Miller Creek

Duff, Elmer, Wang, Kelly, Simmons, and Decker rode through the night, following the creek as it flowed through loamy soil and rock outcroppings, past grasslands and stands of live oak, mesquite, and Ashe juniper. It babbled as it broke over the rocks, resulting in little whitecaps that were somewhat fluorescent in the moonlight.

Wang returned from riding ahead.

"Did you see anything?" Duff asked.

"*Shi.* The cabin is near. There are men outside."

"They have men outside standing guard?" Duff asked.

"I don't think they are standing guard," Wang said. "I think they are waiting to attack us. I think they know we are coming."

"Now how 'n the hell could they possibly know that we're comin'?" Elmer asked. "Are you sure about that?"

"*Shi.* The men are in positions so that they will be able to shoot at us as we approach."

"Damn. That means someone has told them we were comin'," Elmer said. "But who would have done that? Who could have known?"

"In that case, lads, 'tis my suggestion that we dismount and tie our horses here," Duff said. "We're less likely to be seen if we approach on foot."

"Yeah," Elmer agreed. "That's a good idea."

"Wang, since you aren't armed, I'm going to ask you to stay here with the horses. I'm afraid we would be in a great deal of trouble if our horses were to run off."

"*Shi.* I will stay," Wang agreed.

"Take your rifles, men," Duff said. "With Rosalie in the cabin, we need to shoot as accurately as we can."

The cabin near Miller Creek Draw
Clyde Dooley and eight more men were waiting for the expected attempt to rescue the governor's daughter. They were all in good defensive positions, which provided cover and concealment. A tenth man materialized from the dark, and because he was expected, his appearance caused no alarm.

"What you doin' back here, Beans?"

Dooley asked. "Have you seen somethin'?"

"They's a-comin', just like you said they would," Beans replied. "I seen 'em."

"How many are there?" Dooley asked.

"Five of 'em. And that MacCallister feller is with 'em."

Dooley smiled. "Yeah, well, he don't have no idee we're here, so we can kill 'im easy. 'N more 'n likely, Kendrick will give us a reward for that, seein' as he's been a-wantin' that one kilt from the beginnin'. Get ready, men. We'll start shootin' soon as they ride up."

"They ain't ridin'," Beans said. "They're afoot now, so we won't hear 'em all that easy."

"Where are their horses?"

"They left their horses down at the first bend."

"Morris?" Dooley called in a harsh whisper.

"Yeah?"

"Go up on the ridgeline and follow the creek back to the first bend. Their horses is there. Run 'em off."

"What if they's someone watchin' the horses?"

"Kill 'im."

"Dooley, if them five men ain't got to us yet, they'll hear the shootin' 'n likely know somethin' is up," one of the other men said.

"You're right. Tell you what. Peters, you go with Morris. That'll be two of you agin whoever it is they left there. The two of you ought to be able to kill 'im without makin' no noise. 'N that'll still leave us with eight men. Eight of us ought to be able to handle five, most 'specially if they don't know we're here."

"All right."

Duff, Elmer, Kelly, Dawkins, and Simmons had closed to approximately five hundred yards of the cabin when Duff held up his hand.

"What is it?" Kelly asked. "Why are we a-stoppin'?"

" 'Tis thinkin' I am that perhaps we should wait for first light," Duff said. "In the daylight, there will be less chance that the wee lass would be hit by a stray bullet."

"Yeah, I think you're right," Elmer agreed. "I figure it'll be daylight in another hour, so we may as well wait."

Wang was sitting down with his back against a tree when he heard something . . . a sharp snap that stood out against the sound of rushing water and wind-pushed leaves. Standing, he moved back into the darkest

299

shadow, kept his eye on the horses, and waited.

"What the hell? There ain't nobody here," Peters said in a harsh whisper. "I thought you said someone was here."

"I said there might be someone here," Morris said.

"Maybe they figured if they tied the horses, they wouldn't run off on 'em. This'll be easy. We'll just let the horses go."

Wang stepped out of the shadows just as the two men approached the horses. "I will not allow you to untie the horses."

"What the hell?" Morris shouted as he reached for his pistol.

Peters stopped him. "Dooley don't want no shootin', remember?"

Morris nodded. "You got a knife?"

"Yeah," Peters said.

"Pull it. The two of us ought to be able to handle one Chinaman."

As the two men approached Wang, Peters made a low swipe with his knife. Wang avoided it easily, then hit Peters in the neck with the edge of his hand, collapsing the trachea. Peters dropped his knife and put both hands to his neck, struggling for breath before he died.

The interaction happened so quickly that Peters was dying before Morris even knew what was happening. Realizing that the odds had changed, Morris dropped the knife and reached for his pistol. Using the heel of his hand, Wang broke Morris's nose, sending bone fragments into his brain, killing him instantly.

Wang had done his job so efficiently and silently, neither Dooley and the men who were arrayed in their ambush positions nor the Ten Guns from Texas were aware of the drama that had already taken place with the horses.

Duff and the others gradually approached the cabin until they heard someone call out, "There they are!"

A ripple of gunfire came from the Fence Busters, all of whom enjoyed a superior defensive position.

Duff withheld fire until he located the position of everyone who was firing at him and his men. He counted eight flame patterns scattered across a long row of rather large rocks, none of which were in front of the cabin. He was reasonably certain that the men who had opened fire could be engaged without putting anyone inside the cabin in significant danger.

Aiming just over the top of one of the rocks where he had last seen a muzzle flash, he held the aim until he saw what he was looking for. A head came up just far enough for the shooter to take aim. Duff squeezed the trigger and saw the man's rifle slide down in front of the rock. He didn't see the body, but he had seen a little spray of blood fly up above the rock.

The guns continued to roar and the sky was soon filled with birds, who, frightened by the noise, were flying away. The intensity of the shooting, the rising cloud of gun smoke, and the acrid smell of spent powder filled the air.

Bullets whizzed by overhead, most of them sounding like angry bees as they passed by. The very close ones made a popping noise as they fried the air. There was also the high keening shriek of a bullet hitting a rock, then careening off, its whine echoing and echoing back from the nearby bluffs. In addition, there were the shouts and curses of anger and defiance between the two lines as the men who were engaged in the desperate battle were trying their best to kill each other.

Duff killed a second man, while out of the corner of his eye, he saw a third go down. As one Fence Buster tried to improve his position, Duff shifted his rifle to aim at him, but before he could get his shot lined up, he heard a shot from his right, and that man went down, as well.

"Dooley?" someone shouted. "Dooley, they done kilt four of us! We need to get the hell outta here."

"What about Morris and Peters?" Dooley replied.

"They didn't come back, did they? Hell, it's more 'n likely they're both dead, too."

The man had just finished pleading his case when Duff heard a shot coming from Elmer's rifle. The result was another Fence Buster who had abandoned his position and tried to run, only to be brought down. He stumbled forward a few steps before falling.

"Sumbitch, Dooley! Now Marvin is dead! They's only three of us left!"

"Give us the girl!" Duff shouted. "Give us the girl, and we'll quit shooting!"

"The girl ain't here," a frightened voice called back.

"Where is she?" Duff asked.

"I don't know where she is! We got word you was comin', and they moved her some-place else. We was supposed to set up an ambush 'n kill you when you come after her."

"Come out with your hands up," Duff ordered.

Two of the men did come out, both of

them holding their hands in the air . . . though both of them were still grasping their rifles.

"That's only two of you. Where's the third?" Duff asked.

"There ain't no third man. They's just the two of us. I'm Beans, he's Rand."

"I heard you call out to a man named Dooley," Duff said. "Where would he be?"

"I . . . uh . . . don't know," Rand said.

"Elmer, if Mr. Dooley does nae come out by the time I count to five, I intend to kill the man on the left, and I'll be for askin' you to kill the one on the right. Then we can look for the wee lass ourselves."

"All right. Start a-countin'," Elmer replied, raising the rifle to his shoulder.

"Dooley, come out, now!" Rand shouted in a frightened voice. "Come out now, you yellow coward! Don't you dare stay back there 'n let me 'n Beans get kilt!"

"I'm comin' out," a voice said from behind the most distant rock.

"Come out with your hands in the air," Duff ordered.

Dooley stepped out, holding both hands over his head. One hand still clasped a rifle, though he was holding it in one hand by the forestock.

"Toss the weapon aside," Duff ordered.

Dooley did. "Don't shoot."

"Who's in the cabin?"

"There ain't nobody in there," Dooley replied.

"Elmer, look inside and make certain the girl's not there."

"No need to look. She ain't there," Dooley said.

Duff called out, "If anyone is in there, let out a yell. We'll kill all three."

"There ain't nobody there, I'm a-tellin' you. Peabody, him and some of the others took the girl soon as we heard you was comin'."

Elmer stepped in through the door, was gone for a moment, then came back out. "He's right. She ain't there."

"Where is she?" Duff asked.

"I don't know where they took her."

"Kelly, hurry back and get Wang, would you?" Duff ordered.

Kelly nodded, then started back down the trail.

"How did you know we were coming here?" Duff asked Dooley.

"Someone told Peabody."

"Who told him?"

"I don't know who it was that told 'im. All I know is, someone told 'im that you was told where the girl was, 'n that you'd

305

more 'n likely be a-comin' for her. So Peabody left us here to take care of you, 'n he 'n a couple others took the girl somewhere else."

Kelly and Wang came then, leading three horses each.

"Did you get visitors back there, Wang?" Duff asked.

"Shi."

"Where are they now?"

"Dead."

Even though he'd fought and been bested by Wang once, Decker couldn't believe it. "They was two of 'em. You ain't tellin' me that the Chinaman kilt both of 'em, are you? I mean, I didn't even hear no shootin'."

"I told you Wang doesn't use guns," Duff said.

"Wait a minute," Dooley said. "Are you a-tellin' me that this here Chinaman took out both Morris 'n Peters without usin' no gun?"

"I know it wasn't a fair fight, just two of them against Wang," Duff said. "but don't blame yourself. How could you know that Wang can defeat any five men?"

"What are we goin' to do with these three?" Simmons asked.

"I suggest that we take them into Merrill Town," Duff replied. "The folks in and around Merrill Town are most likely to be the ones that's suffering the most from men like these. It might do them good to see them put in jail."

"Once we get 'em there, they'll more 'n likely hang, don't you think?" Elmer asked.

Rand and Beans both put hands to their necks and pulled on the collar.

"It could be. What happens to them will be up to Sheriff Wallace," Duff said.

Neither Duff nor Elmer noticed the smug look that passed between their three prisoners.

The Double D Ranch

"What do you mean you are now charging ten dollars a head?" Kendrick asked. "We have agreed upon five dollars."

"I never planned on you kidnapping the governor's daughter. That has made my position much more precarious," Dobbins replied.

"You knew the risks when we entered into this arrangement," Kendrick said.

"You have greatly increased the risks, and I think it's worth more money now."

"All right," Kendrick said. "But this time I want an agreement signed between the two of us. I don't want you coming back to me later and asking for even more money."

"I would be foolish to sign such an agreement. Why, you could show that to someone and it would be evidence that I was a party to this."

"Yes, it would. But if you expect any more money from me, you are going to have to sign the agreement."

"All right. What do you want the agreement to say?"

"Get the pen and paper. I'll dictate it."

A moment later, Dobbins sat at the desk in his office, pen poised, ready to write.

"By these presents, I hereby agree to the terms between myself and Dirk Kendrick," Kendrick dictated.

Dobbins made the entry. "What next?"

"Sign it."

"Sign what? This doesn't say what the terms are."

"You said yourself that if you wrote out the terms this document could be used as evidence," Kendrick said. "This is only between the two of us. Nobody else will ever see it. I just want to make certain that you don't raise the price of doing business again."

"Yeah, all right," Dobbins said as he signed the paper.

"Date it," Kendrick ordered.

Dobbins added the date.

"There now . . . what the hell?" The expression on Dobbins's face went from confusion to shock. He didn't have time to register panic before Kendrick shot him.

Then, with Dobbins's body lying dead on the floor, Kendrick completed the agreement.

I, by use of this document, transfer all land, buildings, equipment, and livestock constituting the Double D Ranch.

CHAPTER TWENTY-FIVE

Merrill Town

When Duff and the others rode into town that afternoon, their entrance aroused the interest of all the citizens of the community. Dooley, Beans, and Rand had their hands tied behind their backs, riding on horses that were being led.

"What you got them men tied up for?" someone shouted.

"Where are you a-goin' with 'em?" another called out.

"We're a-takin' 'em to jail," Decker called back. "Where do you think we're takin' 'em?"

By the time the nine riders reached the jailhouse, they were part of a regular parade. The citizens of the town, drawn by curiosity, hurried down the street, along each side, as well as behind the procession.

One of the citizens had hurried ahead to notify the sheriff of the approaching caravan, and he and Deputy Bullock were waiting outside the office.

"What is this?" asked Sheriff Wallace.

"Sheriff, 'tis three prisoners I have for you," Duff said.

"What do you mean, you have three prisoners for me? By what authority do you claim such a right?"

"We're deputies to the governor," Elmer said. "And our authority is in any county in the entire state, includin' this here 'n. And we've brung you three no-accounts just like Duff said. 'N you'll either take 'em or else we'll take over your jail 'n throw 'em in there our ownselves."

"What am I supposed to hold them for? What crime have they committed?" the sheriff asked.

"They kidnapped the governor's daughter," Duff said.

"Is that a fact?"

"Aye."

"How come I haven't heard anything about the governor's daughter being taken?"

" 'Tisn't general knowledge yet."

"D' ya hear that?" one of the citizens said. "The governor's daughter has been took."

"Who took her?" another asked.

"Accordin' to MacCallister it was these three sumbitches they just brung in."

311

Word spread quickly through the rest of those who had hung around long enough to find out what was going on. Most of the onlookers had drifted away once the parade was finished, but a few stayed on so they could get the word and share it with the others.

"Did you get the girl?" Sheriff Wallace asked.

"Nae, she wasn't there. These three say she was taken from the cabin before we got there."

"Well now, that's a shame, ain't it?"

"Aye, 'tis at that, but I was thinkin' that you might be able to find out if you ask a few questions. You'll have the opportunity, seeing as we will be leaving these prisoners with you."

Sheriff Wallace stared at the three men who were still bound and mounted. "I'll do what I can. Deputy Bullock, get 'em down, 'n get 'em inside."

"What you goin' to do with 'em, Sheriff?" one of the citizens of the town asked.

"Find out if the girl's still alive," another said.

"She better be. If these men kilt that girl, they need to be strung up," yet another said.

"Sheriff, you got to protect us!" Dooley said in a frightened tone of voice.

"Get on inside, Dooley," the sheriff said. "There ain't nobody goin' to be hangin' you."

"Do you know these men?" Duff asked, surprised to hear the sheriff refer to Dooley by name.

"Yeah, I know 'em," Sheriff Wallace replied. "They ain't none of 'em ever give me no trouble before this."

"Yes, I believe you said the same thing about Mr. Woodson and Mr. Jenkins right after they tried to kill me," Duff said.

"Yeah, I did say that. Because neither one of 'em had ever give me trouble before. Could be, MacCallister, that you're the kinda man that brings out the worst in folks. Have you ever thought on that?"

"Sheriff, do you know why an Englishman wears a monocle?" Duff replied.

"What? No, I don't. Why would you ask me somethin' like that?"

"Because it is apropos to this situation," Duff replied. "An Englishman wears a monocle so he will only see half of what he can't understand. It is clear to me that you understand nothing of what you see."

"I don't understand," Sheriff Wallace said.

Duff chuckled. "My point precisely."

Poke and Jug were among those who had

seen Dooley, Beans, and Rand brought into town.

"They didn't get the girl," Poke said.

"You know what that means, don't you? That means we won't be a-gettin' the rest of our money," Jug said. "Wonder how come it is that they didn't get her?"

"You heard what the Scotsman said. He said they moved her."

"I wonder where at they took her?" Jug asked.

"I don't know. But if we could find out, we could tell the governor 'n still get our money," Poke said.

"I know how we can find out," Jug suggested.

"How's that?"

"All we got to do is go to Blowout 'n just keep our eyes and ears open."

"I don't know," Poke said. "Kendrick spends more time there than he does out at the Blanco Cabin."

"Yeah, well, that's just what I'm a-talkin' about. If he's there, there'll be others there, too, and someone's goin' to say somethin' 'bout where the girl is. Then we can go back 'n see the governor 'n collect the rest of the money. Besides which, if we are there, Kendrick for sure ain't goin' to be suspectin' us of bein' the ones that told where the girl was. He'd never think we'd come there if we done such a thing."

"Yeah, I guess you're right. Only the rest of the money ain't enough," Poke said.

"What do you mean?"

"If we're takin' a risk like that, I think it ought to be worth at least a thousand dollars apiece, rather than just a hunnert," Poke said.

A huge smile spread across Jug's face. "Yeah. Hey, Poke, you ever been to Californy?"

"What? No. Why the hell did you ask that?"

"On account of, oncet I get the thousand dollars, that's where I'm aimin' to go," Jug said.

Poke grinned. "Yeah. Yeah, that's a good idea. What do you say we go to Blowout?"

After Duff and the others left the sheriff's office, they rode on down the street to the CSS *Alabama* Saloon.

"Hey, Gleason," Kelly said quietly. "What was MacCallister talkin' about back there, what with seein' half what you understand 'n all that? Does he always talk like that? I mean, sayin' things that's so highfalutin can't nobody know what he's talkin' about?"

"Kelly, let me tell you somethin' 'bout

Duff MacCallister. I've been most all over the world, 'n I've seen more men than just about any ten people has ever seen. 'N I tell you straight out that Duff MacCallister is the smartest man I ever know'd," Elmer replied. "Just pay attention to him 'n you might learn somethin'."

"He sure is smart, all right," Kelly said as the six of them reached the saloon and tied up at the hitch rack.

"MacCallister!" Prescott bellowed as the six men set foot inside the saloon. "Good to see you back."

"Hello, Mr. Prescott. Would you be for setting all these fine gentlemen up with the beverage of their choice?"

"Sure, 'n I'll be glad to do just that. And who might these men be?" Prescott replied.

"We are the Ten Guns from Texas," Elmer said.

"I beg your pardon? Ten guns from Texas?"

"Five of us, two guns each. Five times two makes ten. 'N seein' as we're in Texas, that's Ten Guns from Texas," Elmer explained.

"But there are six of you."

"Wang don't count, on account of he don't carry no gun," Elmer explained further.

"The Chinaman . . . uh . . . that is, Mr.

Wang," Decker said, "he don't need no gun. I seen him kill two men with only a-usin' his hands. Well, I didn't actual see it, but I seen 'im do it after he had already done it."

"How could you see it, if you didn't actually see it?" Prescott asked, having a hard time following the conversation. "And who is it Wang killed?"

"Decker's right. Wang kilt two of them what snatched up the princess," Simmons said.

"The princess?" Prescott asked, more confused than ever.

"The governor's daughter has been taken," Duff said. "They are holding her for ransom."

"Oh, yes. I've heard about that," Prescott said.

"It was the Fence Busters that took her," Elmer said.

"Damn! How much are they askin' for?"

" 'Tisn't money they're asking for," Duff said. "They want the governor to reverse the law that now makes it illegal to cut fences on public land."

"The governor can't do that, can he?" Prescott asked. "I mean all by himself. He had to have the legislature pass it in the first place, so won't he have to have the legislature unpass it?"

"Aye, 'tis my understanding that he will have to get the legislature to repeal the law."

"Well, don't you think he can talk 'em into doin' that?"

"I suppose he can, but the governor fears that if he does that, the Fence Busters will always be able to force him into things. I think 'tis a good decision he has made not to give in to them."

"And you're lookin' for her?"

"Aye."

"In that case, your first drinks are on the house," Prescott said. "What'll you have?"

As soon as Prescott served up the drinks, the Ten Guns from Texas took them over to a table.

"The girl wasn't at the cabin, so what do we do now?" Elmer asked when they were seated.

"It might be wise to go out to the Slash Bell," Duff said. "Bellefontaine has dealt with these people for a long time now. He might have an idea that would be useful."

"Yeah," Elmer said. "That's a good idea."

"Drink up, m' lads. Our task remains undone, so we'll take the next step in our mission to rescue the damsel in distress." Duff held his glass up.

"To the Ten Guns from Texas," Kelly said.

"Ten Guns from Texas," Decker repeated,

lifting his own glass.

"My word, Elmer, you've actually brought these blokes around," Duff said with a little chuckle.

A few minutes later, Deputy Bullock watched from the alley across the street as the Ten Guns from Texas rode out of town. He looked after them for a long moment until he was reasonably sure he knew where they were going. Then he rode back to give his report.

"They're gone," Bullock said, stepping into the sheriff's office a short while later.

"You sure?" Sheriff Wallace asked.

"Oh, I'm damn sure. I seen all six of 'em ridin' away. Looks like they was all a-headin' out toward the Slash Bell."

"Yeah, that's where they would go all right, especially since Bellefontaine's always stickin' his nose in ever'one's business." Sheriff Wallace got up from his desk, took the ring of cell keys down from the wall, then walked into the back of the jailhouse and unlocked the cell door.

"All right, Dooley, Beans, Rand. MacCallister 'n the others are gone. Looks like they're headed toward the Slash Bell, so don't go that way."

"Don't worry 'bout that," Beans said.

319

"We've done run into that bunch once, 'n we don't plan to do it again."

"You tell Kendrick I let you fellas go," Sheriff Wallace said. "But tell 'im he needs to look out for MacCallister and that bunch with him."

"Ten Guns from Texas," Bullock said.

"What?"

"That's what they're a-callin' themselves, the men that's with MacCallister. They're callin' themselves Ten Guns from Texas."

"They's ten of 'em? They was only six that come out to the cabin," Beans said.

"That's all they is now," Bullock said without any further explanation.

"You tell Kendrick now," Sheriff Wallace repeated. "You tell him that I let you men go."

"We'll tell 'im," Dooley said as he, Rand, and Beans strapped on their guns.

CHAPTER TWENTY-SIX

Blowout

No gilt-edged mirror hung behind the bar of the Pair of Kings Saloon, but there was a real bar and an ample supply of whiskey. There were also several large jars of pickled eggs and sausages on the bar, and towels tied to rings were placed every few feet on the customers' side to provide the patrons with a means of wiping their hands.

The saloon had an upstairs section at the back. At the moment, Penny was taking a customer up the stairway with her.

Poke and Jug were standing at the bar, nursing a beer.

"You was right," Poke said. "All we had to do to find the governor's daughter was to come here. I mean she's here, walkin' aroun' free as the breeze. Ever'one in town knows that."

"She ain't really free," Jug said. "It ain't like she can go nowhere."

"Yeah, but that's good, ain't it?" Poke said. "I mean as long as she can't go nowhere, why, when we go back 'n tell the governor that she's here, she'll still be here when someone comes for her."

"I suppose so," Jug replied. "But I'm beginnin' to think that comin' here wasn't such a good idea."

"Why not?" Poke asked. "You're the one that come up with the idea. You ain't changin' your mind now, are you?"

"No, I ain't changin' my mind. But we got to be real careful 'bout what we say."

"Yeah, you're right about that."

"Hey, Poke, I just got me an idea. 'N it's a good one, too."

"What's your idea?"

"Why don't we take the girl to the governor ourselves?"

"How are we goin' to do that?" Poke asked.

"It'll be easy. You know the girl won't give us no problem, if she thinks we're takin' her back to her daddy. 'N he might give us even more money if we was to show up with her."

"Hey." Poke was getting into the spirit of the conversation. "What if we was to do this? What if we was to take the girl, then hold her until the governor give us a lot of money? Maybe even ten thousand dollars!"

"Yeah," Jug said. "She'll think we're takin' 'er back, 'n we will be, if the governor's willin' to pay for it."

"When you want to do it?"

"We'll do it tonight, when ever'one is either asleep or drunk," Jug suggested.

At that moment, Kendrick pushed in through the swinging batwing doors.

"Damn, there's Kendrick," Poke said. "Wonder what he wants."

"No tellin'," Jug replied. "Just keep quiet 'n don't say nothin' to 'im at all, unless he says somethin' first."

Poke and Jug stared into their drinks as if by that action they could avoid any interaction with Kendrick. Their attempt to avoid him didn't work, however. He walked right up to where they were standing and addressed them directly. "Hello, boys," he said affably. "What are you two doin' in Blowout?"

"Nothin' much," Jug said. "We come here from time to time. You know that."

"Yes, I do know that. But I would think that now, given the circumstances, that Blowout would be the last place you would want to visit."

"Why? What are you talking about?" Poke asked nervously.

"Oh, I'm sure you are quite aware of what

I'm talking about. But tell me, did you two boys enjoy your visit with the governor?"

"The . . . the governor? W-what do you mean? W-why would we visit the governor?" Jug asked, stuttering in fear.

"Oh, I don't know. Perhaps it was to give him some information that he wants . . . like where his daughter might be. I heard he was going to pay you boys five hundred dollars apiece."

"Nothin' of the kind. It ain't nowhere near that much . . . uh . . . what I mean is, why should he pay us anything?" Poke replied, his voice reflecting as much fear as had Jug's.

"Peabody, you and Cahill may come in now," Kendrick said.

Two more men stepped into the saloon. They were holding pistols, and the pistols were pointed toward Poke and Jug.

"What's this all about? W-why are you two boys pointin' them guns at us? W-what are you a-plannin' on doin'?" Jug asked.

"We're going to put you in jail," Kendrick replied. "Then we're going to hold a public trial."

"What? Now, hold on there," Jug said, holding his hand out toward Kendrick as if, by that action, he could push him away. "What do you mean you're a-goin' to hold a public trial? This here town ain't got no law. You don't have the right to do nothin' like that."

"On the contrary, gentlemen, I do have the right. Oh, I will be the first to admit that I assumed that right when I usurped the leadership position of this town, but as surely as a king has civic and judicial authority over his realm, I have such authority over my domain. Blowout" — Kendrick made a circular motion with his hand — "is my own personal principality. I would be remiss in the responsibilities I have assumed if I did not deal with this act of treachery that the two of you have committed."

"I don't know what you think we done," Poke said, "but if you want us to leave town 'n not never come back no more, why, we'll do that. Won't we, Jug?"

"Yeah, sure," Jug said. "We won't never come back. I can promise you that."

"Mr. Peabody, these two gentlemen are under arrest. Please take them to jail."

"Come on, you two," Peabody said to Poke and Jug, waving the barrel of his pistol.

"Now, hold on there!" Jug said again. "There ain't no need for you to do this. We done told you we're willin' to leave town 'n not never come back."

"It's too late for that," Kendrick said.

"You should never have come to town in the first place."

Kendrick, Peabody, and Cahill left the saloon with their two prisoners and walked down the middle of the road. Kendrick wanted everyone in town to know that he was in charge, and being in charge meant that he was also the law.

Rosalie, who was out walking around, saw the five men, two of whom were holding their hands up, and she wondered what it was about.

"Miss Ireland, come here, please," Kendrick called out when he saw her.

Rosalie hesitated.

"Please don't make me send someone to bring you to me by force," he said, his voice a little more resolute than had been his first summons.

Frightened at being called, she walked over toward Kendrick and the others, all of whom had stopped in the middle of the street.

"Jug, Poke, do you know who this young lady is?" Kendrick asked.

"No, I ain't never seen her before in my life," Jug replied.

"What about you, Poke? Do you recognize her?"

"No. Why should I?"

"Why should you? Because she is the reason you will have to pay the ultimate price for your betrayal. This is the governor's daughter."

"The governor's daughter?" Poke asked.

"Yes. The one for whom you double-crossed all your friends when you told the governor where he could find her."

"What are talkin' about?" Jug asked. "We didn't tell the governor nothin' 'bout his daughter bein' here."

"That is only technically correct," Kendrick said. "You didn't tell him she was here, because you didn't know it. But you did tell him that we were keeping her in the cabin at Miller Creek Draw. I know you told him, because I have an eyewitness who saw and heard you talking to him."

"You're just tellin' us that to see if you can make us confess, but we ain't a-goin' to confess to somethin' we didn't do," Poke said.

"Take them to jail," Kendrick said, and at his urging, the men moved on.

Once Jug and Poke were put in jail, Kendrick called a meeting of the Fence Busters at the Rustic Rock restaurant. He had considered holding the meeting in the saloon, but decided there would be too many distractions if they met there, so after ordering the three diners and the employees out, he invited his men to take a seat.

"How many are here, in town?" Kendrick asked.

"There's twenty-two of us," Peabody said.

"Only twenty-two?"

"Well, I left Dooley and nine more back at the cabin where we was keepin' the girl," Peabody said. "And I expect that by now, they've already took care of this fella Mac-Callister 'n whoever he has with him. We got Shardeen 'n three more men with him a-movin' some more cows to the Double D. And there's ten or so out at the Blanco River camp."

"So, at the moment, our total strength stands at just less than fifty," Kendrick said, adding the numbers as Peabody laid them out.

"Yeah," Peabody said.

"Very well. Let's get the meeting started, shall we?" Kendrick said.

"You men all quiet down now," Peabody said to the others. "Kendrick has some things he wants to talk to us about."

With the men paying attention to him, Kendrick stood up to address them. To the casual observer it could have been anything from a prayer meeting to a political rally to a business meeting. It was the latter, but the business was cattle rustling and murder.

"When we took the girl, I sent the governor a message, telling him that I wanted him to take back the bill he got passed that made it a felony to cut fences on public property."

"Hell, Kendrick, what difference does it make whether it's ag'in the law to cut fences on public property or not?" one of the men asked. "It's already ag'in the law to cut fences on private property, but that ain't stopped us none."

Some of the other men laughed.

"It's not the same thing," Kendrick said. "We're representing the New York and Texas Land Company. They are a legitimate organization, paying us to find public land that they can claim and sell. It is good that they are paying us, but what is even more important is the fact that they are providing us with the cover we need for conducting our own operations."

"Which is stealin' cattle, 'n even I know that ain't legal," a man named Harris said.

"I prefer to say that we are acquiring cattle that have been freed as a result of the fencing being cut. And right now, gentlemen, we have freed more than ten thousand head of cattle, which are gathered at the Double

D Ranch. At the moment, the price of cattle at the Kansas City Market is averaging fifty dollars a head. Now for any of you who may not be all that proficient in math, I can tell you that means that we have a net worth of half a million dollars."

A few low whistles sounded in the room.

"I intend to get another twenty thousand head before we market them, at which time our little organization will have assets of a million and a half dollars. At that point, we will cease to do business, and divide up the money in accordance with the agreed-upon arrangement. I will take half that sum, and the remaining funds will be divided equally among you. That should come out to approximately fifteen thousand dollars," he concluded with a smile.

"Fifteen thousand! You mean, fifteen thousand *apiece*?"

"I do indeed mean that."

"Damn! I didn't have no idea there was that much money in the whole world!" someone said, and the others laughed nervously.

"But, as you can see, it's all tied together. In order to do this, we must have the cover of the legitimate business of the New York and Texas Land Company, and if the law against cutting fences on public land isn't rescinded, I fear the New York and Texas Land Company might stop doing business. If they stop, we'll have no option but to stop as well. That's why it is absolutely imperative to have this law against fence cutting repealed. And at the moment, keeping the governor's daughter is our only way of ensuring this."

"How come she's here in town?" someone asked. "How come she ain't still up at the cabin?"

"In the message I sent to the governor, I warned him not to get the Texas Rangers involved. He hasn't, but he has hired Mac-Callister, as Peabody just pointed out, to lead a posse of private citizens."

"How many in the posse?" Taylor asked.

"According to my sources, there were five of them," Kendrick said. "Six, if you count the Chinaman, but I am informed that he doesn't carry a gun."

"It don't really matter whether the China-man carries a gun or not," Peabody said. "He can kill you just as dead without a gun as he can with a gun. You might remember that he was the one that kilt Perkins when we run into 'im at the Slash Bell."

"Yeah, but they was only three of 'em then. You said they was six of 'em now.

331

Where did they get the other three?" Taylor asked.

Kendrick smiled. "You may find this hard to believe, but they got the other three from prison."

"From prison?"

"Yes. Governor Ireland signed the pardons."

"Who did they get?" Muley asked.

"Right now, the only name that I know is Roy Kelly," Kendrick replied.

"Roy Kelly? I ain't never heard of him," Peabody said.

"I've heard of 'im," Muley said. "During the war, he rode with Bill Anderson."

"Bill Anderson? Bloody Bill Anderson? Well, I've sure heard of him," Peabody said.

"Who ain't heard of him? Bloody Bill Anderson was one mean sumbitch," Taylor said. "And that means that if this feller, Kelly, rode with him then he's more 'n likely just as mean."

"Yes, well, the last I heard Quantrill and Anderson are both dead," Kendrick said. "And it is more than likely that MacCallister, Gleason, the Chinaman, and the three pardoned prisoners are dead as well."

"What makes you think that?" Taylor asked.

"Mr. Peabody, I'll let you tell of the plans

we made for them," Kendrick said.

Peabody chuckled. "We don't have to worry no more about MacCallister 'n his bunch. I left Dooley 'n nine others back at the cabin. Good men they are, too, 'n ever' one of had 'em a good place to wait for the ones comin' to rescue the girl. I expect MacCallister and the ones with him was all shot down in the first minute or so."

"How do you know?"

"They's only one way to approach the cabin, 'n that's to come right up alongside Miller Creek. The draw there is no more 'n forty feet wide, 'n it's got steep walls on either side of it. Dooley 'n his men have a natural fort, what with the rocks 'n all. Once the shootin' started, MacCallister 'n that bunch with him wouldn't have had no place to go. Hell, it woulda been like shootin' cows in a slaughter pen."

"So you see, gentlemen, we no longer have to worry about Mr. MacCallister," Kendrick concluded.

"Yeah, but didn't we think the same thing with Jaco 'n Dawson?" Taylor asked.

Kendrick chuckled. "It is said that a smart man learns from his mistakes, a brilliant man learns from the mistakes of others. I have learned from the mistake made by Jaco and Martell. They failed to use overwhelming force. This time, we made certain that maximum force was used. I am satisfied that we will have no more difficulty from Mac-Callister."

"Yeah, well, I know I sure feel better with him gone," Peabody said.

"Now, gentlemen, let's get on with the subject of this meeting," Kendrick said. "I plan to organize a trial for Poke and Jug."

"Why are you goin' to do that?" Muley asked. "Whyn't we just kill 'em, 'n be done with it?"

Muley didn't say anything about it, but he was quite nervous over the prospect of a trial. He recalled talking about the governor's daughter with Jug, and he was sure that was how Jug and Poke got the information. If there was a trial, and it was learned that he had been talking to them, he feared he might wind up alongside Poke and Jug.

"No, we will have a trial," Kendrick said. "A trial will serve two purposes. One, it will present a semblance of organization and authority in the town, with me at its head, and two, it will serve as an object lesson and a warning to anyone in town who might get it in their head to try and overthrow the government I have established. A trial is very necessary."

"Yeah," Muley said, feeling a weakness in his stomach. "Yeah, I guess you're right."

CHAPTER TWENTY-SEVEN

While the meeting was going on in the Rustic Rock, Rosalie Ireland, who, as Kendrick had promised, had the freedom to go anywhere she wanted in town, stepped into the Pair of Kings Saloon. She had never before been in a saloon and had always been curious about them, so, she asked herself, *why not?* There was nothing "normal" about her life right now, anyway.

Her appearance so startled the customers that all conversation came to a halt, and everyone turned to look at her. She immediately wished that she hadn't come in, but it was too late. Four or five women were already in the saloon, all wearing dresses so scandalously revealing that Rosalie couldn't help but wonder how they were even able to keep their dresses on.

One of the girls walked over to her. The girl was young, and Rosalie decided she was probably pretty behind all the garish makeup.

"Honey, we have all heard that as long as you are in Blowout, you are free to go anywhere you want," the girl said gently, "but I don't think you want to come in here. This isn't a place for your kind."

"My kind? And what, may I inquire, do you mean by *my kind*?" Rosalie asked, a little piqued by the comment.

"Why, your kind. You know. You are a lady." The girl smile. "And you are so beautiful, fine, elegant, and decent and all," she added genuinely. "You ain't nothin' at all like none of us." She looked down as if embarrassed to say so. "We're prostitutes, ever' one of us. 'Course, we call ourselves soiled doves, but that ain't nothin' more than another word for the same thing."

Despite the fact that she had been brought to Blowout against her wishes and had been told that any attempt to escape would be futile, Rosalie couldn't help but feel some sympathy for this young woman. Rosalie realized that the woman might even be younger than she was.

"What is your name?" Rosalie asked.

"My name is Glitter," the girl replied. "Glitter Bright."

"Oh, what a lovely name," Rosalie said.

"You like it?" Glitter asked.

"Yes, I think it is a very nice name."

"I'm glad you like it. I made it up my own-self," Glitter said with a broad smile. "My real name is Melba Rittenhouse, but that ain't a very pretty name, 'n in this business, you need to have a pretty name."

"Glitter, do you know who I am?"

"Why, yes, ma'am. Ever'one in Blowout knows who you are, Miss Ireland. We know you are the governor's daughter."

"And do you also know that I was brought to this town against my will? That I am being held prisoner here?"

"Yes, ma'am. We know that, too."

"Well, do you approve of that?"

"Oh, Miss Ireland, it ain't my place to approve or disapprove. Neither me nor none of the others who work here don't have no say at all on what goes on in this town. It's like I told you. I'm just a prostitute."

"But this . . . this is outrageous. The entire town knows I am a prisoner here, and yet no one will do anything about it."

"There ain't nothin' nobody *can* do about it, Miss Ireland. Mr. Kendrick, he controls the whole town. Oh," Glitter said. "Here he comes now. I don't want him to see me talking to you. He said he don't want nobody gettin' too friendly with you. Please don't be mad at me for walkin' away from you."

"I'm not angry with you," Rosalie said.

Glitter managed to separate herself from Rosalie before Kendrick actually stepped into the saloon. Without so much as a glance in Rosalie's direction, Kendrick started directly toward his table in the back corner of the saloon. It was different from the other tables in that it was larger and the chair sitting on the opposite side with its back to the wall was a large, high-backed, padded leather chair. That was the chair Kendrick took.

Rosalie was well aware of how she stood out in this saloon, but she put that aside as she walked back to confront the man who held her fate in his hands.

"Well, I see you found the saloon," Kendrick said. "I do hope you are enjoying your stay in my town."

"There is no way I can enjoy my stay here, as long as I'm not free," Rosalie replied.

"Oh but you are free. Have you been restrained in any way? Tied to a chair, perhaps? Or locked in a room?"

"No."

"And, just to show you what a nice man I am, I have instructed all the merchants in town to give you anything you want. Go to the restaurant and order anything you want to eat. I know you didn't have a change of clothes with you when we took you, so feel free to go to the store and pick out anything you want. You won't have to pay a cent for it. You are free to go anywhere in town that you wish."

"That's just it. I don't want to go anywhere *in* this town, Mr. Kendrick. I want to go *out* of this town."

"There is nothing more I would rather do than let you go, Miss Ireland. But I can't do that until your father agrees to repeal the fence-cutting law."

"You know that he can't do that on his own. That was a law passed by the state legislature. My father is a governor. He is not a king. He can't just snap his fingers and repeal a law."

"Then he's going to have to do all that he can to persuade the legislature to repeal the law, because you will be our guest for as long as that law is on the books."

"You, you are an awful man!" Rosalie said.

"I'm sorry you think so, Miss Ireland," Kincaid said. "I'm not really like any of the men you have encountered before. I'm well educated; I have an appreciation for the finer things in life. It's just that, under the present circumstances, I have to set aside my finer qualities in order to accumulate enough wealth to enable me to live the life of a gentleman."

"You are no gentleman," Rosalie said resolutely.

"You have never seen me under the right circumstances, so there is no way you could know, is there?"

"That's where you are wrong. I know," Rosalie said, and turning away from the table, she caught a glimpse of Glitter as she started toward the door. She tried to read the expression on Glitter's face. Was it fear? Sympathy? She couldn't tell before she left the saloon.

"Weasel," Kendrick called to the bartender after Rosalie left. "I intend to use this place as a courtroom, so from now until I say otherwise, all sales of spirits will be suspended."

"What?"

"Don't sell any more liquor until I say that you can," Kendrick clarified.

"Yes, sir." Weasel, like every other businessman and -woman in Blowout, had no option but to respond to every order and whim of Dirk Kendrick.

The trial for Poke and Jug, if it could be called a trial, soon commenced. Kendrick was sitting in his padded chair behind his special table, acting as a judge.

Two other tables were moved up to the front of the improvised courtroom, the one to Kendrick's left, occupied by the prosecutor. Sitting behind the forward most table to his right were Poke and Jug and their defense counsel.

"Gentlemen" — Kendrick glanced toward the bar girls who were gathered in a frightened cluster near the silent piano — "and ladies, I will be acting as the judge during this tribunal. I am not without experience in this area. I'm sure that many of you are quite aware that I graduated *summa cum laude* from Harvard with a degree in law. I am a member of the bar of the state of New York and am therefore qualified to act as judge in this hearing.

"I have appointed Carl Peabody as prosecutor, and Rex Welles as defense counsel. In doing so, I have leaned toward the defendant since Mr. Welles is a member of the bar of the state of Texas, while Mr. Peabody certainly is not.

"You, you, and you," Kendrick said as he began pointing to various men who were present for the trial. He pointed out twelve of them. "You gentlemen will constitute the jury. If you would, please, drag your chairs over there and line them up in two rows of six."

Once the jury was empaneled and seated, Kendrick turned to Peabody. "Mr. Prosecutor, you may make your case."

"Your honor!" Welles said quickly.

"What is it, Mr. Welles?"

"Do you intend to start this trial without *voir dire*?"

"I do."

"But that's highly unusual, Your Honor."

Kendrick laughed out loud. "Mr. Welles, we have assembled a court in a town without law, appointed as prosecutor someone who is barely literate, and as defender, a lawyer who was disbarred for drunkenness and corruption, and you say it is highly unusual that we are not having *voir dire*?"

"I-I see your point, Your Honor," Welles said in acquiescence.

"I am glad that you do. Now, sir, if we may continue?"

Peabody was sitting at the prosecutor's table, picking his nose.

Kendrick frowned. "Mr. Prosecutor?"

No response.

"Peabody!" he said sharply, when there was still no answer.

"What?"

"Make your case."

"Do what?"

"Begin the prosecution."

343

"Oh, yeah." Peabody stood up and looked toward the jury. "These two owlhoots here" — he pointed to the hapless defendants — "went to the governor 'n told 'im where we was keepin' his daughter that we took. On account of that, we had to leave the cabin where we was holed up 'n bring her here.

"That's the same thing as treason, and people that commit treason has to pay the penalty. As the prosecutor, I'm askin' this court to hang both of 'em."

"Counselor for the defense?" Kendrick said.

Welles took a swallow from the bottle of whiskey he had been working on, wiped his mouth with the back of his hand, then stood unsteadily to begin his defense. "You have accused my clients of a heinous crime — treason — and if they are indeed guilty, they should be expected to pay the maximum penalty. But!" — he paused for effect, then looked directly at Jug and Poke before turning back to the "jury" — "how do we know they went to the governor to give him such evidence?"

He held up his finger in order to illustrate a point. "Gentlemen of the jury, has someone come forward to say that they, personally, saw Mr. Poke and Mr. Jug talking to the governor?

"As far as we know, nobody has made such a claim. And if they have made such a claim, they are not here to bear witness against my clients, for if they were, I would have, under the legal tenets of discovery, been made aware, both of their statements, and of prosecution's intention to call them as witnesses.

"It is clear, therefore, that no such people exist. Therefore, I would point out to you that Article three, section three of the United States Constitution clearly states that *No person shall be convicted of treason unless on the testimony of two witnesses to the same overt act, or on confession in open court.*

"We now know that no such witnesses exist, or if they do, they have no intention of testifying. And it is for certain that my clients have not confessed to the crime.

"*Ergo, ipso facto,* you cannot find Mr. Poke and Mr. Jug guilty of treason. And, since treason is clearly the charge, and the only charge, as specified by the learned . . . uh . . . as specified by the prosecution, you, gentlemen of the jury, have no choice but to find the defendants innocent."

Welles, with a smug smile on his face, sat back down at the table with Poke and Jug, then grabbed the bottle of whiskey and turned it up for another long, Adam's-apple-bobbing drink.

Kendrick looked over toward the jury and right at Felker, whom he had appointed as the jury foreman. "Mr. Foreman, how does the jury find?"

"Objection, Your Honor!" Welles said. "The jury has not yet adjourned for consideration."

"Objection overruled," Kendrick replied. "You clearly have not made your case, and adjournment for consideration would just be a waste of time."

"Your Honor, you are prejudicing my case!" Welles complained.

"You are out of order, Counselor," Kendrick replied. "Mr. Felker, what is the verdict?"

"We find them guilty," Felker said.

"Would the bailiff bring the defendants before the bench?" Kendrick asked, and when nobody responded, he looked toward Cahill. "That would be you, Mr. Cahill. I appointed you bailiff."

"Oh, yeah," Cahill replied. "Get up there, you two."

Jug and Poke stood in front of the "bench."

"Mr. Jug and Mr. Poke —"

"Don't you want to know our real names?"

Poke interrupted.

"Not particularly. Jug and Poke are good enough. You two have been given a trial and found guilty of the crime of betrayal of the loyal band of brothers here assembled. As a result of that finding, I sentence you to be taken from here to a place where some contrivance may be assembled to facilitate the sentence of this court, which is to be hanged by your neck until you are dead."

"No!" Poke shouted. "If you're goin' to kill us, at least shoot us. Don't hang us!"

Kendrick rapped upon the table with the butt of his pistol. "This court is adjourned."

CHAPTER TWENTY-EIGHT

Rosalie was on the second floor of the Del Rey Hotel in a front room that overlooked the street. She had to admit that her accommodations were considerably more comfortable than they had been in the cabin. Her physical situation had improved, but her psychological situation had not. She couldn't help but wonder and worry about what was going to happen to her. She didn't know if her father would acquiesce to the demands of the people holding her or not. She did know that he would be doing everything possible to rescue her. And she knew that her father could muster considerable assets when needed. That thought brought her some comfort.

As she lay on the bed with her contemplations, she heard a lot of shouting and laughing coming from the street. Curious as to what it might be, she stepped up to the window to look outside. Several people were gathered in front of the livery stable just across from the hotel. A long board extended from the loft of the livery, out into the street. The board was supported on the street side by a pole.

Rosalie had no idea what was going on until she saw a wagon pass under the crossbeam. At first, the crowd blocked her view of the wagon, but when it got into position, she could see that four men were standing in the back of it. Two seemed to be bound up by ropes, their arms tied to their sides.

"What in the world?" she asked aloud. As she watched, two ropes with nooses were thrown over the crossbeam, and the two men in the back of the wagon who weren't bound fitted the nooses around the necks of the two men who were, then they jumped down, leaving only the two bound men.

"My God!" Rosalie said aloud. She realized that they were the two men she had met in the street, the men who had told her father where she could be found. They were about to be hanged, and it was her fault!

"No!" one of the men shouted. "You can't do this! You ain't got no right to do this! That warn't no real court!" His voice was loud and filled with fear

Rosalie, feeling tears of remorse, sympathy, and even a degree of responsibility, made fists so tight that she could feel her fingernails cutting into her hands.

"My name is Paul Connelly! It ain't Poke! It's Paul! Paul Connelly," the other man said. "If I'm goin' to meet my Maker, I want Him to know who I am!"

Not wanting to watch the actual execution, Rosalie turned away from the window, just as the team was lashed, causing them to pull the wagon forward. She heard the wagon move forward, and then a thumping sound, which she knew had to be the men reaching the end of the rope.

"Woowee! Look at 'em swing!" someone shouted.

Rosalie returned to her bed and lay there. With a shock, she realized that she could see the silhouettes of the two men swinging back and forth on the wall of her room, shadows cast from the late afternoon sun.

When Dooley, Rand, and Beans rode into town an hour later, they saw a couple bodies hanging from the crossbeam that protruded out from the livery. A hand-lettered sign was nailed to the upright.

**POKE AND JUG
THESE TWO TRAITORS WAS HUNG
CAUSE THEY COULDNT
KEEP THEIR MOUTHS SHUT**

They rode on down to the Pair of Kings saloon, tied their horses out front, then pushed in through the swinging batwing doors. Seeing Kendrick playing solitaire at his table in the back of the room, they walked back to see him.

"Ah, good to see you boys." Kendrick was holding a red eight, looking for a play. "Where are the others?"

The three men looked at each other, didn't reply.

"Never mind. I'll see them later. What did you do with MacCallister and the others after you killed them? I hope you didn't just leave the bodies there."

"MacCallister ain't dead," Beans said.

"There ain't none of 'em dead," Rand added.

"What do mean, none of them are dead? You were forewarned that they were coming, weren't you? All you had to do was set up an ambush."

"Yeah, well, it warn't nothin' like that," Dooley said.

"All right. Let me see if I have this straight," Kendrick said. "You were forewarned, you had plenty of time to find a defensive position, they had to advance in the open, and you had every opportunity to fire upon them from ambuscade, but the ten of you ran away?"

"They didn't nobody run away," Dooley said.

"Then how is it that you are here? Where are the others?" Kendrick asked.

"There ain't no others. This here is all there is of us. The others was all kilt," Beans said.

"Are you telling me that you three are the only ones left alive?" Kendrick said in disbelief.

"Marvin, Morris, Peter, 'n the others is dead," Rand said. "They was all kilt by MacCallister 'n the ones that come with 'im."

With a disgusted shout of anger, Kendrick swept the cards off the table. "They killed seven of you and you killed none of them?"

"Nary a one," Beans said.

"Then why, may I ask, are you three still alive? What did you do? Did you run away and abandon the others to their fate?"

"No, it warn't nothin' like that. The others was already dead before we got took," Dooley said.

"Before you were taken? What do you mean, you were taken? Are you saying you surrendered to them?"

"Yeah, well, as it turned out, we didn't have no choice. They had us covered, 'n if we hadn't surrendered, they would have kilt us," Dooley said.

"It would have been better had they done so. If you were captured by them, how, may I ask, did you get here? Did they let you go?" Kendrick looked at them in horror. "Good Lord, you didn't lead them here, did you?"

"No, we didn't lead 'em here," Dooley said. "What happened is, we got took to jail. But then, Sheriff Wallace, well he up 'n let us go after MacCallister 'n the others left town."

"Sheriff Wallace? You were taken into Merrill Town."

Dooley nodded. "Yeah."

"You said Wallace let you go after they rode off. Where did they go?"

"I don't know for sure, but Bullock thought they might have been goin' out to the Slash Bell Ranch," Beans said.

Kendrick sat for a long moment, drumming his fingers on the table as he glared at the three men. "I assume that as you three rode into town, you did see Poke and Jug hanging out there, didn't you?"

"Yeah," Rand said. "We seen 'em."

"Good. I'm glad that you saw them because I want you to know that that's what happens to people who cross me."

"Look, Kendrick, we didn't cross you," Dooley said. "We done just what you told us to do. We waited there for 'em to show up, 'n when they showed up, we commenced a-shootin' at 'em."

"But you didn't kill any of them." Kendrick's response wasn't a question. It was a statement of contempt.

"No," Dooley admitted. "We didn't kill none of 'em at all."

"I suppose I should have paid heed to the old proverb, never to send boys to do men's work," Kendrick said with a disgusted sigh.

"It warn't like that, Kendrick," Dooley said. "It warn't like that at all. Them fellers could shoot, 'n I ain't never seen nobody who can shoot as good as MacCallister. It don't seem to make no difference to him how far away he is from whatever it is he's a-shootin' at. Why, he hits it purt' near ever' time he pulls the trigger."

"Pick up the cards," Kendrick ordered.

The three men complied.

With the cards recovered, Kendrick shuffled them, then dealt himself another hand of solitaire. "Where did you say MacCallister and the others went?"

"Bullock said he thought they was goin' out to Bellefontaine's place," Dooley said.

"Find Peabody and send him to me."

■ ■ ■ ■

A tall, slender man with a mane of sandy blond hair that hung beneath a black, silver-banded hat was leaning casually against one of the posts supporting the porch roof of the feed store next to the livery. He had watched the hanging and was still there, drawn by morbid curiosity. It wasn't that he hadn't seen men die violently before. In fact, Ethan Quinn had been responsible for the violent deaths of at least twelve men, including the two cowboys he had killed but a few days earlier. He'd rolled a cigarette and had just lit it when he saw Peabody standing with the others.

"Hey, Peabody," he called. With the lit cigarette in his hand, he made a motion toward the two hanging men. "This is quite a piece of work."

"What are you doin' out here, Quinn? Ain't you ever seen anyone hang before?"

"Can't say as I have. It wasn't pretty to watch."

Peabody smirked. "It ain't supposed to be. That's why folks get hung . . . as a warnin' to others."

"Yeah, well, it's the law that does that, ain't it? I didn't think there was any law in

Blowout, which is why I come here in the first place."

"Well, there is a kind of law here," Peabody said. "You might call it an outlaw's law."

Quinn laughed. "Outlaw's law. That's pretty good."

"Hey, Peabody," Dooley said, coming up to the two men then. "Kendrick wants you."

"What's he want me for?"

"He didn't say. He just said he wants to see you."

"I saw you and Rand and Beans ridin' in a few minutes ago. Where are the others?"

Dooley grimaced. "Dead."

"Dead? What the hell do you mean, dead?"

"I mean dead. MacCallister 'n his bunch kilt 'em all."

"MacCallister 'n his bunch? How many of 'em was there?"

"They call themselves Ten Guns from Texas," Dooley replied, without giving any further information. "I expect you'd better go see Kendrick. He don't like to be kept waitin', 'n I can tell you right now that he ain't in a very good mood."

Peabody nodded. "All right. I'm a-goin'."

"Hey, Peabody," Quinn called out as Peabody started toward the saloon. "If you had seven killed, plus Poke and Jug, it would seem to me like it's about time for you to be recruitin' some more men. Tell Kendrick I'd be interested in joinin' up."

"You should know by now that if Kendrick wanted you to join up with us, he'd ask you," Peabody replied.

"Yeah, but that was before he lost nine men."

"Only seven. Poke and Jug don't count. They done some work with us, but Kendrick never trusted them enough to let 'em actual join." Peabody glanced toward the still hanging bodies. "Turns out, he was right."

Reaching the saloon, he stepped inside. He had no idea what Kendrick wanted with him and was a little apprehensive about being summoned. He stopped at the bar and bought a shot of whiskey to calm his nerves.

Kendrick was ensconced in the same leather chair from which he had conducted trial earlier in the day.

"You wanted to see me?" Peabody asked, walking over with the drink in his hand.

"Yeah, have a seat."

Still nervous, Peabody sat.

"Did you hear what happened to the ten men you left back at the cabin?"

"Yeah, Dooley told me they was seven of 'em got kilt."

"That was your responsibility, Peabody. I

357

left you in charge."

"Wait now, just a minute here," Peabody said, holding his free hand out toward Kendrick. "It warn't me. It was Dooley that was in charge when they actual come. You told me you wanted the girl brung here from the cabin, 'n that's what I done. I left Dooley in charge. It ain't my fault he got seven of his men kilt."

"Fifteen," Kendrick said.

"Fifteen? What do you mean fifteen? We only left ten there, 'n three of 'em is here in town, right now."

"I'm talking about how many of our men MacCallister has killed so far."

"Yeah," Peabody said. "Yeah, I see what you mean, now. Countin' the men that was kilt at the Slash Bell 'n the two on the road — but wait, that's only thirteen."

"Fifteen. As it happens, he also killed Jenkins and Woodson back in Merrill Town."

"Damn. We need to do somethin' about him."

"That's why I sent for you. I want Mac-Callister killed, and I'm willing to pay good money to have it done."

"What do you mean by good money?"

"Twenty-five hundred dollars, to be divided up by the men who actually carry out the assignment."

"What if one man does it?"

Kendrick shook his head. "Killing Mac-Callister is more than a one-man job."

"Still, twenty-five hundred dollars is a lot of money," Peabody said. "I might even be interested in trying it, for that much money."

"No, I don't want you trying it, and I don't want to use any of the Fence Busters for the job. We can't afford to lose any more men, and if they aren't killed, but are merely caught, I don't want any chance that it will come back to us."

"You're sayin' you want to kill MacCallister, but what about the others?"

"The others?"

"Yeah, you know — the ones that's callin' themselves Ten Guns from Texas. To hear Dooley talk, they're an army all by themselves."

"Ten guns from Texas?"

"That's what Dooley called 'em."

"Dooley didn't say anything to me about ten guns. Where would he have gotten the extra men? There's MacCallister, Gleason, and the Chinaman. And the information I got said that the governor would be pardoning three men from prison."

"Yeah, well, I don't know nothin' about that. All I know is that Dooley said they was ten guns. If there's that many of 'em, it's

359

not goin' to be all that easy to take care of 'em," Peabody pointed out.

Kendrick shook his head. "The only one we're going to have to take care of MacCallister. If we kill him, I guarantee you, we won't have any trouble from the others."

"You mean like, cut off the head of the snake," Peabody said.

"Why, yes," Kendrick said. "That is exactly what I mean. Now, do you have anybody in mind for the job? Even though MacCallister is the only one we have to kill, he has shown that he's going to take a lot of killing. I think we will need at least five men for the job."

"With the kind of money you're offerin', I don't think it will be all that hard to find five men to take care of MacCallister oncet 'n for all."

"It's not enough just to find five men; you'll need to find someone to lead them. If you can find such a man, we'll give him a thousand dollars and divide up the remaining fifteen hundred among the others."

"Damn, Kendrick, for that kind of money, I'll lead 'em," Peabody said. "I can do it. I know I can."

Kendrick shook his head. "No, you're too valuable to me, I don't want to risk you in this. Besides, you know my plans. Once we get through all of this and get the cattle sold, there'll be enough money for us to go anywhere in the country we want. We'll be far enough away from Texas to be away from the law, and we'll have enough money to live like kings."

"Yeah, you're right," Peabody agreed. "All right. I do have someone in mind. How about Quinn?"

"Quinn. Yes, I have given him some consideration. And I believe he has expressed some interest in joining us, hasn't he?"

"Yeah, I just spoke to him, 'n he asked me to ask you if he could join up with us."

"So, he has come around and is finally ready to ask us, is he? Well, that's a rather fortuitous turn of events, isn't it? Quinn may be just the man we're looking for."

"Yeah, well, don't forget he's kilt a lot of men," Peabody said. "There don't nobody actual know just how many he has kilt. I thought you said someone like that was a . . . what did you say . . . a loose cannon?"

"As a matter of fact, I did say that. But now it seems that I have need for the services of just such a man. How better to deal with a killer than to use a killer? Do you think he will cooperate?"

"Yeah, I know he will. Most especially if

we tell 'im that he can join up with us."

"All right. Tell him he can join. No, wait, don't tell him that right away. Tell him that this is a test. If he can do this job for us, I'll take him into our group. Do you think he'll go for that?"

Peabody smiled. "Yeah, he'll go for it."

Kendrick looked up toward the door and saw Quinn coming into the saloon. "Speak of the devil, our friend has just come into the saloon. I'll leave now. I think it might be better if you spoke to him alone. Buy him a drink and get his confidence."

CHAPTER TWENTY-NINE

Peabody watched Kendrick leave, then he called out to the bartender. "Weasel! Mr. Quinn's drink is on me. Quinn, come over here. Let's talk."

A moment later, Quinn was sitting at the table with Peabody.

"You asked me to talk to Kendrick for you, 'n I done that."

"And?" Quinn asked, interested in the remark. "What did he say? Will he take me into the Fence Busters?"

"Yeah, he will, but only if you'll agree to do one special job for him."

"What job would that be?"

"Wait, you ain't heard all the details about it, yet. He'll give you a thousand dollars, and he'll also take you into the Fence Busters."

"A thousand dollars?"

"Yes. And another fifteen hundred dollars for you to divide up among your men."

"What men?"

"Why, the men you'll get to help you if you decide to do the job," Peabody explained.

"Will I be in charge of these here men I round up?"

"Yes, you will be totally in charge."

"All right. You tell Kendrick I'll do it," Quinn said.

"You ain't heard yet what the job is."

"I expect he'll be wantin' me to kill someone, seein' as how that's what I'm most good at."

"Yes, that's exactly what we want you to do."

"All right. Who is it he's a-wantin' me to kill?"

"His name is MacCallister."

"MacCallister? Wait a minute. Ain't he the one Dooley was talkin' about? The one that kilt all Dooley's men?"

"Yes, that MacCallister. But of course, he had ten guns with him. Kendrick is only interested in killing MacCallister, though. He figures if MacCallister gets kilt, we won't have to worry none about the others. Are you still interested in taking the job?"

"Damn right I am," Quinn said. "And I'll get the job done, too. You just tell me where he is. That's all I need to know."

"I believe he and his men are staying out at the Slash Bell Ranch," Peabody said. "I know that he 'n Bellefontaine have come to be real good friends."

"The Slash Bell? Where is that?"

"It's just outside Merrill Town, but I'd think twice about tryin' to hit MacCallister out at the ranch. There's not only his men stayin' there. Bellefontaine has plenty cowboys out there, as well. What you need to do is catch him at a time when he ain't at the ranch. I know that Bellefontaine 'n his cowboys go into Merrill Town a lot. More 'n likely MacCallister will be goin' there his ownself."

"Yeah, that's what I'm a-thinkin', too. All right. I'll go to Merrill Town and check things out," Quinn said. "Don't worry none 'bout me. I'll check things out pretty good before I make any move."

"You'll need to pick up some men to help you."

"If I need anyone, I'll pick 'em up in Merrill Town."

"Why would you pick them up there? Why not get the men here?"

" 'Cause outside them that's already a part of the Fence Busters, I don't figure there's anyone here that would be worth a damn in a fight. If they was, they'd already be in the Fence Busters."

Peabody laughed. "I don't see as how I can argue with you on that, Quinn."

Rosalie was having lunch at the Palace Café, the other restaurant in town, when she saw Kendrick coming in. She stared at her plate, hoping that if she didn't meet his eyes, he wouldn't come to her.

Her ploy was unsuccessful. She felt, rather than saw, him approach her table.

"May I join you, Miss Ireland?" he asked, even as he was pulling out the chair.

"Do I have a choice?"

Kendrick chuckled. "No, not really."

"Then why did you even ask?"

"I was just being polite."

"If you were being polite, you would let me go."

"We have already discussed that. I'll let you go when your father accedes to my demand."

"When do you intend to cut those poor men down?" Rosalie asked.

"I'll cut them down before nightfall. I want everyone to have a chance to see them. You are an intelligent young lady. I'm sure you realize that a public execution is not as much about the people who are being hanged as it is to provide an object lesson for the people who see it and learn by it."

"I'm sure those two poor gentlemen were comforted to know that they weren't the purpose of their hanging."

Kendrick laughed out loud. "You have a good sense of humor."

"Why did you hang them? What did they do?"

"You do recall that we had to move you from the cabin where we were keeping you. That is because those two men, Poke and Jug, went to see your father and told him where you could be found."

"Oh. That means I am the reason they were killed."

Kendrick frowned. "Well, not because of anything you did personally, my dear. However, indirectly, you were the cause of their demise."

"Mr. Kendrick, I have been told that you are supposed to be a lawyer."

"Oh, but I am, my dear."

"Then I don't understand. Aren't lawyers supposed to uphold the law? What gave you the right to hang those men?"

"You may have heard that we held a public trial for them. Even in this town, we have laws. It's just that our laws are unique to our citizenry and, you might say, our situation."

"You should be ashamed of yourself."

"I feel no shame, Miss Ireland. I believe it is a man's destiny to maximize his potential in any way he can. In my case, I have found ways to utilize my education and my intellect to attain my goal. Yes, the road there will, from time to time, be strewn with let us just say *unpleasant* diversions from the straight and narrow. But once that goal is achieved, it is my intention to leave Texas and establish residence in some other place as a wealthy man. There, I will be a law-abiding citizen and, no doubt, become a pillar of the community."

Rosalie frowned. "Do you really think you could put all this behind you?"

"Yes, I am certain of it. Now, I would like to ask you a question. Do you know a man by the name of MacCallister? Unfortunately, I can't give you his first name since MacCallister is the only name I know."

"MacCallister? No, I don't think so. Why?"

"What about a man named Gleason? Both men would be in conjunction with your father."

"Gleason? Wait, yes. Mr. Gleason saved my father's life during the war. I just met him the other day, and now that I think about it, I believe the name of the man who was with him was MacCallister."

"I told you that the two men it became necessary for me to hang had gone to your father with information as to your location. Your father had been cautioned not to send the law after you, so he got around that by dispatching MacCallister, Gleason, Kelly, and some others to go to the cabin to rescue you. But, because I had advanced warning that they were coming, I was able to move you before they got there."

"You knew they were coming to rescue me?"

Kendrick nodded. "Yes."

"How did you know that?"

"Really, now, Miss Ireland, you don't expect me to tell you that, do you?"

"What happened? Did your men" — she paused before she completed the question — "kill Mr. Gleason and Mr. MacCallister?"

"On the contrary, Miss Ireland, none of your would-be rescuers were killed or even wounded, but MacCallister, Gleason, and the men with him killed seven of my men. You should consider yourself quite fortunate you weren't there. MacCallister and his men came in shooting like mad fools, and had I not made provisions to move you to safety, it is very possible that you would have been killed in the cross fire."

"Why did you ask me if I knew them?"

"I'm trying to locate them now. I was hoping you would be able to help me out."

"Even if I knew where they were, do you think I would tell you? Why, they risked their lives to save me. I would do nothing to bring harm to them."

Kendrick applauded quietly and smiled across the table at her. "Good for you, Miss Ireland. If you had information, I would have appreciated you telling me, but I must say that I respect you the more for your loyalty."

"You are a strange man, Mr. Kendrick."

"It is too bad that we had to meet under conditions that have been so unpleasant for you," Kendrick said. "It would have been much better for us to meet three years from now, when this is all behind me, and I am the epitome of the decent and wealthy citizen. I think you would welcome my attention."

"What?" Rosalie gasped. "Surely, Mr. Kendrick, you are not suggesting that there could ever be something between us?"

"Oh, don't discount the possibility, my dear. I think you would find me quite charming, under the right circumstances."

Slash Bell Ranch
Elmer, Wang, Kelly, Decker, and Simmons

ate in the bunkhouse while Duff had dinner with the Bellefontaines in the big house. He'd learned their son was a cadet at the United States Military Academy in West Point, and their daughter was attending school at the Lindenwood School for Women in St. Charles, Missouri. Mrs. Bellefontaine had presided over the dinner, then discreetly withdrew as the men retired to the library.

Duff accepted the offer of a cigar and a glass of Glenfarclas Scotch.

"I can't help but feel guilty about the governor's daughter," Bellefontaine said, holding a match to the end of Duff's cigar. He then lit his own and took a few puffs before he spoke through the smoke that wreathed his head. "If I hadn't insisted that he get the law passed about cutting fences on public land, she wouldn't have been taken."

"Nonsense. It isn't your fault at all," Duff said. "And I'm sure she hasn't been harmed. It would nae serve Kendrick's purpose to harm her in any way. I just wish I knew where they were keeping her."

"I've heard that the Fence Busters keep a cabin on the Blanco River. I don't know that they have taken her there, and even if they had, I'm not sure exactly where the cabin is, other than somewhere on the Blanco River. Eighty miles, and the cabin could be anywhere along the whole course of it. And to tell the truth, I'm not even sure about that. I have heard, however, that they do have such a place. If you were to ask a few questions around town, you might find someone who has a better idea."

"Yes, that's a good idea," Duff said. "In fact, I know just where to start."

"You are going to question the men you captured at the cabin where they were holding Miss Ireland," Bellefontaine said. It wasn't a question. It was a statement validating what Duff was about to say.

"Aye," Duff replied.

"Good idea, that's exactly where I would start, as well."

The next morning, Elmer learned that a steer was about to be slaughtered to provide meat for the ranch. He asked Sam, "How do you plan to kill it?"

"The way we kill all our beeves. We've got a catch stall that we put them in, where it's too narrow for them to turn, then Tim smacks them right between the eyes with a sledgehammer. It's the most humane way of doin' it, 'cause it kills 'em right away, faster than shootin' 'em would."

"Before you do that, I would like to talk to my friend, Mr. Wang, for a few minutes."

Sam frowned. "You want to talk to Wang before we kill the steer?"

"Yeah."

"Why? What does he have to do with our killing a steer?"

"Just hang on a second, 'n I'll let you know," Elmer said.

He and Wang exchanged a few words in Mandarin.

"What the hell are they jabberin' in?" one of the cowboys asked.

"That's called Chinese," Kelly said. "Elmer can talk Chinese."

"He can? Damn, I ain't never know'd no white man that could jabber in Chinese. I know some that can talk Mex, 'n even some that can talk a little Injun, but I ain't never met no one who could talk Chinese. What is it they're a-talkin' about?"

"I don't have no idea," Kelly said.

"*Shi,*" Wang said, nodding his head in the affirmative.

Elmer walked over to where Post, Kelly, and the others were standing as they had watched in curiosity the conversation between him and Wang.

"What was that all about?" Post asked.

"I've talked my friend Mr. Wang into

givin' us a little show," Elmer said a moment later. "There is no need for O'Leary and his hammer. Wang can kill the steer with his bare hand."

"What? The hell he can," Post said.

"Believe me, he can," Elmer said.

"Yeah, well, even if he can, and I have no idea how he could do such a thing, I just told you that we want to do it in as humane a way as possible," Post said. "There's no sense in letting the creature suffer."

"It'll be as quick as O'Leary hitting the cow with a sledgehammer," Elmer promised.

Post, O'Leary, and all the Slash Bell cowboys laughed. Post noticed, however, that Kelly, Simmons, and Decker didn't laugh.

"What the hell? You boys don't think he can do it, do you?" O'Leary asked the three men who had come with Elmer and Wang.

"I don't know that he can," Kelly said. "But by damn, I don't know that he can't, neither."

Post snorted what might have been a laugh. "For a moment there, I thought you were being serious," he said to Elmer.

"I'm serious enough to put a little money on it," Elmer replied.

"How much?"

"It depends on how many of you want to bet," Elmer said, "and how much you want to bet. I know what a cowboy's wages are, 'n I wouldn't want to be takin' away money you might use to have a drink or a nice meal in town. But I'd be willin' to cover ever'one's bets."

Word quickly spread that Elmer would cover all bets, and all the cowboys but Post and O'Leary — fifteen of them — put two dollars apiece down. Post and O'Leary put down five dollars each.

"That's forty dollars, Gleason. Can you cover it?" Post asked.

"I can. There's no need for me to, but I can." Elmer put forty dollars down on the table. He looked over at the three men who had come with him. "You boys want in on this? And if you do, which side?"

"Elmer, you know there ain't a one of us that's got a nickel to our name," Kelly replied. "Even if I did, I don't think I'd want in on this. I'm not sure the Chinaman can do what you say, but I wouldn't want to bet ag'in 'im, neither. I think I'll just watch."

"Yeah," Decker said. Simmons nodded his agreement.

Duff and Bellefontaine were summoned for the "show" and fifteen minutes later, they joined the cowboys, Elmer, Kelly,

Simmons, and Decker to watch Wang's demonstration.

"Which one is it you're a-wantin' to kill?" Elmer asked.

"We'll get 'im over here," O'Leary said.

A moment later, the steer was in a stall, then hooked up in a harness so he could be lifted up to be butchered after he was killed.

"There he is," Post said, pointing the animal out to Wang. "What are you going to do? Choke him to death?"

The others laughed.

"When do you call it off and admit that it is all a joke?" Bellefontaine asked with a chuckle.

"Oh, it's no joke," Duff replied.

Wang stepped in front of the steer, then held his open hand down by his side. He took a few deep breaths, then raised his hand over his head. *"Kiayah!"* he shouted, bringing the knife edge of his hand down to the steer's head, striking it right between the eyes.

The steer shuddered once, then fell down, lying perfectly still.

"Holy cow!" Post shouted.

"You mean dead cow, don't you?" Elmer replied with a little chuckle.

"I've never seen such a thing in my entire life!" Bellefontaine said. "How the hell did you do that?"

"*Wushu* is here," Wang said, pointing to the side of his head. "Not here." He held out his hand.

"Can all Chinamen do that?" O'Leary asked.

"Only those who have studied for many years," Wang replied. "I began to study when I was a small boy."

"How long did you study?"

"My study has not stopped."

"Yeah, well, there ain't none o' you goin' to learn how to do this just by jawin' about it," Post said. "Get this cow cut up. That is, if you're wantin' to eat anythin' over the next couple weeks."

CHAPTER THIRTY

Merrill Town

"Sheriff Wallace, I would like to talk to your three prisoners, please," Duff said when he stepped into the sheriff's office later that same day.

"It isn't visiting hours," Wallace replied.

"Perhaps that is so, Sheriff, but this will nae be a social visit. I just need to get some information from them."

"Do you expect me to let just anyone come in off the street and question my prisoners?"

"Nae, but as I showed you when I brought the prisoners to you, I'm nae just anyone off the street. I am a constable, duly authorized by the governor himself, with authority and jurisdiction throughout the state of Texas. That means in this town and in this county. Now, will you be for letting me talk with your prisoners? Or do I take you prisoner and lock you in your own jail for obstructing justice?"

"What are you talking about? You can't do that," Wallace replied.

"Oh, but I can and I will, if you dinnae let me talk with the prisoners."

"They aren't here."

"You have moved them? Why would you do that?"

"I didn't move 'em." Sheriff Wallace was quiet for a moment, then he added, "I let 'em go."

"You let them go? And would you be for telling me, my good man, why in the name of Robert the Bruce would you have let them go?"

"Because I didn't have nothin' to hold 'em on. I wasn't a personal witness to anything they may have done. I don't know how you do things in England —"

"It's Scotland, you *dobber*, not England," Duff said, barely controlling his anger.

"Yes, well, here in America, we do have laws. And the law says I can't keep anyone in jail without charges being filed. And, as no charges were filed, I made the decision to release my prisoners."

"Bloody hell. They weren't your prisoners. They were mine, and as such, it was nae your decision to make." Duff glared at Wallace so intensely that the sheriff couldn't meet his gaze. Duff turned on his heel and left. His next destination was the CSS *Alabama* Saloon.

"Mr. MacCallister, good to see you again!" Prescott poured a shot of Scotch.

Duff lifted the drink and held it out in salute toward Prescott. "To all the lads who sleep in the sea."

"A noble toast, my friend," Prescott replied. "A noble toast."

Duff tossed the drink down, then set the empty glass on the bar. Prescott picked up the bottle to pour another.

"Nae," Duff said, putting his hand over the glass. "One is enough. Tell me, Mr. Prescott, what do you know of a group of disreputable gentlemen who call themselves the Fence Busters?"

"I know that when you call them disreputable gentlemen, you are only half right. They are disreputable, but they aren't gentlemen."

"I've heard that they are headquartered in a cabin on the Blanco River. Do you know if there is any truth to that?"

"I can't vouch for it, for a fact, but I've heard that same thing mentioned so often that there must be some truth in it. Why do you ask?"

"You do know that they are the ones who

took the lovely wee lass that is the governor's daughter?"

"I suspected as much."

"A few friends and I are looking for her."

"I pray that you find her. You sure you don't want another drink?"

"No thanks. I'll have a cup of coffee, though."

"It's a good man who knows to appreciate, and not abuse a fine liquor," Prescott said. "I'll just step into the kitchen and get you a cup."

After Prescott stepped away, Duff used the mirror to study everyone in the room.

Four men were playing poker at one of the tables, the game being kibitzed by an attractive young bar girl. At another table, three men sat drinking, engaged in earnest conversation. A smiling cowboy was sharing a drink with a bar girl at another table, while three more tables were occupied by solitary drinkers.

One of the solitary drinkers got up and left just before Prescott returned with the coffee.

Quinn was leaning against the bar of the Hog Pen Saloon, clasping his beer mug with both hands. He had come to town the day before, first to see if he could find out any information about MacCallister, and also to recruit some men for the job he was planning.

So far he had recruited no one, but shortly after he had arrived, he told a man named Creech that he was looking for MacCallister. He thought back to that conversation.

"What for?" Creech asked. At one time, he had been a cowboy for Bellefontaine, but he was fired when it was learned that he had stolen a couple beeves to sell.

"What do you care why I'm lookin' for 'im?"

"I don't care why you're lookin' for 'im. I was just wonderin' is all. And bein' as he's a friend of that sumbitch Bellefontaine, that means he sure as hell ain't no friend o' mine."

"Maybe I'm lookin' to kill 'im," Quinn said.

"I think you're funnin' me."

"What makes you think I'm just funnin' you?"

"MacCallister ain't been here all that long, but from what I heard, he ain't that easy to kill."

Quinn smiled. "If he was easy, it wouldn't be no fun to kill 'im now, would it?"

"You mean you're serious?"

"Will you help me find him? I'll make it worth your while."

"You'll pay me for it if I find 'im for you?"

"Yes."

"How much?"

"One hundred dollars."

"All I have to do is find 'im and point 'im out to you, 'n you'll give me one hunnert dollars? Hell, yeah. Damn right I'll help you find 'im," Creech replied exuberantly.

Quinn had neither seen, nor heard from Creech since their conversation.

He took another swallow of his beer, then made a face. "Hey, Hog Jaw. What the hell do you put in this beer, anyway? It tastes like horse piss."

The bartender moved down to Quinn, picked up his mug, and took a swallow. "Damn, you're right. I've got to talk to the Dutchman about that. Today is the day he is supposed to use mule piss." Pouring the rest of the beer out, Hog Jaw held the mug under the barrel, pulled the handle, and refilled the mug. He set the glass with a high standing head in front of Quinn. "See if this one isn't just a little better."

Quinn chuckled. "You're full of horse crap, you know that?"

"That's what my ol' mama used to tell me," Hog Jaw replied with a smile.

"Tell me, Hog Jaw, have you ever heard of a feller by the name of MacCallister?"

"You mean the Scotsman?"

"Scotsman. Yeah, I reckon he is a Scotsman at that. Have you ever heard of 'im?"

"Heard of 'im? Why, Quinn, I seen 'im in action. He kilt Woodson 'n Jenkins right here in this saloon. 'N he was a-standin' right there where you're a-standin' now when he done it."

"What do you mean he kilt 'em both? You mean at the same time?"

"Yes, sir, at the same time."

"Hog Jaw?" someone called from the other end of the bar.

" 'Scuse me," Hog Jaw said as he walked away.

Quinn lifted his mug to see if the beer tasted any better than the first. Before he could take a swallow, however, he saw Creech come into the saloon. "Where the hell you been? I thought maybe you'd rode out of town or somethin'."

"No, I been doin' what you told me to do. I've been keepin' my eye open for that feller we talked about, 'n now I got somethin' to tell you."

"Not here, standin' at the bar," Quinn replied. "Grab a beer and come to the table."

Quinn left the bar and found a table by the stove, which, being summer, was cold. He watched as Creech ordered a beer, then came over to join him."

"What have you got for me?" Quinn asked as Creech sat down.

"He's here in town, right now," Creech said.

"How do you know he's in town? Did you see him? Do you know him?" Quinn replied.

"Yeah, I seen 'im. He's down there in the *Alabama,* right now. I can't say as I know 'im to talk to, but I know what he looks like. I seen 'im the other day with Bellefontaine 'n that Sam Post." Creech took a swallow of his beer, then made a face. "Damn, this tastes like horse piss."

"Mule piss," Quinn corrected. "What about MacCallister? Was there anyone with him?"

"You talkin' about the older feller and the Chinaman? No, there warn't neither one of 'em with 'im. None of the ranch hands was with him, neither. He's just over at the *Alabama* all by hisself, standin' at the bar, not talkin' to nobody 'cept sometimes Prescott."

"You're absolutely positive it's him?"

Creech nodded his head. "Oh, it's him all right."

"Good."

"So, now that you found 'im, are you plannin' on killin' 'im?"

385

"I'm not just plannin' on killin' 'im, I *am* a-goin' to kill 'im," Quinn replied easily.

"What about the one hundred dollars?"

"What one hundred dollars?"

"You know what one hundred dollars! I'm talkin' about the money you promised me if I'd find MacCallister for you. Well, I found 'im, 'n I told you where he was. So I want my money."

"I'll give it to you after."

"If you got it, I'd like it now."

"Look here, Creech. You ain't tellin' me you don't trust me, are you? 'Cause I don't think I'd like to hear that."

"Oh, I trust you all right. It's just —"

"It's just what?"

"What if it's you that gets kilt, instead o' MacCallister? Iffen that was to happen, they wouldn't be no way I'd be able to get my money."

Quinn laughed out loud.

"What is it you're a-laughin' at?"

"You, Creech. I'm laughin' at you. I'm just real touched 'bout you worryin' 'bout me, but you don't need to worry none 'bout it. I ain't been kilt yet, 'n I don't expect to be kilt this time, neither. I tell you what. I'll buy you another beer when I leave, but I can't pay you now, 'cause I don't have a hunnert dollars. But I'll pay you when I get my money."

"What do you mean, when you get your money?"

"I'm gettin' paid for killin' 'im."

"You plannin' on killin' 'im all by yourself?"

"Yeah, why? Are you offerin' to help? If you are, I could maybe go another hunnert dollars."

"Not even if you said five hunnert dollars," Creech replied. "I've heard enough about MacCallister that I don't want to have nothin' to do with 'im. Why, do you know he kilt four men right here in this very saloon the other day?"

"Four men, huh? Are you sure it was four, 'n not just two?"

"Oh, you already heard about it, right?"

"Yeah."

"Well, maybe it was only two men. But still, if I was you, I'd get some men to help me."

Learning that MacCallister was in town all alone, Quinn was convinced that he wouldn't need anyone else. And if he didn't use anyone else, he would have a legitimate claim to the entire twenty-five hundred dollars Kendrick was offering.

Quinn walked over to the bar, ordered another mug of beer, and told one of the bar girls to deliver it to Creech, who was still sitting at the table.

Leaving the Hog Pen, Quinn walked down the street to the CSS *Alabama*. If he was going to kill MacCallister, he at least needed to know what he looked like. He didn't want to shoot the wrong man, after all. Kendrick wouldn't pay for the wrong man.

Quinn giggled at his thought, and was still smiling as he pushed through the batwing doors and stepped into the saloon. He moved up to the bar. "What are you serving for beer? The reason I ask is down at the Hog Pen, Hog Jaw is servin' horse piss."

"Well, if I could get away with it, I'd serve the same thing," Prescott said, drawing a mug for him. "After all, that is cheaper."

Quinn paid for the beer, then looked out over the floor. When he saw someone sitting at a table alone, drinking coffee, he stared closely at him. He had the strongest feeling that it might be MacCallister. "Who's the feller drinkin' the coffee?"

"Why are you askin'?"

"No reason," Quinn replied. "It just don't seem to me like a man would come to a saloon to drink coffee. You'd think he'd want a man's drink."

"Yeah? Well, I wouldn't say anything about him not being a man if I were you. Not if you want to live much longer, that is."

"Is that a fact?"

"Yes, sir, that is a fact. You see, mister, that there feller is Duff MacCallister. I reckon you've heard of him, haven't you?"

"Can't say as I have."

"Well, there are quite few who would still be alive if they had heard of him before they tangled with him."

"Fast with a gun, is he?"

"Fast with a gun? Well, now that you mention it, I don't know if he is fast or not. I don't know that those men were killed in what you might call an actual gunfight. I think mostly they were killed just because MacCallister was a lot smarter than they were."

"Are you sayin' he shot 'em in the back?" Quinn asked, surprised by the bartender's remark."

"Now don't you be putting words into my mouth, 'cause I didn't say nothin' at all like that. What I said was, he's smarter than anyone who has ever tried to kill him."

"I'm thinkin' that one of these days, MacCallister might run into someone who is smarter than he is."

"That's a strange thing for you to say. What makes you think that?"

"No particular reason," Quinn replied.

"It's just that gunfighters like him always do."

Prescott shook his head. "No, you don't understand. MacCallister isn't like the kind of man you are talking about. He's not what you would call a gunfighter. And he doesn't go around starting fights, but he does seem to have a knack for endin' 'em."

"Show me someone who has a reputation for killin' a lot of people, 'n I'll show you someone who's picked more 'n a few fights."

"What makes you such an expert in this?" Prescott asked, obviously getting a little annoyed with his customer.

"You might say I'm in that business," Quinn replied.

"Oh? And what business would that be?"

"The business of killin' people," Quinn replied with a humorless smile.

"Who are you, mister?"

"Quinn. Ethan Quinn."

Prescott blinked once, but he didn't respond to Quinn's remark.

"I see you've heard of me."

"Yeah, I've heard of you."

"I thought maybe you might have." Quinn finished his beer, then left the saloon.

CHAPTER THIRTY-ONE

Walking across the street, Quinn stood in front of the leather goods store, keeping his eye on the front door of the CSS *Alabama* Saloon.

When he first went into the saloon, it had been his intention to challenge MacCallister man-to-man, but he'd started thinking about the number of men that MacCallister had killed, just since arriving in Texas. Quinn realized that a direct challenge might not be the smartest thing he could do. All Kendrick wanted was for MacCallister to be dead, and dead was dead, no matter how he was killed.

Quinn smirked. And, he thought, the twenty-five hundred dollars would spend just as well, no matter how he killed him.

Prescott watched the door of the saloon until he was certain Quinn was gone, then he walked over to the table where Duff was still drinking his coffee. "Mr. MacCallister, did you happen to notice the man that just left here?"

"A slender man with long yellow hair?"

"Yeah, that's the one. His name is Ethan Quinn, and he has a bit of a reputation as a gunfighter. I just thought I'd tell you that he was askin' a lot of questions about you."

"Thank you, Mr. Prescott. I appreciate the information."

Elmer Gleason, a little bored staying out at the ranch, decided to ride into to town to look up Duff to see if he had been able to find out anything. Besides, two sets of eyes and two sets of ears would be better than one. He passed the blacksmith shop as he came into town. The ringing of the smithy's hammer filled the street with sound.

He was pretty sure that Duff would be in one of the two saloons, so he decided he would check the CSS *Alabama* first.

Across the street, Quinn saw a rider coming down the street toward him, but paid no attention, other than just keeping an eye on him. He didn't want the rider between him and MacCallister when MacCallister stepped outside. Quinn knew that he would have only a second to maintain the advantage over the man he intended to kill.

He smiled when he saw MacCallister push through the swinging doors and step out onto the wooden porch in front. The timing was perfect. Quinn would have a shot at him before the approaching rider could pass between them. He saw MacCallister pause to look up and down the street, and that gave Quinn the opening he needed. Taking advantage of the momentary distraction of his target, he pulled his pistol, then raised it toward the man he intended to kill.

The approaching rider saw Quinn raise the pistol and aim it at Duff. *"Duff! Look out!"* Elmer shouted at the top of his voice.

Duff's reaction was instantaneous. He dropped to one knee just as Ethan Quinn fired. He felt the concussion of the bullet as it fried the air by his ear and slammed into the door frame just behind him.

"Damn!" Quinn shouted in anger. He cocked his pistol and aimed again, but he didn't get the opportunity for a second shot.

Even as he was cocking his pistol, Elmer and Duff were shooting at him. Elmer's bullet hit Quinn in his side, and would have, no doubt, prevented the gunman from shooting a second time. At the same time, Duff's bullet plunged into Quinn's heart. Quinn fell facedown, his feet still on the porch of the Merrill Town Leather Goods store, and his face in the dirt of Bratton Road. His right arm was outstretched, his hand still wrapped around the gun.

The shooting, happening as it did right in the middle of town, drew a crowd as people came pouring out of the businesses lining the street, the Rustic Rock Restaurant, the Del Rey Hotel, Sikes Hardware, and Buckner Ragsdale Mercantile.

"Damn! You know who that feller is? That's Ethan Quinn!" someone said.

"What happened?" another asked.

"He got hisself shot. That's what happened."

Sheriff Wallace and Deputy Bullock hustled onto the scene, and after taking a look at the Quinn's body, Wallace looked around. "Who done this?"

"I did," Duff replied.

"Me too," Elmer added.

"Both of you? You mean it was two of you against this one man?" Wallace challenged.

"Sheriff, they didn't have no choice," one of the bystanders said. "I seen it all, 'n Quinn, he's the one that started it. He shot first."

"Who did he shoot at?"

"Why, he shot at him." The man pointed to Duff.

394

"If he was shootin' at MacCallister, what were you doin' shootin' at Quinn?" the sheriff asked Elmer.

"I shot 'im, 'cause I seen that he was 'bout to shoot at Duff," Elmer replied.

The sheriff smirked. "Then you can't claim self-defense, can you?"

"He doesn't have to," another man said. "Clearly, this man's act is justifiable homicide, as it can objectively be proven to a trier of fact and beyond all reasonable doubt that Quinn intended to commit violence against Mr. MacCallister. A homicide in this instance is blameless."

Wallace turned to the speaker. "What business is this of yours?"

"I am a lawyer, Sheriff, an officer of the court. As such, I have taken an oath to support the Constitution and laws of the United States and of Texas. The actions taken by these two men are fully justified."

Blowout

"Are you telling me Quinn was killed?" Kendrick asked.

"Yes sir. I seen 'im shot down my ownself," Creech replied.

"What about the men who were with him?"

"There warn't no men with him," Creech

395

said. "He was all by hisself. But MacCallister, he warn't all by hisself. They was another man, a feller by the name of Gleason, 'n he was also a-shootin' at Quinn."

Sitting at his table in the Pair of Kings, Kendrick drummed his fingers on the table, then turned to look at Peabody sitting across from him. "I thought you told me Quinn was the consummate gunman."

"The what?" Peabody replied.

"You led me to believe that Quinn would be able to deal with Mr. MacCallister."

"Well, if he had done what we told 'im to do, if he had got him some men with 'im, more 'n likely MacCallister 'n Gleason would both be dead now."

"Perhaps." Kendrick turned his attention back to Creech. "I thank you for bringing me the news."

Creech cleared his throat.

Kendrick frowned. "What is it?"

"Uh, Quinn, he promised me a hunnert dollars if I found MacCallister for 'im. I found 'im, but Quinn didn't give me no money. He said he would pay me later."

"And you are telling me that, because?"

"I thought maybe . . . that is . . . I was kinda hopin', you'd give me the money."

"I am under no obligation to honor any contract entered into by the late Mr.

396

Quinn."

"Yes, sir. I just thought —" Without completing the sentence, Creech started to turn away from the table.

"However," Kendrick said.

There was a hopeful sound to the word, and Creech turned back toward Kendrick's table.

"You did bring me word of Mr. Quinn's demise. I suppose, under the circumstances, that should be worth something." Kendrick took out a twenty-dollar bill and held it out toward Creech.

The expression on Creech's face registered his disappointment.

"But if you don't want it," Kendrick said, pulling the money back.

"No, sir, I want it! And it's mighty grateful I am for it, too," Creech said quickly, reaching out to take the money." Grasping the money tightly, he left the saloon.

"We have to do somethin' 'bout MacCallister, or he's goin' to be big trouble," Peabody said after Creech left.

"There is *no going to be* about it. He has already proven to be trouble," Kendrick said.

"What are we goin' to do about him?"

"We do have an ace in the hole," Kendrick said.

"What's that?"

"We've got the girl."

"Yeah, but we've had her all along."

"We just haven't been imaginative enough with our handling of Miss Ireland. Perhaps if MacCallister knew that the girl was not enjoying a comfortable stay with us, we might be able to draw him into acting injudiciously."

"What do you mean, the girl not enjoying a comfortable stay with us? What do you have planned?"

"Suppose we had a lottery among the men, and the winner would be granted the opportunity to . . . let us say, enjoy Miss Ireland's feminine charms? They would be second, of course. I would be first."

"Kendrick, are you saying what I think you are saying?" Peabody asked, a broad smile spreading across his face. "You mean, laying with her?"

"That is precisely what I mean."

"How 'bout if the winner was to be third? I mean, seein' as I'm your right-hand man, maybe I could be second."

"All right. I can see that."

"When are we goin' to do it?" Peabody asked anxiously.

"Not right away," Kendrick said. "First, MacCallister has to realize that the threat is there. Otherwise, we lose our advantage."

"How is he going to find out?"

"Get Creech back in here. I think if I would give him another eighty dollars, fulfilling Quinn's contract with him, he would be willing to carry the message for us."

Glitter Bright was sitting at a table nearby, but because the girls who worked the Pair of Kings had become as ubiquitous as the furnishings, neither Kendrick nor Peabody paid any attention to her. She'd overheard every word of Kendrick's plan.

Her first thought was one of sympathy for the governor's daughter. She felt bad about the young woman being a prisoner in the first place, but as she thought what the girl would be facing, she was even more concerned. She thought about warning her, but what would that accomplish, besides getting herself into danger, as well?

Maybe if Rosalie knew the danger she was in, she could hide.

But they would find her, and if they did, they might also find out that Glitter was the one who had warned her. Glitter kept thinking. What if both of them left town?

Glitter went upstairs to her room, then began putting things into a cloth bag. A moment later, she went back downstairs carrying the bag. "Weasel," she called over to the bartender. "I'm takin' some things down to the laundry. You got anything you want me to take?"

"No, thanks. I got it took care of yesterday. When are you comin' back?"

"Prob'ly not until late. I'm goin' out to see Mr. Tadlock."

Weasel chuckled. "Why do you waste your time with him? That ol' man ain't never goin' to marry you."

Glitter smiled. "You're jealous of him, ain't you, Weasel?"

"Maybe I am, a little."

"How come you ain't jealous of any of the men that take me upstairs?"

"On account of I know they ain't none of them that's ever goin' to think of marryin' you."

"You're a sweet man, Weasel. I just wish we'd met somewhere else, before this."

Weasel nodded.

"You take care, Weasel," she said as she left.

Weasel stared at the empty door. *Take care?* That was a strange thing for her to say.

Glitter thought of what she had said to

400

Weasel. She meant it. She really did have feelings for him. She also felt a sense of sadness because she knew what he didn't — that she had no intention of ever seeing him later or of ever returning to Blowout.

Leaving the saloon, she walked across the street to the Blowout Livery.

"Hello, Miss Bright," the stable man said.

"Hello, Mr. Statler. Would you get the buckboard ready and park it in front of the hotel in about half an hour?"

"I'll bet you're going to see Tadlock," Statler replied with a knowing grin.

"You're just too smart," Glitter replied.

"I sure don't know what you see in that old coot. Why he's so ugly he'd make a train take five miles of dirt road," Statler said, laughing at his own joke.

"Money, Mr. Statler. Money," Glitter said, rubbing her thumb and forefinger together.

"All right. I'll have the rig down there in about half an hour."

CHAPTER THIRTY-TWO

Although Rosalie did have the freedom to go anywhere in town she wanted to go, she had explored all of it, so she was content to spend her time in the hotel room, leaving only for meals. When she heard a knock on the door, she was frightened. "Who is it?" she called hesitantly.

"Miss Ireland, it's me, Glitter Bright. Please let me in."

Rosalie recognized the voice and wondered why she might be there, but remembered that the girl had seemed frightened of Kendrick. Thinking she might be in trouble, Rosalie opened the door.

"Thank you," Glitter said, stepping in quickly and closing the door behind her. "I don't think anyone saw me. At least, I hope not."

"Are you in trouble?" Rosalie asked. "Can I help?"

"I'm not in trouble. You are," Glitter replied.

Despite her situation, Rosalie laughed. "Well, yes, I am in trouble. But you didn't have to come here to tell me that."

"No, I mean you really are in trouble. More trouble than you think," Glitter said.

"Oh! What kind of trouble?"

"Kincaid wants to . . . uh . . . well, just trust me, you need to get out of here. I'll have a buckboard in front of the hotel in a few minutes, and I'll drive you out of town."

"But won't you get into trouble for helping me?"

"I would if I came back to town," Glitter said. "But I ain't comin' back. I'm runnin' away with you."

"Oh, Glitter, I don't know. If they see me riding in a buckboard with you, they'll know something is wrong."

"No they won't, because they won't recognize you."

"How will they not recognize me? Everyone in town has seen me by now."

"Yes, but not the way you're going to look when we leave."

Opening the sack she was carrying with her, Glitter dumped the contents on the bed — a dress, a camisole, and various bottles and tins.

"What is this?"

"This is what you're going to wear. You're going to be a soiled dove."

"Oh, no. I can't!"

"You ain't really goin' to *be* a soiled dove, but you're goin' to look like one. Honey, if I'm goin' to help you leave town, you don't have no choice. You're either goin' to have to wear this or you're goin' to be stuck here. And believe me, you don't want to be stuck here. I've heard what they've got planned for you."

"All right," Rosalie said. "I'll do whatever you say."

Glitter and Rosalie stepped out onto the front porch of the hotel. Like Glitter, Rosalie was wearing a dress that exposed not only most of her legs, but also the top halves of her breasts. Her lips were a crimson glare, her cheeks were pink, her eyes were lined, and her eyelids were painted blue.

Statler was sitting in the seat of the buckboard in front of the hotel. His eyes opened wide when he saw Glitter and Rosalie. "Well now, who is this?"

Rosalie held her breath because she knew that Statler had seen her before.

"This is one of Weasel's new girls," Glitter said. "Her name is Fancy. Fancy Bliss. I'm takin' her out to meet Mr. Tadlock."

"How come I ain't seen her before?"

"She just come in yesterday."

"Well, Fancy, I'll be callin' on you, soon. Yes, ma'am, I will."

"Why, Mr. Statler, you are making me jealous," Glitter teased.

"Am I? Well, don't you worry none about it, Glitter. I'm man enough for both you ladies. Somethin' Tadlock sure ain't." Statler jumped down from the buckboard.

"My, Glitter, does this gentleman always carry on in such a fashion?" Rosalie asked, assuming a very strong Southern accent.

"Oh, Fancy, you have no idea," Glitter said.

"You'll just have to look me up when I get back," Rosalie said, flashing a flirtatious smile toward Statler as Glitter snapped the reins against the back of the team.

The buckboard left at a rapid pace, Glitter holding the team at a trot.

"Hello, Mr. Felker!" Glitter called as they drove past Felker and Conroy, both of whom were standing on the corner.

"Where you goin', Glitter?" Felker yelled back.

"I'm takin' Fancy out to introduce her to Mr. Tadlock! Wave at the men, Fancy!"

Rosalie pasted a smile on her face and

waved at the two men who had been so instrumental in her initial capture.

"Whooee, you're a purty thang. I'll be callin' on you for sure when you get back," Conroy said.

"They are two of the men who captured me, and they didn't even recognize me," Rosalie said after they left town. "How can that be?"

"They've never seen you dressed like that before," Glitter said with a little laugh. "And with all the paint on your face, 'n you smilin' 'n all, that helped, too. You'd be surprised at how much a smile changes a person's face. Why, as many people as has seen me workin' there in the saloon 'n all, I can put on proper clothes 'n go downtown without face paint or a smile, 'n folks don't even recognize me."

Rosalie reached over to put her hand Glitter's arm. "Glitter, I can't tell you how grateful I am for what you have done."

"Well, I thank you for that, but I ain't done it yet. We ain't quite out of it till we get somewhere safe."

Merrill Town

When Rosalie and Glitter came into town they drew a lot of attention. It wasn't that no one had ever seen a woman dressed in such a way before, but no one had seen a woman dressed like that in public. Even the bar girls dressed conservatively when they were out in public.

"Everyone is looking at us," Rosalie said.

"Yes, well, I hope we are giving them a good show," Glitter replied with a little laugh.

"Where are we going?"

"I think we should go to the sheriff's office," Glitter said. "We should certainly be safe there, and he can get word to your papa that you have been found."

"Yes! Yes, I think that's a wonderful idea!" Rosalie said. "Oh, Glitter, I'm going to make certain that Papa rewards you."

"I don't need a reward for doin' what's right."

Wang Chow was at Ma Ling's Chinese Restaurant enjoying a meal. Other diners were there as well, and while Wang wasn't the only Chinese person present, he was the only Chinese diner.

"Wooee, look out there, Freddy," one of the men said to his dining partner. There's somethin' you don't see ever' day. Two soiled doves that's as pretty as them two, just ridin' right down the street in the open, like that."

Like the others, Wang looked through the front window to see a buckboard passing by. And as the man had stated, there were two very attractive and very scantily dressed women.

"One is *jinu,* one is not," the young Chinese waitress said.

"Tell me, Maylin, why do you say one is not a prostitute?" Wang asked, speaking in Mandarin.

"The young woman on this side is uncomfortable with her clothes," Maylin said. "I think such clothing is new to her."

He watched the buckboard stop in front of the sheriff's office, then saw the two young women go inside.

The sheriff and his deputy were drinking coffee and eating a piece of pie.

"Who are you? What are you two doing in here?" the sheriff asked as Rosalie and Glitter approached his desk.

Rosalie read the sheriff's name from a sign that sat on his desk. "Sheriff Wallace, my name is Rosalie Ireland. This is my friend, Glitter Bright. She helped me escape from the outlaws who were holding me captive. Would you please send a telegram to my father and tell him I am safe?"

"What do you mean, safe?"

"Didn't you hear my name? I'm Rosalie Ireland. My father is the governor."

"Are you tryin' to tell me that the governor's daughter is a soiled dove?"

"She ain't the one that's the soiled dove, Sheriff, I am. I'm Glitter Bright, and I'm from over in Blowout. Kendrick 'n his men captured Miss Ireland 'n was holdin' her prisoner. I dressed her like this so we could get away."

"Wait a minute. Are you saying you two run away from Dirk Kendrick?"

"Finally, you understand," Rosalie said. "Now, will you please send a telegram to my father and ask him to come get me?"

Sheriff Wallace stroked his chin as he studied the two women. "What do you think, Bullock? You think they're tellin' the truth?"

"I think they prob'ly are tellin' the truth," Bullock replied. "I don't know why they'd lie 'bout somethin' like that."

A big smile spread across Sheriff Wallace's face. "You know what? It looks like a gold mine just dropped in our laps."

"I'm sure my father will be most grateful to you, and I expect he will want to reward you," Rosalie said, "but I would hardly call it a gold mine. You must know that he is not a very wealthy man. I hope you aren't disappointed."

"We won't be," Wallace said. "Come back here with me, both of you."

Rosalie frowned. "Come where?"

"I'm going to put the two of you in jail."

"What?" Glitter replied. "Why in the world would you do something like that?"

"Believe me, you'll be much safer here," Wallace said.

"Do you really think that's necessary?" Rosalie asked. "Couldn't we just wait here until Daddy sends someone for us?"

"I don't want to take a chance on anything happenin' to you," Wallace said. "You're my responsibility now."

Rosalie nodded reluctantly. "All right. If you think so."

The two women followed Wallace into the back of the jail, which, mercifully, was empty. He opened the door to one of the cells, and after the two stepped inside, he locked the door behind them.

"What are you doing that for? Why are you locking us in?" Glitter asked.

"Like I said, you'll be safer this way."

"I don't like this, Sheriff. I'm not comfortable being locked in like this."

"Well, missy, I don't care whether you are comfortable or not," Sheriff Wallace replied with a triumphant smile.

Curious as to why they went to the sheriff's office, Wang watched for a few minutes longer. He saw the sheriff and the deputy leave the office, though the two young women had not yet come out.

A moment later, the sheriff and his deputy rode out of town at a rapid trot. The two women were still inside the sheriff's office, and Wang became even more curious.

Finally, curiosity got the better of him. He left Ma Ling's and walked down to the office. The front door was locked.

Something about that didn't ring true. Moving quickly, he hurried back to his horse, then started toward the Slash Bell to get Duff, Elmer, and the others.

Blowout

"Thank you, Sheriff Wallace," Kendrick said. "You have been most helpful and will be rewarded for your service."

"I was hopin' you would say somethin' like that," Wallace replied. "Are you goin' to Merrill Town to get her back?"

"I don't have much choice, do I? Without her, I have absolutely no leverage with her father."

"I'll be ridin' in with you," Wallace said. "By now, most folks have figured out that I been in cahoots with you, anyhow, so I may as well come out in the open about it."

Kendrick smiled. "I appreciate your support, but it would be better if you didn't ride in with me. We will be riding into town from the west. I want you and Bullock to ride in from the east. For the time being, it will better serve our purposes if not everyone knows of our alliance."

"All right."

"And you say that Glitter is there as well?"

"Yeah. She's the one who brought the governor's daughter in."

"I see. Well, she will just have to pay the price for her betrayal. Peabody?"

"Yeah?"

"Go out to the cabin and get anyone who is out there. When we go into Merrill Town, I want to go *en masse.*"

"All right," Peabody agreed.

"Dooley, you round up everyone that's in town and bring them here to the saloon. This will be our organizing point."

With the two men dispatched to carry out their assignments, Kendrick stepped up to the bar, thinking to arrange for Weasel to serve a beer to all of his men before they left.

But Weasel wasn't there.

"Penny, where's Weasel?"

"I don't know," Penny said. "He left a few minutes ago."

Merrill Town

When the Ten Guns from Texas rode into town, they went straight to the sheriff's office. Finding the front door of the office still locked, Duff stepped back, raised his foot, and kicked the door in.

"Oh!" they heard a woman's voice call out from the back of the office.

Leaving Wang and the others out front, Duff and Elmer hurried toward the cells.

"Miss Ireland?" Duff called, but he got no answer until he reached the cells. There he saw Rosalie and another young woman clinging to each other in fear.

Rosalie recognized Duff and Elmer. "It's all right, Glitter. I know these two men," she said in relief, turning their expressions to joy.

"It's good to see that you are safe, Miss Ireland. Don't lose heart. I'll get you out of here and back to your father," Duff said.

"Mr. MacCallister?" Roy Kelly said, stepping into the cell area. "There's a fella out front that needs to talk to you."

"All right. Send him in.

Kelly stepped aside, and another man came through the door.

"Weasel!" Glitter said with a happy shout. "What are you doin' here?"

"Sheriff Wallace and Deputy Bullock come ridin' into town awhile ago. They told Kendrick that you 'n the governor's daughter is here. He ain't happy about it, 'n Glitter, he ain't none too happy 'bout you helpin' Miss Ireland escape, neither."

"Won't he be just as unhappy with you for warning us?" Rosalie asked.

"I reckon he will be, but I've had about as much of that crook as I care to take," Weasel replied. "And I don't plan on lettin' anything happen to you, neither."

CHAPTER THIRTY-THREE

"Me 'n the others done looked ever'where, 'n we can't find no keys to the cell nowhere," Decker said.

"I'm sure he took the keys with him so that no one would be able to let the two young women out," Duff said.

"Oh! Does that mean we are stuck here?" Rosalie asked.

"No, ma'am, it don't mean that at all," Elmer said. "I'll go see the smithy 'n borrow a metal saw from 'im. I'll have you outta there in no time atall."

"You won't have time for that," Weasel said. "I've been here a couple minutes already, 'n I know damn well they ain't more 'n ten or fifteen minutes behind me. I gotta tell you, Mr. MacCallister, Kendrick sent out to the river cabin to get ever'one gathered together, 'n right now that'll be at least thirty men."

"Does he think he needs that many people

to recapture one young woman?"

"It ain't just that. He's plannin' on takin' over the whole town. He already controls Blowout. He wants Merrill Town, too. 'N he especially wants you."

"We need to get ready for him," Duff said.

"We gotta get these women outta here first, don't we?" Elmer asked.

"Maybe not," Weasel said.

"What do you mean?" Duff asked.

"Before I opened up my saloon in Blowout, I lived here in Merrill Town. This here jailhouse is the strongest buildin' there is. You could leave the two women here, 'n there won't be no chance of 'em gettin' hit by a stray bullet. Bein' made of granite blocks 'n all, it ain't likely goin' to burn, neither."

"Good idea. Miss Ireland, when they come into town, I want you and the young lady to take the mattresses off, then crawl under the beds. Move up as close as you can to the wall and put the mattresses on this side of you. That way if a stray bullet comes in through the window and strikes the bars, there'll be no chance of you getting hit by any ricochet."

"But we'll still be locked in," Rosalie said.

"Aye, but 'tis this promise I'll be making you. As soon as it is all over, we'll get you out 'n back to your father."

"But what if —" Rosalie didn't finish the question, but it wasn't necessary.

Duff knew she was going to ask, what if Kendrick prevailed in the fight. He chuckled. "Here, lass, we'll nae be worring about that, now."

Rosalie laughed nervously. "You're right," she said, summoning up as much courage as she could muster.

The men left the cell block and returned to the office.

"You know, Mr. MacCallister, if Kendrick has thirty men, like Weasel said, the odds are going to be stacked against the five of us," Kelly said.

"Six," Wang said.

"How can we count you?" Kelly said. "You don't have a gun, 'n there ain't no way they're goin' to just stand there 'n let you walk up to 'em and hit 'em in the head like you done that steer. Or even like you done them two men back at the cabin when we first come to rescue the girl."

"I believe Mr. Wang will find a way to be useful," Duff suggested. "But the odds are still a little long." He looked at the man who had delivered the warning that Kendrick and his men were coming. "Weasel, is it?"

"My real name is Deschamp, but all my

friends call me Weasel."

"Weasel, you said you lived here for a while. Do you know the men of this town? Do you have any idea who we might be able to count on in a fight?"

"There's a few that I know fought in the war." Weasel chuckled. "Onliest thing is, some of 'em fought for the North 'n some fought for the South."

"Would they fight on the same side to save their town?" Duff asked.

Weasel nodded. "Yes, sir, I'm sure they would. Ken Prescott, he was goin' to be the first one I would get. He was a sailor man, fightin' for the South. Hog Jaw Lambert would be my second choice. He fought with Sherman."

"All right. I want you to get them and any others you think we can count on. Bring them to see me down at the CSS *Alabama* Saloon. In the meantime, tell all those who will nae be joining us in the fighting to stay off the street and in their houses until the fighting is over."

"You round up all the fightin' men," Kelly said. "Me 'n Decker 'n Simmons will get the other folks off the street."

Duff nodded. "Aye, good idea, Mr. Kelly. That will greatly expedite the preparation."

■ ■ ■ ■

It took Weasel no more than ten minutes to round up those who said they would fight. Everyone was armed, a couple with pistols only, one with a rifle only, and two with shotguns.

Duff always carried two rifles with him, a lever-action Winchester, .44-40, and a Martini-Henry .577-450 caliber. This was a British rifle known for extreme range and accuracy. As the men gathered, he fitted a scope to it.

"You pretty good with that gun, are you?" Prescott asked.

"Is he good?" Elmer replied. "Why, I've seen him shoot the leg off a fly from a hunnert yards."

"Missed the fly, did he?" Kelly asked, and the others, including Duff, laughed.

"Knowing the town as you do, perhaps you would have a suggestion as to the most advantageous position for me to pick out targets of opportunity," Duff said to Prescott.

The barkeep laughed. "Targets of opportunity. I ain't never heard that said before, but I reckon it's easy enough to figure out what you're a-sayin'. Best place I can think of would be up in the church belfry."

"Nae," Duff said, shaking his head. "I'll nae be killing from a church."

"All right. The next best place would probably be from the loft of the livery. You'd have a good view of 'em when they come in, no matter which way they might be a-comin' from."

"Thanks."

"It is more than likely they know we are coming," Kendrick said. "Glitter worked for Weasel, and Weasel disappeared shortly before we left town. I'm quite sure he has come to town to warn MacCallister and the citizens of the town of our approach."

"Damn!" Dooley said. "You mean we'll be goin' ag'in the whole town? They's only twenty-nine of us!"

"It is obvious, Dooley, that you have no understanding of the psychology of the masses," Kendrick said.

"The what?"

"Simply put, the citizens of the town will cower in fear, depending upon someone else to defend them. Only a few will answer the call, and because of that, the numbers of the actual combatants who will engage us will be quite small. But even if they outnumbered us, we would prevail, for it is as Euripides once said, 'Ten men wisely led are worth a hundred without a head.' I am in command, so we, as I am sure you will all agree, are wisely led."

The residents of Merrill Town who did not answer the call to arms either left town or took shelter in their homes or in other buildings. The streets, which normally would be crowded with commerce, were empty. The small community had turned into a virtual ghost town. From his position in the loft of the livery stable, Duff stared in the direction from which he expected Kendrick to approach, though from time to time he checked the opposite end of the street as well, just to be sure.

A gust of wind rustled up a dust devil, which darted and danced across the empty street before it rattled the painted tin sign in front of White's Drug Store. A dog, perhaps sensing something was amiss, ran across the street, then climbed under the low-lying porch in front of Blum's Clothing.

From the loft, Duff could see the nine other men he had positioned around the town. Elmer was just inside the door of McGill's Feed and Seed, Kelly was at the corner of the Elite Dress Shoppe, Decker was lying behind the watering trough in front of Malone Hat Store, Simmons was on the roof behind the false front of the Hog Pen, Hog Jaw was just behind the batwing doors of the same building, while Prescott was just inside the CSS *Alabama*. Ziegenhorn had taken up a position on top of his real estate building, Doc Dunaway was at an upstairs window of the Del Rey Hotel, and Alfred Sikes stood just inside the door of his hardware store. That made ten of them, ten men waiting to do battle with what could be as many as thirty men, perhaps even more.

As he thought about it, Duff couldn't help but chuckle. Elmer had been saying all along that they were ten guns from Texas. As it turned out, he was now correct. They were, legitimately, ten guns from Texas.

Duff had not counted Wang among those who were in position to defend the town, but neither had he discounted him. Shortly after he had assigned everyone their position, Wang had left town, not to avoid the fight, but to take the fight to the Fence Busters, doing it his own way.

Wang Chow had ridden one mile in the direction from which Weasel had indicated the men would come. He glanced around, looking for a position from which he could engage them, when he saw the perfect place — a large live oak tree with a limb that extended out over the road leading into town. He tied his horse off so that it was out of sight, then climbed the tree and moved out onto the limb.

No more than five minutes after he was in position, Wang saw riders coming toward him, led by one man, and proceeding down the road in a fourteen-rank column of two abreast. Unseen by the approaching riders, he waited until the last two men passed under him, then he jumped down from the tree, landing with perfect precision with one foot planted just behind each saddle. This left him poised on both horses.

Even before the two riders realized someone had dropped down behind them, Wang took them out. Striking them with the same power he had used to bring down the steer, he broke their necks with quick silent blows from the knife edge of his two hands.

Quickly, Wang leaped down to the ground, pulling the two men off their horses, cushioning them as they left the saddles so that the men riding ahead of him didn't hear them fall. Even with their saddles empty, the two horses continued to keep pace with the column before them.

The column rode on, totally unaware that their strength had been decreased by two men.

Duff saw the approaching riders at the crest of a hill at least half a mile out of town. He counted them through the scope and saw that there were twenty-seven. He also saw that two of the horses were without riders, and he smiled, realizing that Wang had already begun his work.

As the riders reached the crest of the hill, they spread out along the ridge. The newly positioned men pulled their pistols, and one of the men — Duff assumed he was Kendrick — rode back and forth in front of the group, apparently giving them directions.

Duff drew a bead on Kendrick, thinking that if he killed their leader it would disorient them immediately, but Kendrick rode behind an outcropping of rocks and was out of view. He switched his aim to another.

"Hey, where's Davis 'n Cooter?" Peabody asked. "Their horses is here, where are they?"

"Maybe they're takin' a piss," Taylor said.

"Davis! Cooter! Get back here and get mounted!" Kendrick called.

"Maybe they fell off," Beans said, chuckling at the suggestion.

"Yes, well, we don't have time to be concerned about that now," Kendrick said. "We are about to ride into Merrill Town, and when we do, I want you to shoot everyone you see — man, woman, and child."

"Women and children, too?" Taylor asked.

"Yes," Kendrick said. "I know that sounds harsh, but those of you who were in the war know that war is harsh. And as Sherman showed on his march to the sea, absolute war leads to absolute victory. Our tactics will instill shock and fear among the citizens of the town, and that will lead to a quick capitulation."

Suddenly there was a sound like the buzzing of a bee, then a *thock.* It sounded as if someone had hit their open hand with a fist.

"Uhnn!" Logan said aloud.

Looking toward him, the others saw a big, blood-pumping hole appear in the center of his chest. He fell from his horse.

"What the hell was that?" Dooley asked.

"Somebody shot 'im," Beans said.

"Who? I didn't hear no —" That was as far as Rand got before he, too, fell from his horse with a bleeding hole in his chest.

"Kendrick, we got to get outta here!" Peabody shouted. "They's someone close by that's got a bead on us!"

"Impossible!" Kendrick said. "It's all open ground between here and town! There's no place for a shooter!"

"Maybe not, but we've had two men shot."

"All right," Kendrick said. "Forward men, at a gallop!"

CHAPTER THIRTY-FOUR

Duff could hear thundering hooves as the riders approached the town, drunk with the power their numbers gave them.

"They are coming!" Ziegenhorn shouted. His position on top of his office building was the closest to the edge of town. "Kendrick and his men are coming fast!"

"Everyone stay calm!" Duff shouted from his position in the open loft window of the livery. "Pick your shots and make them count!" He raised his Martini-Henry rifle to his shoulder, aimed, and fired. Another of Kendrick's advancing men tumbled from the saddle.

The approaching riders were too close and coming too fast for Duff to use his rifle anymore, so he jumped down, and with his rifle in one hand and pistol in the other, he ran across to the feed store and stepped inside just as gunfire ripped through the street. So many shots were fired at the same time that he had no idea where they were all coming from.

"Use this! She's loaded!" Elmer said, tossing over a double-barreled shotgun. Duff stepped through the front door and fired, knocking one of the approaching riders out of the saddle.

The street continued to ring with gunfire, not only from the feed store, but from every other place Duff had positioned his men. Realizing that by being mounted they were easy targets, Kendrick ordered the Fence Busters to dismount. The riders leaped from the horses and took cover where they could, behind watering troughs, porches, and the corners of buildings.

Elmer fired a Winchester, jacking the lever down to eject the empty cartridge and push in a new .44-40 round. Duff saw him take down one of the Fence Busters just as the outlaw raised up from behind a watering trough to take a shot.

A bullet from one of the Fence Busters dug a trench along the doorframe of the feed store, sending splinters flying, a few of them striking Duff in the face. He spun around, his face dotted with bits of blood.

"Duff!" Elmer called out in alarm.

"It's nothing!" Duff called back. Because the shotgun was empty, he raised his pistol.

Seeing one of Kendrick's men running from one place to another, trying to improve his position, Duff shot him down.

"Stay here and keep firing!" he shouted as he headed out the back door. He ran down the alley and saw Sheriff Wallace step out of the doorway just in front of him.

"Sheriff?" Duff called. "I'm glad you're back."

"Are you now?" Wallace replied with a sneer. He fired at Duff, and Duff fired back. Sheriff Wallace missed, Duff didn't. Out of the corner of his eye, he caught a glimpse of someone else running. He dropped to one knee and fired. His bullet shattered the hip of the runner, sending the man sprawling in the dirt.

He heard the crashing of glass, and realized that some of Kendrick's men were concentrating on the CSS *Alabama* Saloon. Prescott was in there alone, so, turning, Duff ran back up the alley.

Just as he went in through the back door, Deputy Bullock spurred his horse through the batwing doors up front. Duff and Prescott shot at the same time, knocking Bullock from his saddle.

"I always knew Bullock was a sorry excuse for a deputy!" Prescott said. "I wonder where Sheriff Wallace is?"

"The constable is in the alley out back," Duff said.

The gunfire had begun to trickle down until there were only a few popping sounds here and there, most that were fired by men who were frustrated at no longer being able to find a target.

"Duff MacCallister!" a voice called.

Duff didn't recognize the voice.

"MacCallister! I'm Dirk Kendrick! Do you know who I am?"

"Aye, the name has certainly become a familiar one."

"You seem to have been quite effective in reducing the number of my men. I still have men left, though, and if we continue with this battle, I fear that some of the innocent citizens of the town may be killed. I have an offer, if you are amenable!"

"And what would that be?"

"You have been quite the nuisance ever since you arrived in Texas. I believe if you could be eliminated that things would go back as they were. Suppose the two of us meet in the street, right here, right now? If I prevail, I would expect your men to leave Miss Ireland in my hands, so the governor and I can continue the negotiations we had begun. If you prevail, you will let my remaining men withdraw in peace."

Duff chuckled. "That's some proposal."

"What do you say, MacCallister? Just the two of us?"

"All right."

Cautiously, Duff stepped out and looked around. Gun smoke lay over the town like a low-lying cloud, and his nostrils burned with it. The street was littered with bodies. Among the dead, he recognized Simmons, who had ridden with him, as well as a couple of the townspeople, including Ziegenhorn and Doc Dunaway. There were also several bodies strewn about who were wearing blue kerchiefs around their neck.

Slowly, the survivors of the battle came out from their fighting positions — Elmer, Kelly, Decker, and Hog Jaw among them.

Seven of Kendrick's men also came out into the street, looking around warily.

"Where are you, Kendrick?" Duff asked.

A man stepped out of the bakery. It was the first time either of them had actually seen one another, and they stared across the street at each other for a long moment.

"I didn't think you would actually come out," Kincaid said.

"Why not? If we can end it here and now, I think it worth the risk."

"How do you want to do this?"

"Are you familiar with the *code duelo,* Mr.

Kincaid?" Duff asked.

"I am, sir."

"Then you are aware that, as the challenged party, the details are up to me."

"Yes, I am aware."

"As neither of us are native to the American West, I am going to assume that you are no more proficient in the art of the fast draw than I am. Therefore, I suggest that each pistol be emptied of all ammunition except one shell, and that the chamber bearing that bullet be placed in the proper position so that it will fire when the trigger is pulled. I will choose Mr. Elmer Gleason as my second. You may choose a second of your choice. Our seconds will examine both pistols, to ascertain that they are properly loaded."

"I'll choose Carl Peabody."

"Once the weapons are properly charged, we will stand back-to-back and advance a mutually agreed-upon number of steps, then turn and fire. Do you agree to those terms?"

"I do, sir."

The survivors on both sides of the fight had come into the street. Duff's supporters stood on the north side of the street, while Kendrick's supporters were gathered on the south side.

The pistols were prepared and examined, then handed to the belligerents. The two men stood back-to-back, their arms crooked at the elbow, the pistols pointing into the air.

"Thirteen steps, Mr. Kendrick?" Duff asked.

"Yes, quite appropriate, I would say."

"Your second may count the steps."

Peabody began counting out loud until he reached thirteen. At thirteen, Duff and Kendrick turned to face each other.

"Now, Dooley!" Kendrick shouted.

Duff saw a man standing on the roof of the bakery across the street, aiming a rifle at him. Even as Dooley pulled the trigger, he was tumbling forward. A throwing star embedded in Dooley's back flashed in the sunlight.

Briefly, Duff caught all of that out of the corner of his eye. Concurrent with Kendrick's shout, his and Kendrick's pistols had discharged as one.

Because he was hurried and had counted on Dooley to kill Duff, Kendrick's shot whizzed harmlessly by. Duff's shot plunged deep into Kendrick's chest.

Kendrick looked at Duff with an almost whimsical smile. "Damn. I had plans. Big plans." His sentence ended with a cough, then he fell back into the dirt, the pearl-handled pistol still connected to his hand only because his finger was still hooked through the trigger guard.

Austin

"You say that the Hill Country Cattlemen's Association is taking care of getting all the rustled cattle back to their rightful owners?" Governor Ireland asked.

"Yes, all the ranchers agreed to that, including Glitter," Duff replied.

"Glitter, yes, she is the prostitute who helped my daughter escape."

"Oh, she may have been a prostitute when she helped Miss Ireland escape, but now she owns the Double D Ranch. It turns out that an old man she had befriended was actually her grandfather, and he had proof that Donald Dobbins was her father. With Dobbins dying intestate, his ranch now belongs to Glitter."

"That's good," Governor Ireland said. "Rosalie has announced her intention to be maid of honor when Glitter marries Weasel. I think it would be a bit more acceptable to people, thinking of her participating in the wedding of a ranch owner, rather than the wedding of a prostitute." He laughed. "Though in truth, I don't think it makes any difference to Rosalie whatever Glitter is. And good for her, I say."

"When is Fitzhugh's trial?" Elmer asked.

"There won't be a trial, as such," the governor replied. "Fitzhugh wants to avoid the public scandal. He has confessed to providing information to Kendrick, and the judge will be sentencing him in a closed hearing. He has been with me since I was an associate justice for the Texas Supreme Court. I would have never suspected he would betray me."

"Yeah? Well I didn't trust the squirrely lookin' traitor from the moment I first saw him," Elmer said.

"Oh. At your suggestion, Mr. MacCallister, I have asked Captain Brooke to send a couple men into Blowout to provide them with some law until they can elect a new sheriff."

"Good idea. Weasel informs me that there are some decent people in Blowout. They just need some stability until they can get back on their feet."

"And I've appointed your friends Roy Kelly and Hugh Decker as sheriff and deputy sheriff to fill out the terms of Wallace and Bullock." The governor shook his head. "To think that less than a month ago, both those men were serving sentences in the state penitentiary."

Elmer nodded. "They're good men, Colonel. Both of 'em are, 'n you can count on that."

"Given the role they played in my daughter's rescue, I don't doubt that. By the way, Elmer, are you sure you want to go back to Wyoming? If you would like to stay, I know I can find a position for you."

"A position, is it?" Elmer replied with a chuckle. "Tell me, now, Colonel, is a position better than a job?"

"Of course it is."

"Well, then here's the thing, Governor. I've already got me a position up in Wyomin'. 'N I like that position just a whole lot."

Turn the page for an exciting bonus short story . . .

INFERNO
A LAST GUNFIGHTER STORY

by William W. Johnstone
with J. A. Johnstone

(Note: This story takes place before the events in the Last Gunfighter novel The Drifter.)

Frank Morgan smelled the smoke before he saw it. That was a mite unusual, but at the time, he was riding upward through a ravine at the edge of the Cap Rock, the time-eroded escarpment that divided the High Plains from the rest of Texas, and that restricted his view of the landscape.

He reached the top of the ravine and came out on the prairie and saw the smoke, sure enough. Big billowing clouds of the thick gray stuff rolling across the Texas plains, driven by a hard wind that threatened to pluck the hat from his head. He reached up to hold it on as a frown settled onto his weathered face.

The fire was coming toward him, leaping across the prairie at a dizzying speed, but it was still about a mile away, he figured. Although he could see the southwestern end of it, the wall of flames and smoke stretched off to the northeast farther than he could see.

Morgan had a good horse under him, a hammer-headed dun that he had been riding for a while. It took him only a second to realize that he could gallop hard to the west and get safely out of the way of the blaze.

The settlement that was smack-dab in the fire's path didn't have that option.

Even with the threat that faced him, Morgan paused for a moment at the sheer horror of it. The flames were eight or ten feet tall and devouring ground at a terrifying rate. He could see some of the townspeople scurrying around like ants, panic-stricken by the fire's inexorable approach. Some of them clustered around the public well, hauling up buckets of water to fling onto the buildings in the futile hope that they might turn back destruction. Others leaped onto horses and fogged it out of there, escape their only thought. Still others tried to load a few belongings onto wagons, buggies, and buckboards, bartering time to flee against their possessions.

Poor stupid idiots, thought Morgan. Everything they had, including maybe even their lives, was about to be snatched away from them through no fault of their own, and there wasn't a damn thing they could do about it.

He didn't have to worry about anything except saving his own life. He turned his horse and heeled it into a run, leaning forward over the dun's neck as he urged it on to greater and greater speed.

The wind shifted a little in Morgan's favor, taking away any chance that the fire might blow on past the settlement without destroying it. Not that there had ever been much of a chance to start with.

He looked over his right shoulder and saw that he was getting clear of the danger. He kept the dun running hard for another few minutes, just to be sure that another sudden wind shift wouldn't send the flames in his direction again. It wasn't long before he was well clear and could rein in. He turned his mount so he could watch as the blaze reached the town and the gray smoke turned black and billowed even more as the buildings went up, one after the other.

Morgan could have just ridden on. There was a reason he was known throughout the West as the Drifter. Ever since a young man, when he had gotten a reputation as a fast gun, he had been on the move most of the time, always riding, never staying in any one place for very long. At first, maybe he had been searching for happiness, but as man after man fell to his blazing speed and unerring accuracy with a Colt, every opportunity to settle down ultimately had been lost.

Now in middle age, Morgan drifted, one of the last of his breed, seeking only to be left alone. Wanting only to not have to kill yet another snot-nose punk out to make a name for himself.

So it was an unaccustomed impulse that sent him riding toward the ruined settlement after the fire had roared on through and finally burned itself out when it reached the edge of the Cap Rock.

He came to a stagecoach road that cut a path through the charred landscape and followed it into town . . . or rather into what was left of the town, which wasn't much. The walls of the adobe buildings were still standing, but their interiors were burned out. The frame buildings were gone, right down to the ground, except for their foundations and the occasional partially consumed timber. The insides of buildings were just heaps of ashes. The conflagration must have been incredibly hot. It reminded him of towns that had been bombarded by artillery and then set afire during the war. He saw burned bodies lying here and there, which accounted for the sickly sweet stench in the air.

The people who had gotten out in time were trickling back in, some on foot, others on horseback or in wagons. They wandered around, dazed, staring in disbelief at what was left.

The wind had finally fallen still, too late to save the settlement, and an eerie quiet lay over the scene, broken only by a faint crackling from the places where some of the ruins still burned.

The hush was shattered by a harsh, incoherent scream, followed by a woman's agonized voice. "Gone, all gone!" she cried. "The boys, too! They're dead! Dead! Damn you! Damn you to hell!"

Morgan turned his horse and saw a middle-aged woman pounding frenzied punches into the chest of a man who stood there looking stunned as he absorbed the punishment. Stocky, with thinning white hair and a neatly trimmed beard, his expression was that of a man who'd been shot in the gut. He looked like he was dead and just didn't know it yet.

Morgan had seen that expression all too

many times. He hadn't liked it then, and he didn't like it now.

"Your fault, your fault, your fault!" the woman screamed at the man as she continued hitting him.

He made no attempt to stop her. Finally, grief overwhelmed her and she fell to her knees, then toppled over onto her side and lay there in the ashy dust, covering her face with her hands as she sobbed.

The man finally seemed to become aware of Morgan sitting on the dun a few yards away. He looked up at the Drifter and asked in a dull voice, "Who're you, mister?"

"Just a fella who's passing through." Despite the hard shell he usually cultivated around him, Morgan wasn't an unfeeling man. "I'm sorry for your loss. Sorry for all the losses here. I saw the fire coming, but there was nothing I could do to help."

The man shrugged. "Wasn't nothin' anybody could do once the fire was lit."

"You mean once the fire started, don't you?" Morgan asked with a frown.

"Nope." The man shook his head. "That fire was started a-purpose." He looked around at the destruction surrounding them. "My wife's right. This is all my fault. I founded this town. I was the mayor. This was my *home,* and I burned it down."

■ ■ ■ ■

The man's name was Al Bowman. He sat in the shade of a still-standing adobe wall and nipped at the bottle Frank Morgan had taken from his saddlebags and given to him.

Bowman made a face at the raw bite of the whiskey. "I'm not really much of a drinkin' man. And while I appreciate it, mister, I got to say it don't help much."

"Nothing will but time," Morgan said as he hunkered on his heels in the shade.

Bowman shook his head. "Not even that'll do it. Some things can't be forgive or forgot. My wife lost our home and three of our boys. Tell me how time's gonna help that."

"You lost your sons in the fire?"

"Three of the four. I grabbed the youngest and went lookin' for the other three, but I couldn't find 'em nowhere. They were off somewhere in town. You know how boys are, always underfoot except when you're lookin' for 'em."

Morgan nodded.

"God, it tore my heart out to leave without 'em," Bowman went on in a choked voice. "But them flames were practically on top of us already, and there was nothin' else I could do." He took another swig of the

445

whiskey. "I tell you, though, mister, I'm already startin' to wish I'd stayed and died with 'em."

Morgan shook his head. "One more death wouldn't have done anybody any good."

"You don't know, mister," Bowman whispered. "You just don't know."

Morgan had no answer for that. Nobody knew what was in another person's heart. "What you said earlier about it being your fault . . . even if somebody set the fire, it wasn't you, was it?"

"No, but I caused it. It wouldn'ta happened if I hadn't done what I did. I told the Locklin brothers to get out of town. I got a posse together and we cornered 'em with shotguns in the saloon and told 'em to get out of Flat Rock. We had the drop on 'em, so they didn't have much choice. But Steve Locklin said nobody talked like that to the Locklin brothers and got away with it. He said we'd be sorry." Bowman heaved a sigh. "I reckon we are."

Locklin . . . Morgan recognized the name. Steve Locklin and his brothers Asa and Rance all thought they were slick on the draw, and they had the kills to prove it. Their arrogance and greed had led them to become outlaws, and they had murdered and plundered their way across the Lone

446

Star State. The Texas Rangers had been on their trail for a while, but the Rangers were spread thin and the Locklin brothers had fast horses as well as fast guns. They had escaped from every trap the lawmen had tried to set for them.

"Jed Ainsley came foggin' in just as the smoke started to rise," Bowman went on. "He was ridin' into town for supplies from his spread northwest of here. He spotted Steve Locklin with a torch, settin' fire to the grass. The wind was so high Jed knew the fire would come straight for us, so he took off hell-for-leather to warn us. The Locklins saw him and opened up on him, and Jed caught a bullet. He kept on anyway. Of course, it didn't make a bit of difference. Poor son of a gun died for nothin'." Bowman gestured vaguely to a blackened corpse that hardly looked human anymore. "There he lays, over yonder."

Morgan's jaw tightened. He wasn't a man given to brooding and pondering, but this was a rare occasion when he felt himself torn inside. Nothing was more feared by frontier folks than a prairie fire, and one look around Flat Rock was enough to see why.

Anybody who started such a blaze, especially through resentment or carelessness, was lower than dirt in his eyes. The fury he felt as he looked around, seeing what had happened, warred with his long-ingrained desire to just be left alone and continue drifting.

"They wasn't our blood, you know," Bowman mused, breaking into Morgan's thoughts.

"What?"

"The boys. They was adopted, I guess you'd say. We took 'em in to raise when they was orphaned, because nobody else would. Our own kids are grown and gone. But that didn't matter to my wife. She loved 'em like they were our own."

"You saved one," Morgan pointed out.

"Yeah, but —" Bowman couldn't go on. He made a choking sound and just shook his head.

Morgan rubbed his jaw. Clearly, no words he could say were going to offer any comfort to the man, and the whiskey wasn't helping, either.

So he did the only other thing he could. "You know where I can find these Locklins?"

Bowman's drooping head came up as he frowned in surprise. "You ain't . . . you ain't thinkin' about goin' after them, are you, mister?"

448

"Anybody left alive in this town who's up to the job?"

A bitter laugh came from Bowman. "There was nobody here who was up to that job even when everybody was still alive."

"You don't want them to get away with this, do you?"

"God, no! But I didn't think there was anything anybody could do."

Frank straightened to his feet. "Maybe I can."

Bowman blinked as he looked up at Morgan, a dark shape with the afternoon sun behind him. "Who are you, mister?"

"Name's Frank Morgan," the Drifter said.

Bowman's breath hissed between his teeth. He scrambled up. "Morgan! You mean you're Frank Morgan, the gunfighter?"

"Some call me that."

"What are you doin' in this part of the country?"

"Passing through, like I told you," Morgan said. "Now, can you tell me where to find the Locklins or not?"

Bowman rubbed his mouth as a look of desperate hope came into his eyes. "I've heard rumors that they're hangin' around a road ranch and stage station about ten miles north of here, on the trail to Lubbock. Place called Vinegar Hill. Don't ask me why; there ain't many hills in these parts."

Morgan nodded. "Much obliged." He turned toward the dun, which stood nearby waiting patiently with its reins dangling.

Bowman took a quick step after him. "Wait a minute. Are you really goin' after 'em?"

Morgan looked around at the burned town. "I figure if I don't, it's liable to stick in my craw."

"Then I got just one request of you, Mr. Morgan . . . take me with you."

Morgan's mouth tightened as he gestured toward the woman who had finally gotten up and was wandering aimlessly in circles. "Don't you think you ought to be trying to comfort your wife?"

"She don't want no comfort from me. She just wants things to be back like they were, and that's somethin' no man can do. Nor God, either, I reckon. Like the Good Book says, the movin' finger has writ, and the page is turned. All that's left now is settlin' the score."

"It's your choice," Morgan said. "I don't tell any man how to live his life."

"I don't care about livin'," Bowman said. "Just dyin'. I want to be there to see it when those damn Locklins cross the divide."

Morgan swung into the saddle. "Up to you to keep up, then," he said as he turned the dun and prodded it into motion, heading north out of Flat Rock.

He figured Bowman would give up the damn fool idea, but he had underestimated the man's determination. When he looked back a few minutes later, he saw that Bowman had gotten hold of a horse somewhere and was riding after him, bouncing awkwardly in the saddle. Morgan shook his head and slowed the dun so that Bowman could catch up to him.

Morgan noticed the revolver stuck behind Bowman's belt and gestured toward it. "Where'd you get that?"

"Made the town marshal give it to me. He didn't care anymore. Said he was ridin' out and never comin' back. I thought I might need a gun. I thought I might help you."

Morgan bit back a curse. The last thing he needed going up against three gun-wolves like Steve, Asa, and Rance Locklin was some grief-stricken townie "helping" him. For a moment, he seriously considered reaching over and walloping Bowman. The best thing might be to knock the man out until the showdown with the Locklins was over.

But there was a look of such pathetic eagerness in Bowman's eyes that Morgan couldn't do it. He didn't think Bowman was going to find what he was really looking for at Vinegar Hill, but short of violence, the man wouldn't be stopped.

"When we get there, stay out of the way," Morgan said. "This is my kind of work, not yours."

"I'll only take a hand if I need to," Bowman promised.

They rode the rest of the way in silence, because really, what was left to say?

Coming in sight of the low, rambling adobe building with the sod roof, Bowman said, "That's it. That's Vinegar Hill." He leaned forward in the saddle. "And those horses tied up in front belong to the Locklin brothers! I recognize them."

"Last chance to go home, Bowman," Morgan told him.

Bowman shook his head. "Got no home to go to. Not after today."

Inside the road ranch, the men either heard the horses or saw them coming, because they ambled out the door and spread out, a sign that they knew what they were doing.

The skinny one with the buckskin jacket and long, tangled hair under a flat-crowned brown hat moved over to the water trough and propped his left foot on it. The short one who was about as wide as he was tall crossed his arms over his massive chest and leaned back against the wall beside the door. The third man, about as tall as the skinny one but heavier, with a dark mustache drooping over his mouth, went the other way and stopped by the corral fence. He had a Winchester cradled in his arms.

Steve, Asa, and Rance, in order from right to left, Morgan thought. He had never crossed trails with them before, but he had seen their pictures on enough reward dodgers tacked to trees. Kill-crazy scum, the lot of them, especially Steve. The other two might callously gun down somebody in a robbery, but only Steve was loco enough to set a fire that he knew would destroy an entire town.

"Howdy, mister," Steve called. Grinning, he gestured toward Bowman. "You know you got a turd followin' you?"

Asa made a rumbling sound, and after a second Morgan realized that it was laughter.

"I never knew a turd to ride a horse before," Asa said.

The most practical and pragmatic of the

brothers, Rance, said, "Who are you, mister, and what do you want?"

Never taking his eyes off them, Morgan dismounted without answering. He wanted to be on solid ground as he faced them. "You'd be the Locklin brothers, I reckon."

"That's right," Steve acknowledged. "You got the advantage on us, friend."

Morgan shook his head slowly. "I'm no friend to snakes like you."

Steve's arrogant grin disappeared as he lowered his left foot to the ground and dropped his casual pose. He wore two guns, fancy ivory-handled pistols. Asa was a two-gun man, as well, wearing them butt-for ward in cross-draw rigs that hung from bandoliers crossed over his broad chest. Rance had a Colt, too, but he was best with a rifle, Morgan recalled. He made it a habit to know as much as he could about men he might have to face in a showdown someday. It came in handy.

"You some kind o' lawman?" Steve demanded. "Texas Ranger, maybe?"

"Lawman?" Morgan repeated. "Not hardly. Just an hombre who doesn't like what you did today."

"You mean burnin' out Turdface and his friends?" A bark of laughter came from the man. "Hell, they had it comin'. They

454

shoulda known better than to run the Lock-lin brothers out of town. That's just like spittin' into the wind." Steve laughed again. "And that was some wind earlier today, wasn't it? I never saw flames move so fast in all my borned days."

"So you don't deny what you did?" Morgan asked.

"Deny it? Hell, I'm *proud* of it! It ain't ever' day that a fella can destroy a whole damn town!"

Slowly, Morgan nodded. "You know, Locklin, I haven't enjoyed killing most of the men I've killed, but I think I'm going to enjoy killing you."

Steve's face twisted with anger and hatred. "That's mighty big talk for somebody who won't even tell us who he is. I think you're nobody! I think you're just one more stupid owlhoot who's got it comin' to him!"

Suddenly, Rance spoke up in a worried tone. "Steve, I think I know who this hombre is! I've seen pictures of him! He's Frank Morgan!"

"Morgan!" Steve's eyes widened with surprise. His hands stabbed toward his holsters. "Gun 'im down!"

It was like it always was. Time seemed to slow down for Frank Morgan. With the speed that was as natural to him as breathing, he drew and fired. His first bullet tore out Asa's throat. He had heard that despite his bulky build, Asa was the fastest Locklin brother. Morgan pivoted, crouching as he shifted his aim, and pumped a slug into Rance's chest, driving him over backwards. The rifle in his hands cracked, but the barrel was already tilted skyward. Morgan shifted smoothly, anticipating Steve's shots, and sure enough, a pair of slugs whistled through the air where his head had been an instant earlier. His Colt came to bear on Steve . . . but before he could pull the trigger, more shots roared close by.

Bullets pounded into Steve Locklin's body, making him do a jittery little dance as he backed up to the adobe wall behind him. Al Bowman walked for ward, the gun in his hand blasting two more times as he turned Locklin's face into a ghastly crimson smear.

"*You* had it comin'!" Bowman cried in a tortured voice. *"You!"*

Morgan hadn't even seen the man dismount. All his attention had been focused on his opponents, not the unlikeliest of allies.

As Steve Locklin's corpse slid down the wall to come to rest propped in a sitting position on the ground, Bowman stopped shooting and lowered the gun. "He's dead,

456

isn't he?"

"Considering that's his brains and blood all over the wall, I'd say so," Morgan replied. "I told you to stay out of it."

"I didn't think you were gonna get him in time. I thought he was going to kill you."

Bowman could tell himself that all he wanted to, Morgan thought. The man might even believe it. It didn't really matter.

Morgan punched the empty loads out of his Colt and slid fresh cartridges into the chamber. "Well, it's done with," he said without looking at Bowman. "You can go back to your wife and boy now. Make something out of what's left of your life, Bowman. That's all I can tell you."

"You're not coming back to town?"

Morgan shook his head. "No reason to. Like I've told you, I'm just passing through." He pouched the iron and took up the dun's reins.

"I tell you, there's nothing for me to go back to." Bowman looked at Steve Locklin's body and shuddered. "It doesn't change a thing. Not a damn thing. *He* started the fire, but I'm still to blame for what it did."

Morgan turned the horse. He couldn't talk to the man in the state that Bowman was in. He'd have to find his own way out.

"Thanks, Mr. Morgan!" Bowman called

when the Drifter was about fifty yards away. "Thanks for your help! And Mr. Morgan . . . there's one bullet left in this gun!"

Morgan's head jerked up as the shot rang out over the plains. He twisted in the saddle and looked around in time to see Al Bowman's body slump to the ground.

He had a reason to go back to the settlement after all. He lifted Bowman's body, draped it over the saddle of the horse the man had ridden to Vinegar Hill, and took him home.

When he lowered the body to the charred ground at the feet of Bowman's wife, the woman looked at it for a long moment and then spat on it. "It was his fault. All his fault. Big man who had a job to do. Had to run those outlaws out of town. He had it comin'."

Morgan was getting damn sick and tired of hearing that.

As he rode out of Flat Rock, leaving the devastation behind him, he thought that within days, sprigs of green grass would begin to poke up out of the ground where there was nothing but ashes. Just nature's way of showing that it truly didn't give a damn what happened to people. The world would turn, the rain would fall, and the grass would grow, no matter how much suffering the folks who lived there had to endure. . . .

And the only ones immune to that pain were those who had nothing left to lose.

Like the man called the Drifter.

The employees of Thorndike Press hope you have enjoyed this Large Print book. All our Thorndike, Wheeler, and Kennebec Large Print titles are designed for easy reading, and all our books are made to last. Other Thorndike Press Large Print books are available at your library, through selected bookstores, or directly from us.

For information about titles, please call:
  (800) 223-1244

or visit our Web site at:
  http://gale.cengage.com/thorndike

To share your comments, please write:
Publisher
Thorndike Press
10 Water St., Suite 310
Waterville, ME 04901